Special

Author's

Edition

Shadows of Eagles

Stephen Lodge

Shadows of Eagles

Stephen Lodge

Special Author's Edition

Special Author's Edition

ISBN: 978-1-4357-1824-1
PUBLISHED BY MIRAGE BOOKS

Palm Springs, California

Printed in the United States of America

For all of you from Radford and The Chandler Lodge Morning Meeting–
always behind me:
One Day at a Time

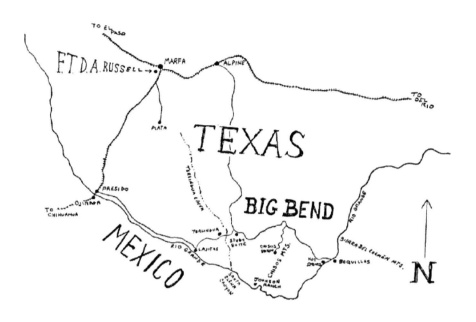

Spring – 1918
Over Chateau-Thierry
Near the French Lines

The steady drone of the Spad 11's Hisso 220-hp finely tuned aeroplane engine–along with the unvarying sameness of the bleak, monochromatic sky–had lulled the young American pilot into a dull disregard. Nineteen-year-old Josh McComb–a Texas-trained pilot with the Aviation Section of the Signal Corps–was returning from a somewhat successful observation mission over German territory when the zinging bullets that seemed to come out of nowhere ripped through the plane's left side, tearing canvas and shattering struts. The machine immediately lost altitude. For several distinct moments Josh listened as the Spad's drone paled off–followed by coughing and sputtering.

In seconds, a shrill blast shook the heavy air around him as a tri-winged Fokker crashed down from above–barely missing McComb's impaired aircraft while the German guns echoed with their deadly pop-pop-pop.

Regaining partial control, the youthful Yank managed to maneuver the French biplane to a much lower elevation, skipping along in obvious trouble–hedgehopping above a muddy battlefield. At once the Fokker dropped in behind and continued to stalk the wounded plane. The youngster sideslipped as best he could but was unable to avoid a smattering from the deadly Spandau machine guns on his tail. McComb took several slugs in his leg.

Before long another volley of German lead found its target, clipping a wing, fouling the underside of the Spad's cowling, stopping the engine completely. The Spad's nose dipped dangerously toward the ground. The landing gear hit first, shearing off entirely, causing the plane to belly in. It slid for some distance until the propeller ground off and the fuselage went tail-up, throwing the injured McComb clear. The Fokker swept through– directly above–pulling into a steep climb as the Spad exploded in flame.

As Josh McComb–with his left leg shattered and bleeding–dragged himself through the muck, the Fokker continued to climb away. Through mudspattered goggles, Josh glanced back over his shoulder and saw the German pilot roll his plane out of its climb, dropping the nose into a death dive.

The horrified youth froze in the position where he lay–belly down in the mire; his eyes fixed on the advancing plane. Instinctively he knew what all seasoned soldiers fear–that the end was finally at hand.

At the last possible moment the Fokker pulled out of the dive, skimming over McComb's location just inches from the ground. A small missile splattered into the mud beside the wounded man. Slowly McComb's hand reached the place in the muck where the object had landed, his fingers groping and searching. Finally, he grasped something–carefully lifting it from the mire. It was a Blue Enamel Cross of the Pour le Merite: The Blue Max. The highest honor ever bestowed on a German aviator.

The enemy pilot circled overhead, watching, it appeared, until he could see that the American flier was all right. The German held up a hand with his thumb up for McComb to see before pulling away. Young Josh looked dazedly off in the direction taken by the Fokker. He, too, raised his hand– slowly lifted a thumb–returning the international gesture of friendship.

Spring – 1944
Presidio County, Texas
Near the town of Marfa

CHAPTER ONE

The dog heard it first.

A moment later the horse's ears perked.

Josh McComb rubbed at the dull pain in his left leg then stroked the strawberry roan's neck, softly toying with her mane. Through his gloves he could feel the blood racing under her skin as all four of her legs shook slightly with impending excitement. From his vantage in the saddle, McComb could see the hair on the dog's back standing at attention, her whiskers bristling. *A good dog, this one,* Josh thought. Half Border Collie half Australian Shepherd—with one blue eye—and the best goddamn personality he had ever come across in a dog in all the years he'd lived in Texas.

Josh finally heard the whistle, as faint as it was. The train was still a good distance away and he didn't want the horse wasting energy before it was time.

"Easy girl, stand easy," he whispered softly.

The mare turned her head, one eye looking back at him. She snorted, almost nodding. She pawed the gravel with one hoof. The hair on the dog's back had now risen even higher.

"Don't be so impatient, dog," he said with a grin. "You'll have your race."

The morning train was their favorite amusement. Both animals looked forward to it like Josh looked forward to that moment when his airplane's wheels lifted off the ground; that instant when he would defy every natural law and separate himself from the earth, ceasing to be just a man for a while. Josh McComb really felt free doing only two things: flying a plane, and letting a good horse run full out.

McComb adjusted himself in the stirrups, still aware of the pain in his leg–a discomfort he'd felt continuously for the past twenty-six years. At times–for brief moments–his mind raced back those several decades: to another time; another war; another world.

The roan's ears perked as the engineer blew the whistle to let them know that he was almost there. The horse blew back, spraying snot. The dog let out a short bark–an excited yip–looking up to her master for a signal. Josh held the reins as tight as he could and the horse seemed to gallop in place. He waited until he could feel the heat of the steam from the approaching iron monster, then he nodded to the dog and she took off at once. Josh dug in his spurs for all they were worth, throwing his hands forward.

"Heeeeyaaaaa!" he yelled at the top of his lungs.

The roan took her cue, shooting out like a pinball, sending a shower of sparks and shale in her wake. Within seconds the horse and rider had caught up with the dog and all were moving even with the clattering wheels.

Josh hunkered low in the saddle, giving the animal her full head. He knew that he wouldn't have to spur or whip her anymore. She knew what she was doing. She even knew how to pace herself. McComb could feel her speed pick up slightly as they began to edge up toward the engine with the dog yapping at their heels.

The dream Oberstleutnant Erich Jurgen Raller was having dealt with floating. He was high above the ground, suspended in the clouds and naked. He was drifting on a warm air-current high above the green meadows of his Fatherland–eyes half-closed–lingering in the smells of his childhood. He could feel the muscles in his face smiling. He sensed the tepid breeze as it lapped the moisture from his skin. Was he experiencing death? Was this what he'd always waited for? Maybe this was heaven. But there was no music, no silver angels. Only this isolated spot in the peaceful sky where he wafted quietly through the balmy welkin like– There it was. Did he hear it? Or was it just imagination? He tried to open his eyes but could not. The sound grew louder. An enemy plane? It was getting closer. He had to open his eyes. He had to see what was approaching. With every bit of strength he raised his lids; his wandering pupils peered through crossed lashes. He recognized the plane at once: the green and gray camouflage with the bull'seye roundel. It was a Vickers-Supermarine Spitfire F.IX and it was coming right at him. The sound of the roaring 1,650 horsepower Rolls Royce Merlin engine exploded inside his head. He saw the flashing flames from the four .303-inch Browning machine-guns and felt the wake of the burning lead as the bullets whizzed past him. Then the pilot fired the two Hispano cannon. As if in slow motion, Raller watched the projectiles zero in on him. And for a fleet second, he thought of Bronco Billy– the American cowboy from the moving pictures he had watched as a boy in Berlin. A distant train whistle, and he was awake.

At first Raller thought he might still be dreaming. The land stretched before him as far and as flat as he'd ever seen before. He felt the motion of the train and the tightness in his muscles as his ears adjusted to the constant clickety-clack of the steel on rail. He blinked. His head rested against the window, his nose pressing the glass. Something caught his attention and he looked down. A cowboy rode along beside him on a horse that ran like the wind. There was a small dog at the horse's heels, barking a silent bark. The cowboy glanced in his direction and smiled, then made a fist with his right hand and gave a thumbs-up sign directly to Raller. The oberstleutnant automatically returned the gesture.

McComb veered off slightly to avoid a telephone pole and the mare's hooves hit level ground with a new burst of speed. He looked over to the train again and could still see the blur of the German's face in the dirt-spattered window. He was a Luftwaffe Officer–Josh could tell by the uniform, what there was left of it–on his way to the prisoner-of-war camp out at Fort Russell, no doubt. The officer was older than most of the other German prisoners Josh had seen, probably close to his own age–old enough to have flown in the Great War like himself. It was a shame, he thought, the Huns were about to lose this war too and were getting so desperate they were having to call up the reserves. He felt sorry for the man for a moment. Then he thought of Homer Leaton–Monroe's boy–and pondered that this kraut might be the sonof-a-bitch who shot Homer down. He put just a little touch of the spur to the mare's flank and moved on up to the next car.

Raller watched the dog, horse and rider for another moment then settled back in the seat. He tried to fold his hands but the cuff and chain prevented it. He closed his eyes again. The whistle blew.

Cecil Sitters stepped out onto the porch of the Casa Grande and eased the thick wooden door closed behind him like he did every morning at exactly six-fifteen. He carried his frazzled boots in his left hand while the callused right held tight to the spur rowels, keeping them from jingling in the early morning air. He slipped across the Mexican tiles in his stocking feet, tippytoeing down the twelve steps that separated the colossal adobe structure from the Texas soil. He sat on the lowest stoop, tugging on the boots. When that task was done he stood up again, pulled his lime-green galluses up over his bony shoulders and buckled his belt. Cecil drew in a deep breath of the dry

Texas air and squinted toward the eastern horizon. He could clearly make out the flat line of the land against the sky in the gray of dawn. And he could tell by the way the salt had come to the surface on his lips that the day was going to be a hot one.

Cecil listened to himself walk as the spurs jingled their familiar tune on the way to the barn. He could smell the damp aroma of fresh-cut hay as he neared the large doors and he only had to break cadence once to skirt a dog pile. He shook his head. *Damn,* he thought, *I just know that Mr. Marcy's ol' hound laid his turds smack dab between the house and the barn on purpose. Just lyin' out there somewhere lickin' his balls an' laughin'. Sum'bitch don't even know c'mon from sic 'em.*

Cecil reached the big barn door and slid back the heavy bolt, eyeing the chipping paint and making a mental note that he and the hired hand, Clete, had better set to it and get started on their annual refurbishing. Then he stuck in his heels and threw back the double doors. They swung open like gargantuan castle gates.

All that could be seen in the darkness was the unretractable axle that connected the two front landing-wheels of the bi-plane. The rest of the monster was covered with canvas. Cecil could make out the shape of the thing. He'd seen it enough times. It was a 27-year-old deHavilland and Cecil's boss, Mr. Marcy, kept her in pinnacle condition. The ranch owner had inherited her from the Army in the late '20s after they'd discontinued the aerial patrols along the Rio. The old D.H.4–as it was called–had seen plenty of action when the banditos were raiding, and for the fifteen-or-so years since, she'd been kept like a racehorse at stud. Marcy used her to keep track of his several herds. Every once in a while he'd take her to El Paso for maintenance or to have her wings re-strung. But that was before Josh McComb had arrived. That was before this new world war had come to the Trans-Pecos.

The medal sparkled in the morning sunlight from where it hung on the plane's windscreen. Cecil still couldn't understand why Josh held so much regard for a dumb ol' German medal. Sometimes, when he really gave it some thought, it could tick him off.

The '35 Ford coupe swung off the dirt and onto the pavement, crossing the Southern Pacific tracks, then made another turn, bringing the gray vehicle abreast of the Presidio County Courthouse. Texas Ranger Captain Red Collinson slowed to a stop and shut off the motor. He looked out the window on the passenger side. He had a full view of the three-story brick building with its splendid tower and dome soaring another forty-feet to where the rising sun had just begun to reflect off the tarnished brass weather vane. He could see the light on in the mayor's office and another bulb burning behind the barred, opaque windowed door leading to the jail annex.

Collinson had been born the same year the courthouse had been built–1882– and had grown up watching the little whistle-stop called Marfa develop into the thriving cattle town it had become by the turn of the century and on into the sprawling community it was now. With the present war on, and the German P.O.W. camp now out at old Fort Russell, Collinson's job hadn't been any easier in the last two years.

He opened the door and stepped out, planting his highly polished Wellingtons on the new asphalt. He bent down to slip his pants-cuff over the boot-top, then stood to his full six foot five inches, tugging at his belt until the three-piece suit he always wore on these occasions felt comfortable. Collinson didn't like wearing suits. He preferred rivet pockets and soft flannel. He still wore his favorite flat-brimmed Stetson though. He didn't give a tinker's damn if it was sweat-stained and wasn't in style and that most of the City Fathers wore the short-brimmed cattleman's model. He'd been wearing the old ten-gallon for as long as he could remember and he'd wear it as long as he was going to live, no matter what the hell they said.

He slipped out his watch and checked the time–six-forty–about an hour too early for his meeting with the city council, the meeting he had set up to try and ease local minds about the German camp thing. The Mayor had asked that it be held at the early hour so he could announce the outcome on Elmer Ellsworth's Farm Report that went on the radio at 8:15 a.m. sharp.

Collinson glanced down the empty street and saw the door open at Packy Corrigan's Cafe. A faint rumble in his stomach suggested he pay ol' Packy a visit.

"Howdy," came the familiar voice from the order window that looked out from the kitchen. "Make yer'self at home, I'll be with ya' in a minute." Collinson could hear the bacon frying and smell the fresh coffee as he stepped up to the marble counter and gently eased his hemorrhoid-swollen rear-end onto the leather cushion. He took out his pipe and pouch and began to load the bowl when the little opening in the wall seemed to fill itself with the smiling, porky face of Packy Corrigan.

"Oh, it's you, Red," he chuckled. "What brings the captain of the Texas Rangers into town so early in the day? And dressed ta' kill, I see."

Collinson continued thumbing his regular tobacco wad into the bowl and began to pack it down. "Meetin' with the mayor and the council," he answered.

Corrigan unplugged the hole in the wall with his face and swung around, entering through the door in one move, bringing the coffeepot and a large cup with him. He poured some of the brew and set it down in front of Collinson. "Oh yeah," he said, "Booger Twiggs told me about it last night. Said you was gonna' set everything straight about what the Army's doin' out at the old fort."

"The Army can do whatever they want to durin' wartime, Packy," said Collinson, tired of the topic by now. "I'm jest' gonna' try ta' calm some fears, that's all."

"Yeah, I know," said Packy, wiping the lip of the coffeepot. "It's a shame ain't it? Man don't have no say 'bout nothin' anymore. Damn income tax withholding is screwin' me too. Hell, do you know how many forms I have ta' fill out now since they passed them new Federal tax laws?"

The ranger gulped down a large swallow and lit his pipe, shaking his head, "I wouldn't want ta' guess, Packy. It's all too tricky fer' me. I jest thank the Good Lord the state sees to it that I got it in my budget ta' hire someone ta' handle my accounting."

Corrigan wagged his finger, "Yer' lucky, Red. I surely wished I knew what the world was comin' to." Then he added, "Want some breakfast? Griddle's hotter'n spit in a campfire an' beggin' fer' batter."

"Let me have some of those buttermilk flapjacks yer' famous for and keep the coffee comin'," said Collinson with a smile.

"You bet," shot back the proprietor as he re-entered the kitchen. "Ain't that often I get ta' serve one of Texas's finest."

Collinson glanced down at the edge of the badge that showed slightly beneath his lapel, "It ain't because I don't want to eat out, Packy," said Collinson wiping his brow. "It's jest' that on what they pay us rangers, we can't afford it too often."

Collinson leaned both elbows on the counter and puffed on the pipe, taking some of the weight off his buttocks. He could feel the cold steel of his Colt .45 as the new position pressed the blued barrel into his stomach. He didn't like wearing a holster when he wore the suit–it made an ugly bulge. So he just tucked the ever-present weapon into his belt and covered it with his vest. It still didn't do much for the line of the suit, but Collinson didn't mind–everyone knew he carried the Colt anyway.

"I hear tell Coke Stevenson's gonna be turnin' over the Big Bend to the Federal Government come November," yelled Packy.

Collinson took another sip. "Governor Stevenson knows what he's doin', Packy. Most folks have wanted a National Park down here fer' a long time."

"Yeah, well," said Packy, "I guess it'll make yer' job easier anyhow."

"Probably not," answered Collinson. "National Park'll attract tourists. More people, more crime."

"Yeah, too bad that's the way it is," said Packy, his spatula making a slick, professional sound on the grill, "'Afore ya' know it, this town'll be as big as Del Rio, I 'spect."

Collinson nodded. "More'n likely, Packy. More'n likely."

The ranger's pipe had gone out like it always did after the seventh puff and he found another Blue Diamond and struck it under the counter. He brought the flame up to the bowl and sucked fire. A chug and a bang from the street turned his attention to the door and he could see Plunker Hancock's Model-A as it rolled by on the way to the ranger office. Plunker was Collinson's second-in-command and his shift started at seven. Plunker was never late. He'd be relieving Lester Suggs who'd had the night duty. Collinson chuckled to himself as he visualized Suggs dozing in the swayback chair as the prim and proper Hancock walked in on him. Plunker would chew the bejeezes out of the older man like always and Suggs would apologize and promise never to do it again. Then the next day Plunker would catch him snoozing in a cell. It was a recurring situation that helped Collinson maintain his sanity. He liked both of the rangers and their constant bickering amused him.

"I hear young Martin Claymore's body's comin' in on the mornin' train," said Corrigan. "It's a shame, ain't it?"

Collinson looked up as Corrigan set the plate on the counter, refilling his coffee cup. "Yeah, Packy, sure is," he said picking up a fork. "That makes about seven boys this county's lost now, don't it?"

"Eight, if ya' wanna' count Monroe Leaton's boy," added Corrigan.

"Almost forgot about him," said Collinson with his mouth full. "That boy was in that all-Negro 332nd, wasn't he? Can't say he never learned how to fly a plane. He was a good pilot, Monroe's boy." Collinson shook his head, "Mighta' made somethin' of himself, too, if he hadn't bought it so early on," he added softly. The ranger said a quiet blessing then flopped the napkin across his lap and forked in a mouthful of bacon.

"Radio's comin' on with the war news at seven," announced Corrigan. "Care ta' listen, Captain?"

"Go ahead," nodded Colinson, "turn it on. They tell me a man in my position has ta' keep up with such things."

"Put yer butt into it, Ceese," grunted McComb as he shouldered the tail section of the deHavilland. Cecil leaned back and pulled as hard as he could on the rope attached to the axle and slowly the big plane started to roll out of the barn and into the bright sunlight. McComb's dog sat nearby, watching.

To the three, trail-worn cowboys who were approaching the ranch after an all-night's ride, the plane's emergence into the yard was quite a sight. First to appear from the shadows was the four-bladed propeller, followed by the first glint off the polished steel exhaust pipes that were affixed to the Rolls-Royce 250-hp Eagle III engine. Next, the double set of wings loomed out of the darkness with their struts and wires standing at various angles, the metal lines taut and humming with every bounce the aeroplane took as it was rolled into the open. The fixed Vickers machine guns stood their sentry up front, and the single Lewis .303 was locked into place pointed toward the tail. She stood as proud as she had the twenty-or-so years earlier and was most likely in better condition. C.D Marcy was a perfectionist, and like everything he owned the D.H.4 was a study in impeccability.

When her tail finally cleared the barn door, Cecil dropped the rope and stepped back puffing. Josh moved around and knelt down, untying the towline. He stood and began coiling the rope as he moved over to where Cecil waited. "What's the matter, pard," he chuckled, "getting' to be too much for ya'?"

Cecil shook his head, "There's a lot more ta' pullin' than there is ta' pushin'," he huffed. "Any mule can tell ya' that."

"I reckon you're right, Cecil," laughed Josh. "Next time, you can push."

Sitters pointed off to the three cowboys who were just dismounting near the corral fence, "Yeah," he said nodding, "next time you can get them squawkers ta' help ya'." He called out to them, "Shorty, Biscoe! C'mon over here an' give us a hand turnin' this thing around." He yelled at the third cowboy, "Turpin! There're some oil-cans in the back of the barn there. Bring 'em out here, will ya'?"

McComb said his howdys to the young cowboys as they sauntered over to lend the two older men some muscle. After the plane was readied, Josh moved to the corral fence with the cowboys and fetched his saddle off the fence with the dog following. The others unsaddled their mounts and turned them out into the enclosure along with Josh's mare. Then all four, followed by the dog scampering in their wake, went on into the barn and to the tack room where they kept their gear.

Josh found his leather jacket, goggles and cap on the hook where he'd left them the day before and shook off the dust. Biscoe, Shorty and Turpin were shedding their chaps when Cecil came in.

"This may sound impolite, boys," he told them, "but Mr. Marcy needs you out at Mescalero Wells this morning."

"Ahhh, c'mon, Cecil," grumbled Turpin.

"Yeah," piped in Biscoe. "We was out all night an—"

"You know as well as I do that work comes first around here," Cecil interjected.

Now the third cowboy tried his excuse, "But we was—"

Cutting him off Cecil said, "You three was nothin' but belly-up to a bar all night, I can tell by yer' stink. Now you wanna' argue, you argue with Mr. Marcy. But I'd suggest you take a hot bath an' gargle with some Witch Hazel before you do. An' while yer' talkin' to 'im, ask 'im fer' yer' final week's wages. 'Cause if yer' not out at the Wells by nine o'clock, all three of ya' will be collectin' 'em before noon."

The threesome grumbled themselves back into their leggings while McComb slipped into his jacket, chuckling to himself. He knew Cecil Sitters well and that he meant business. He just wondered how the old fart could smell the liquor on them when Cecil nosed out like a bad batch of stagger soup himself all the time.

Josh called out, "Ceese, turn me over, will ya'?" He whistled for the dog. "C'mon, dog. We're takin' off."

The dog jumped to her master's voice and Sitters threw a hard look at the hungover cowhands then followed McComb out of the barn.

"They're good boys, McComb," said Cecil once they were outside. "Ya' jest' gotta' be hard on 'em sometimes. They jest' got some growin' up ta' do, that's all."

"I expect that's true," replied Josh as he circled the plane, checking it out thoroughly. "Is she full-up?"

Cecil patted the plane on the lower wing. "Yer' good fer' three and a half hours, maybe more." Then he added, "If ya' get a tailwind."

McComb stepped up onto the wing, pulling his left leg after him with his hand. It was the first time that morning that Cecil had noticed him favor the old injury. He knew Josh still carried close to a half pound of lead above his left knee and he admired the man for the way he was able to ignore it–most of the time.

The dog jumped up after McComb and Josh lifted her over into the cockpit, securing the animal with a harness he kept in the plane for the sole purpose of keeping the dog from falling out.

McComb squeezed into the cockpit beside the dog while Sitters moved around to the front of the machine and waited until all things were ready. Josh nodded and Cecil caught hold of the nearest blade and gave it a turn. The Eagle III sputtered and chirped. Josh nodded again and Cecil repeated the action. This time the engine sparked and Sitters stepped back quickly as the blades fluttered then whirred.

The noise from the big engine was ear-shattering. The backwash from the propeller churned the barnyard dust into hundreds of small tornadoes, causing the horses to plunge and jump. McComb smiled to himself. The dog barked excitedly. Josh could feel the tightness welling up deep down inside. He was aware of every hair on his body alive with electricity. He pulled down his goggles and waited a moment as he revved to a higher R.P.M.

C.D. Marcy heard the roar of the D.H.4's engine when it started up and calmly finished his grapefruit and coffee. He got up from the table and moved out of the dining area and through the vast front room to the door, stepping out onto the porch. He had to shield his eyes from the turbulent dust storm that raged in the ranchyard and could barely make out the shape of the deHavilland and the small figure of Josh McComb beside his dog in the forward cockpit. He did manage to get Cecil Sitters' attention and the older man ran over to the porch to find out what his employer wanted.

"Good morning, Cecil," said Marcy in a loud voice. "Tell McComb to remember that he's still on my payroll and when he and that mutt of his are tired of spyin' on that nest o' Nazis, I want him to take a check on sections eight and nine. See if there might be some strays over there."

"You bet, Mr. Marcy," yelled Cecil over the uproar. He turned and ran back to the plane, climbing up on the wing and repeating the message to Josh. McComb sent Marcy a thumbs-up and Cecil jumped to the ground and backed away.

Turpin, Shorty and Biscoe came through the barn just in time to catch a spray of fine gravel full in the face as Josh turned the plane and began his taxi toward the road that led away from the ranch. The three youngsters moved to the corral fence and were joined by Cecil and they all watched as McComb cleared the gateposts and swung out onto the road.

Josh held his R.P.M. and listened for anything unusual. There was nothing. He looked off to his right and checked the wind sock atop the grain bin. He stroked the dog's head. Finally he released the brakes.

Marcy watched the takeoff from the porch. It was smooth, almost silent with distance erasing the fine pitch of the power plant as the ancient daybomber climbed into the sky. *Josh McComb was a damn good pilot, one of the best,* Marcy thought, as the deHavilland shrunk into a dot on the sweltering horizon. The plane blended into the shimmering heat waves that had already begun to rise over the flat land. *It was too bad McComb was lame like he was, Marcy continued thinking, America could have used him in Europe–or the South Pacific.*

Marcy's look drifted toward the corral where three of his hands were saddling up some fresh horses with Cecil Sitter's help. Those three kids were almost of age, weren't they? Uncle Sam would most likely be calling them up before too long. Marcy hoped he wouldn't have to bury them too, like he was going to bury his friend Willingham Claymore's son that afternoon. Yeah, too bad those things have to happen when there's a war on. Thousands of miles away yet so close. And the dead soldiers returning every so often were constant reminders. So were the arriving German prisoners.

First Sergeant Francis Hatfield waited in front of company headquarters with the staff car's engine running. He took one final drag on his Camel and opened the door, crushing the butt into the gravel beside the runningboard. He didn't use the ashtray. As a matter of fact, Sergeant Hatfield never used the ashtray when he drove for Colonel Purrington. The old man hated the smell of stale cigarettes almost as much as he detested the stench of cow manure; therefore– and because of his rank–Colonel Caleb Purrington had ordered that no man smoke around him. Stopping the local bovines from defecating was a different matter.

Hatfield popped a Sen-Sen into his mouth for good measure just as the double-doors to the staff building swung open with Purrington–in a brisk march–whisking through them. The old man wore his pink whipcord breeches and riding boots, he carried his ever-present leather quirt under his left arm. An anxious aide moved along with the officer and was somehow able to reach the car a split-second before Purrington did, pulling open the rear door and saluting in one single movement. The colonel shot back a swift tap to his cap and slid in, the door slammed with precision behind him. Hatfield's eyes flicked to the rear-view mirror, awaiting his orders. Purrington cleared his throat and settled back. "Take me into Marfa, Sergeant," he ordered. "The County Courthouse; and put your foot into it."

Hatfield popped the clutch, the tires spun. The car swung around the drive and past the infirmary, making a sharp right by the officers' mess then moving through the twin guard-towers. In a little over thirty seconds, Fort D.A. Russell was a blur in the mirror and the car was rolling at well over fifty miles-per-hour down the dusty road that had only been graded several months earlier.

Purrington rode silently for a few minutes before turning around slightly to glance back at his command. The rows of barracks, the work buildings, the Post Exchange and the recreation area looked no different than any of the other old United States Army cavalry forts. Actually, the only variance from most other U.S. Army establishments were the guard-towers, which stood at set distances along the electrified barbed wire that surrounded the entire encampment. Besides, Purrington thought, the whole place looked quite spiffy–in military terms. After all, from what he'd heard, the Germans even liked it there. And that was quite a compliment, considering the way they ran their prisoner-of-war camps.

Wally Bowman watched the olive drab Dodge as it disappeared into the boiling dust cloud on the horizon, then he settled back into the metal folding-chair that was his only means of comfort in the tiny space atop the guardtower. He took out a Lucky Strike cigarette and leaned his Winchester pump twelve-gauge shotgun against the unpainted wall. He flicked open the top of his Zippo lighter and listened to the clear ring the top made as it fell back. He struck the flint and lit the cigarette's tip. *What a godforsaken country,* he thought to himself, his eyes wandering across the vast plateau that lay before him. He shuddered as he remembered the first night in the barracks when he threw back the mattress to find two tarantulas locked in fierce combat on the rusty springs. He'd thought he was having a heart attack. Gawd, the others had laughed at him, turning his fear into anger and embarrassment. Wally Bowman was extremely frightened by any kind of insect and had been all of his nineteen years. He wasn't afraid of anything else and had proved it against man and beast. But a bug, he couldn't even muster up the courage to squish one–not even a piss ant– and now the others knew his phobia and Wally Bowman knew that his stay in this place was going to be miserable. Some jerk had already put a wasp's nest in his footlocker and a five-inch scorpion in his favorite commode. Thank God he'd seen it before he sat down. That would have done it. That would have been the real heart attack for sure.

Bowman stood up and looked down into the compound below. He took another slow drag on his cigarette and watched as the Germans began to line up for roll call. Most of them were dressed in the light gray of the Afrika

Korps and Wally couldn't help but admire them for the way they followed orders. Hell, he thought, they were prisoners and they fell into ranks better than any American Army platoon he'd ever been in. Nazis, the leaders had to be hard-core Nazis. Otherwise those guys would be taking it as easy as they could. Just like he would if he were in their position, faced with sitting the rest of the war out in this desolate land. But the leaders had to be Nazis, and they probably threatened the regular German soldiers every minute of the day to keep them in line. That had to be it. That was the only way they could be so orderly, so easy to guard. He also thought they must have something up their sleeve. He fieldstripped his Lucky Strike and watched the shreds of tobacco drift away on the soft breeze. He picked up his weapon and went back to the chair. He had another hour before his duty was over—one hour and he could sack out again. Gawd, he hoped they hadn't put another bug in his bunk.

CHAPTER TWO

Most of the members of the city council had arrived and were milling around in the big room when Colonel Purrington entered. He recognized several of the men from a previous meeting held out at the post four days earlier–two of them being the Mayor and the captain of the Texas Rangers. The men had come to him out of fear and pressure, they'd said, but Purrington knew that their fear stemmed from the unknown and the pressure from their wives. Still, they had reason to be concerned. Fort D.A. Russell was no longer the lazy cavalry post the little town of Marfa had grown to accept over the years. Recently it had come to be, like many other forts across the nation, an internment camp for the governing of "Civilian Enemy Aliens and Prisoners-of-War," with a great emphasis on prisoners-of-war; especially Germans. What had begun as a helping hand to the British–a plan to catch the overflow of the tiny island's enemy captives–had now blown completely out of proportion. And Purrington agreed to himself that it most likely had done just that, to some extent, because no one would have ever guessed the ultimate number of Germans to enter the United States for the prime purpose of imprisonment. There were already 155 base camps throughout the states, with an additional 511 branch camps–something to test the flexibility of the War Department and the various governmental agencies involved in the jurisdiction of the project. But no one had ever given any thought to how the citizens of the United States of America would react to having the enemy on their soil; actually living side-by-side with the dreaded Nazis. Purrington chuckled to himself. He was about to find out.

Toby Ben Deemer, owner of the Marfa General Merchandise and Hardware, opened the meeting. He called the gathering to order by leading everyone in the Pledge of Allegiance. Booger Twiggs–who was acting secretary and who also ran the local hotel and owned one of the town's two gas stations–dispensed with the reading of the minutes and introduced Mayor Calvin Pyrtle. The applause was sparse so after thanking everyone for being there, Pyrtle read a short statement asking the Army–represented by Purrington–if there were any alternatives to having the P.O.W camp in Presidio County. Purrington replied with a simple, "No." The colonel didn't offer an apology. He just explained to the small group that the camp was going to be there for the duration of the war and that it was being guarded to the best of the Army's ability–including air patrols utilizing an armed airplane borrowed from one of the local ranchers.

Jimmy Dee Luther, who owned the Lumber Company, made it clear that he would shoot on sight any prisoner that used his property for an escape route. Then Mose Landrum suggested forming a vigilante committee—as they'd done in the old days–just in case.

There were some audible "yeas" to Landrum's proposal then everyone quieted down as Texas Ranger Captain Collinson took the floor.

"I think you boys're lookin' at this thing all wrong," he told them. "Havin' this camp here is a damn important part of our war effort. Kinda' like collectin' tin cans, or buyin' war bonds. You're worried about what'll happen if there's a riot out there or if some of them krauts escape. Well, I think you can put your worries aside for now. What you men gotta' remember first is jest' where we are. Hell, it's a ten-hour drive by car to El Paso. Imagine how much time it'd take if you were walkin'? And I hear kraut shoe leather ain't about ta' last that long."

There was some laughter and Purrington had to give the ranger credit. He was turning the meeting into something lighter than it had started out. What the colonel didn't know was that this was the way Red Collinson handled any situation that looked like it might get out of hand. Collinson had once turned a lynching party into a champagne brunch and a Mexican uprising into a fiesta. Red Collinson had been around West Texas all of his life and he knew how the people thought. He was "border folk" to the quick, and he understood the locals' ways where Purrington didn't. The colonel was by the-book U.S. Army and he was glad that the ranger was talking instead of he. Somewhere deep inside Purrington knew that the Marfa citizens wouldn't have listened to him had he gone on any further telling them that the Army could do anything it wanted in their territory. Things they didn't want to hear.

When Collinson was finished, the air in the room seemed cleaner. It was decided that the danger of the camp existing side-by-side with the law-abiding town had been a false fear and that with the city's leaders, the Army, and the rangers working together, the situation could be kept in tow. At 7:55 a.m. the meeting was adjourned.

At 8:15 on the dot, Elmer Ellsworth took to the air with the Presidio County News and Farm Report. His lead story was all about the council meeting. With his gentle voice and reassuring way, Elmer could always put his regular listeners at ease. Elmer, along with the Bell Telephone grapevine, helped assure the good people of Marfa that they were safe from the terrible Hun for the time being.

By the time Red Collinson had shaken hands all around and said his goodbyes, the several streets of Marfa had come alive with the regular passers-by, both foot-traffic and vehicular. Back inside his car, Collinson smiled to himself, turned on the ignition and drove to the ranger office to begin his day.

It hadn't been that easy for Red Collinson in the years leading up to the present. For sure it hadn't been an effortless job, helping to bring law and order to this desolate country. The early days sometimes took on the likeness of a vintage two-reel Western in the ranger captain's mind, what with the endless days in the saddle, the poor pay and the occasional shoot-out. All of the days spent before the Great World War, twenty-some years ago, had become a jumble. A series of black-and-white memories that sometimes replayed over-and-over in the percipient nickelodeon tucked deep between the folds of Collinson's aging brain.

Somewhere around 1917 sepia began to creep into the faded footage. And when someone would ask him about his days working undercover for the Army, he would tell the story about how he was sent into Mexico as a spy to search out the German officers who were teaching the Mexicans military science and tactics. How he had been part of the small band of mercenaries responsible for blowing up a powerful wireless radio station in Mexico City that had been sending vital information to the Central Powers. He also liked to tell about the Zimmerman note and the plot he helped uncover wherein Mexico—with the aid of Germany and Japan—had planned the takeover of Texas and several other southwestern states by force. He'd put a few bullet holes in some Huns on that occasion and it had won him the promotion to captain on his return to the rangers.

During that same time there had been the Chico Cano Bunch to contend with, too. Chico and his brothers, Jose and Manuel, along with their band of cutthroats, were making numerous raids into the Big Bend area and the locals had been desperate for their capture. Collinson had led a small company of hand picked rangers after them and had utilized the Army's two deHavilland bi-planes in a virtual air-war against the marauders. No one had ever known what had happened to Chico, Jose and Manuel—no one; that is, except Captain Collinson. Everyone else just took it for granted that the Cano Bunch had tired of the skirmishes with the U.S. authorities and slipped back across the border. Red Collinson knew different. In his home, just outside of Marfa, on a top shelf, in a dingy basement, there were three Mason jars containing pieces of human scrotum. If ever anyone ventured to ask him about the gang of banditos that had led him on so many chases, Ranger Collinson would answer simply, "Those Cano boys had balls."

His ranger years had taken him places other than the Big Bend and El Paso districts. He'd spent most of the Twenties assigned to curb the liquor traffic along the border all the way to Brownsville and he had survived plenty of brush fights. He had taken part in the Goat War of San Jose and had fought beside Captain Jim Fox and Bud Weaver at El Pourvenir. He had also been part of Senior Ranger Captain William Hanson's National Association for Protection of American Rights in Mexico, and had helped prepare the "Murder Map of Mexico"– something he didn't like to talk about much anymore.

Collinson had lived the transition in Texas from frontier simplicity and directness, to what it was now–contemporary confusion. And there were plenty of times when he yearned for the old days, even though they were fraying around the edges. But Red Collinson still had two years until his retirement and the reminiscing would have to wait. Right now he had ten hours to put in and if this day was to continue like it had started, Red Collinson was more than ready for it.

Erich Raller stood on the long porch of the railroad station and waited. Waited like he had at every stop and route-switch he'd encountered during the long journey across this foreign land. He waited in cuffs, chained to the next man like an animal–a humility Raller had never experienced in any of his forty-seven years.

At first he couldn't understand the treatment. It hadn't been this way during the Great War. He'd been shot down then, too, but those who'd captured him had treated him like the gallant hero he'd been and his release had come almost at once. This current conflict had proved to be pure hell in Raller's mind. He had bailed out of his Messerschmitt 109G-6 somewhere over the English Channel– halfway back to the Abbeville airfield in France–having just shot down his 36th enemy plane. He'd been too jubilant and most likely, too tired, and had not seen the Spitfire stalking him from above. He'd felt the sting of the Browning slugs way before he could fire back with his own 13 millimeter MG 131s. Then his Daimler-Benz engine had taken a direct cannon hit and Raller took to the silk. It still puzzled him why the Spitfire circled and fired on him again as he floated down, helpless in the parachute. Was that how he was supposed to die? Erich Raller, top Wing Commander for the infamous Abbeville Kids; veteran of Major Stempel's Kampfeinsitzer Kommandos? Erich Raller, who had flown side-by-side with Von Richthofen and the young Hermann Goering; who had dined with the Kaiser during the Great War and Adolf Hitler in this one? Erich Raller, who had been awarded the Blue Enamel Cross of the Pour le Merite, whom school children throughout Germany worshipped? Was he supposed to leave this world while being used as target practice by an overjoyed British pilot who didn't even know who Erich Raller was? No. No, he wasn't. He was just captured. And captured while unconscious at that, with no chance to fight it out with his captors or defend his honor.

Three English fishermen had seen his lifeless form splash into the choppy sea and they pulled him out. They thought he was dead and just piled his limp body in a corner on the deck, turning it over to the authorities in Dover. Had they known he was still alive they would more than likely have killed him. Raller considered himself very lucky and never once complained that the fishermen had stolen his leather flying jacket for a souvenir.

He spent a month or so in a series of hospitals, followed by several weeks of interrogation because of his rank and reputation. Then finally–and much to his surprise–he found himself, along with about two-thousand other P.O.W.s, aboard a returning liberty ship, headed for New York City in the United States of America.

While at sea, the prisoners ate as well as their guards, had plenty of tobacco, a warm place to sleep–though it was crowded–and books to read whenever they wanted. There had only been one close call, when they were almost torpedoed by one of their own U-boats. Other than that, there was just the constant seasickness to occupy the time.

Arriving in New York, Raller had been quite surprised to see that the American city was completely void of any destruction whatsoever–a dramatic contradiction to what he'd been told the Luftwaffe had done to the United States. He was also relieved that the Americans didn't systematically interrogate each prisoner like the British had done and had nothing like the infamous "London Cage" on the corner of Kensington Park Gardens and Bayswater Road, where the P.W.I.'s had taken a toll on his body and brain.

Raller had also been amazed that, with the hundreds of Germans and Nazis around him constantly during the voyage, not once had a single member of the Waffen S.S. approached him. It was a well-known fact back in Berlin, that he'd refused to join the Nazi Party but that knowledge was hushed because of his celebrity and even Goering himself had sent him off to France with a warm handshake and nary the bat of an eye. But Raller had known they were with him. Everywhere he'd gone he'd felt their presence. As far back as 1936, when he had flown with the Condor Legion, Germany's contribution to Franco's Nationalist Forces in their battle with the Republicans in Spain's Civil War, Raller had known the Gestapo was watching him. They had been on the ship, too. He knew that. He'd learned their distinct scent whether they dressed in the gray-green of the Wehrmacht–the common soldier–the light gray of the Afrika Korps, or their own slick silver-trimmed uniforms covered in fancy wings and braided cords. He knew they would come, eventually. He was sure that soon one of them would approach him. They knew of his celebrity. He knew they would need him and try and use him as they had attempted before. Only this time Raller didn't know if he would be able to fight them off. He was tired now; he was still recovering from his wounds. And he was older, wiser he thought, and as of late, he'd been pondering on his own life, his beliefs and whether everything he'd ever done might have been for the wrong reasons. He'd almost been glad he had been captured. Now he would have the time to sit it out for a while and rest. Take a step out of himself and look back on his career and study the reasons that had led him to be who he was. He almost looked forward to his approaching incarceration, for then he would have some time to relax and reflect on this recent self doubt.

Raller looked around at the drawn faces of the other prisoners on the platform, then to the few Americans who stood behind ropes viewing them as if they were on display. He felt the iciness of the Americans' stares and could almost smell the suspicion ooze from their pores as they watched the M.P.s herd the disheveled Germans into groups of ten.

When the guard removed his cuff, only to replace the steel manacle with another shackle, Raller felt the sharp teeth bite into his flesh. The M.P. apologized and Raller nodded his forgiveness, understanding that the soldier was just as fatigued as he was.

He took a cigarette from the packet given to him on the train. There were three left. He took one and broke it carefully in two pieces, sliding the larger portion back into the cellophane then lighting the second stub with a crumpled paper match. He blew the smoke through dry lips. His eyes were met by those of another German soldier who had been watching him prepare his smoke; without a word Raller withdrew the packet and handed the man the larger butt. He got a nod for a thank you.

The weather was arid in this part of the country, a parched flatland in comparison with the green forests he'd traveled through the first few days of the train ride. America was a very big country, like taking a trip from the Fatherland to the distant deserts of Africa and still being in the same nation. And he was in Texas, one of the states he'd heard of. Where Gene Autry, Tom Mix and Hopalong Cassidy came from.

Something pulled his attention to the sky: a faint sound–a familiar modulation from the past. He recognized the engine's purr instantly. He'd heard it many times in the air above France some twenty-six years earlier. Raller shielded his eyes and looked toward the sun in the direction from where the sound was approaching.

The plane's silhouette bore down on him like so many had in his lifetime. Winding down and dropping lower all the time, using the sun to cover its advance. Through squinted eyes Raller was able to recognize the aircraft's type, a familiar deHavilland–a D.H.4–one of the finest double-wing aeroplanes ever put out by the British Aircraft Manufacturing Company. Raller knew the plane quite well; he'd sent seven of them down in flames. It had been his eighth encounter with one of them that had shot him out of the sky for the first time, those many years ago.

Raller smiled to himself as the plane swept by the train station, flying parallel to the tracks at about one hundred feet, and he thought for a second that he'd seen the pilot dip his wings.

"OK, you grubby scum-suckers," said the voice, "let's get a move on."

Raller felt the gentle touch of the Winchester pump shotgun's barrel on his arm, bringing his attention back down to earth. Then he felt a tug on his chain as the man in front of him stepped out, following some others, heading for several canvas-covered trucks that awaited the exhausted captives in the dusty parking area.

McComb ruffled the hair on the dog's back then shifted his goggles, tipping the left wing as he passed the railroad station on the outskirts of Marfa. "Lookie down there," he said to the dog. "Them're Germans. They're the enemy. The ones we're fightin' against." He could see several columns of prisoners moving slowly toward the trucks that would be taking them to Fort Russell. For the past six months, aerial surveillance of the P.O.W. camp had become a regular part of McComb's daily routine–with extra flying time on the days when new prisoners arrived from the east.

Near the front of the train, Josh could make out some more commotion beside the baggage car. As soon as he glimpsed the red, white, and blue flag-draped coffin slowly being removed by the local color guard, he knew it was Martin Claymore's son come home from the war. Josh dipped his wings in a final salute to the brave young man.

McComb continued on, flying the length of the main street then he pulled the nose up, kicking a full right rudder. "I want the good people of Marfa to know that they're gettin' their money's worth," he said to the dog with a chuckle. "That Mr. Marcy's personal pilot has his eyes on the dirty Nazi Alemanes and that they'll be safe as long as the 'Big Chicken' is watching out for 'em." McComb laughed to himself again as the plane turned a lazy circle, heading back toward the station. He could see the raw, pink faces turned skyward, hands shielding their eyes as they followed his antics high above the dry pavement. "Big Chicken" was a name given to the deHavilland-4s, mainly because of their size. But Josh flew her like a screaming hawk and he could maneuver the bulky aircraft with the same ease he had flown other planes during his long career in aviation. He liked the D.H.4 and found it much more comfortable than the Stearmans, the Pitcairns, the Waco Taperwings and Curtis Orioles he'd flown as a civilian. And it was certainly a more comfortable craft than the French Spad he'd ridden to the ground during the Great War–at least his mind told him so. That First European War of so many years ago was something Josh McComb would just as soon forget.

The years leading up to the Great War had been his favorite. He'd learned to fly at age twelve in Dallas where a friend of his father's had taught him as a favor to the old man. As soon as he'd soloed, he had started teaching others. As a teenager he'd flown over Mexico for General Pershing during the Mexican Wars and had been lambasted but good by his superiors for attempting to bomb the Villa gang with dynamite–something he'd picked up from Villa's own aviators who were, more than likely, either German or German-trained. Those days had been an adventure, but the young McComb wanted something more challenging.

There'd been many times in the past when Josh had questioned why he'd gone off to Europe with Pershing–where he'd flown observation patrols for the famed Lafayette Escadrille. He'd always chalked it off to his youth and the early excitement of flying. But the armed conflict had proved to be totally different than he'd projected. Every single friend he'd had in those war days had died over France and he himself had taken a leg full of lead and bellied out in a cow pasture after he'd dived, trying to shake a Fokker Tripe Red off his tail. His Spad had been a maneuverable craft and the two planes battled down to hedgehopping when a lucky burst of machine-gun fire ripped the side of the Spad's fuselage and shattered McComb's left leg above the knee. He had pulled himself from the flaming wreckage and dragged himself clear of the explosion when the Fokker dived on him again. He'd known he was going to die as he saw the whirling propeller advancing down on him. But the German never fired his guns. Instead the pilot had pulled up at the last possible second, so close that Josh still remembered his face–and his smile. Then the German pilot had flown by much lower, dropping a medal, and had circled again, rocking his wings, giving the helpless McComb a thumbs-up. Then he had flown off over the horizon leaving the young American with a puzzle that still haunted him to this day. Josh McComb had survived the "Suicide Service," something too few pilots of the Great War could attest to. At times McComb felt good inside, knowing he would not have to fight in this present conflict. He vividly remembered things about the first one that he'd intensely disliked and the list led off with death and killing. He'd had his share of kills. The observation planes he'd flown had all been equipped with a Constantinesco gun gear with its fixed Vickers'. What really bothered him though was the fact that there had been a few times wherein he seemed to enjoy pulling the trigger.

Josh tugged back on the stick and gave the old baby some more gas, checking the fuel mixture then leveling off as the plane flew over the train station once again. He saw that the trucks had been loaded and the dust billowing up from under the carriers told him that they were starting their engines. "C'mon, dog," he told the dog. "Let's finish up an' go to work for Mr. Marcy." He circled around the south end of town in a lazy bypass and picked up the tiny convoy again as they headed down the two-lane blacktop. He trimmed the nose up slightly to slow the craft and followed the trucks all the way to Fort Russell. Once there he kicked a full right-rudder and slipped past the main gate before pulling the nose up and heading back toward the Marcy spread where he had the rest of his day's work cut out for him.

Raller spotted the S.S. officer right away. The Nazi stood two steps behind the American M.P.–who was instructing the new arrivals–and translated. He introduced himself as Dankwart Spengler and he was dressed in cast-off American khakis, topped with a gray cloth cap of the Afrika Korp. His hollow blue eyes found Raller almost at once out of the group of fifty and even though he avoided the man's stare, Raller knew that he'd been singled out. The afternoon was spent mostly in the recreation area, which Raller recognized as a done-over parade ground. The newly arrived Germans were issued necessities and a mattress. They were interrogated shortly and finally shown to their barracks. Raller was assigned to Compound number Two which stood in the middle of Compounds One and Three, with the recreation area on the north and the hospital and garrison echelon on the south. The entire camp, including each compound, was surrounded by eight-foot high double rows of woven-wire and there were guard towers placed at every strategic point along each fence.

Raller chuckled to himself as he flopped onto his bunk in the sweltering barracks building. If this was to be home for the duration, he'd better get used to it. He stripped to his undershirt and settled back, closing his eyes. He listened to the other new arrivals arguing among themselves, searching for their assigned bunks. Raller breathed deeply and could separate new sweat from the old that lingered in the musky room. Within moments, he was drifting through the clouds, high above the green valleys and mountains. Floating. Just floating. Nothing else.

CHAPTER THREE

Monroe Leaton stood silently on the porch of the Company Store looking off at the scattered adobes that were spread out across the ungracious expanse of sand and rock called Terlingua–the only community, of sorts, in the Texas Big Bend region. Several minutes had passed since the sun had dipped behind the distinct rock formation known as Fossil Knobbs. Monroe watched as the Mexican inhabitants lighted kerosene lamps one-by-one in the tiny windows of the stone jacals. He flared his nostrils and swept in the blended aromas of the cabrito and liebre–goat and rabbit–that still lingered as the mesquite fires died out around the town and Monroe thanked the Lord that his stomach had been satisfied once again. He pulled a toothpick from his snakeskin hatband and gently gouged some tiny scraps of gristle from between the few remaining teeth he was still blessed with and listened to his belly digest the food.

From somewhere nearby a guitar played, sending the soft strains of a Mexican war song wafting across the village. Monroe could hear the pots and pans rattle from inside the large building behind him as the cooks and dishwashers closed down the company kitchen.

The few remaining workers would be settling in for the night, preparing for the next day in the mercury mines. They might even attempt a short round of lovemaking with their wives before falling off into a few hours of bliss. Only to be interrupted again when the four o'clock whistle blew them awake and led them back down the shafts and into the darkness of the quicksilver tunnels known as the Chisos Mine.

The gentle flutter of the wind chargers played in Monroe's ears while his eyes drifted across the vast desert panorama that spread to the mountain range etched on the horizon, now disappearing into the settling dusk. The mountains, like the mine, were called the Chisos and where a faint V was still visible in the rugged formation, Monroe could see several dots of light coming from the government C.C.C. camp nestled high up in the basin.

Monroe Leaton had helped build the camp more than several years back and had been saddened by its recent abandonment. All that remained were the few scattered buildings and three or four government employees. Monroe made a mental note to visit the Chisos basin on his next trip down to the

Bend. He liked the mountains. He liked the peace they brought to his soul.

A couple of the Mexican dishwashers came out onto the porch and stopped to chatter for a moment several feet from Leaton. In all the years he'd spent in West Texas he'd never learned Spanish and it always bothered him when the Mexicans spoke it around him. He sometimes thought they did it on purpose and he always knew when they were talking about him, because there was one Spanish word he *did* understand and that word was "Negro."

The two Mexicans that stood on the porch didn't use the word this time and Monroe was glad. They must be talking about the stars he thought, or maybe about their sweethearts down Mexico way. He nodded to the men as their conversation broke up and they moved down the cement steps, heading for their adobes. The Mexicans nodded back. They knew Monroe Leaton and felt sorry for him. For to their way of thinking, he hung from a lower rung than they did. Monroe watched the Mexicans disappear into their huts while he located his Bull-Durham sack in the top pocket of his overalls. He tugged open the pouch with his teeth while expert fingers creased a paper. He poured a neat row of tobacco and rolled, licked and lit in one easy movement, waving the flame out and breaking the match in two pieces from habit. He took a long draw and inhaled deeply, taking the butt away from his mouth and leaving a thin veil of paper on his lower lip. He rolled the adherence into a small ball with his teeth and tongue then spit it to the wind where it vanished into the night. The breeze was warm and it felt good on his exposed arms, sending a gentle chill from his spine to the few hairs on his neck. One of the main reasons Monroe Leaton had stayed on in the area after his hitch with the cavalry was up had been the weather. Mississippi, where he'd grown up, was just too wet for him. It seemed like it never stopped raining back there and the roofs he'd always found himself under invariably leaked.

Because of his background with the mounted troops, Leaton found it easy to hire on with the eager Yankees who had come to the Big Bend in droves to try their luck trapping during the Twenties. He'd scouted for them and made sure they learned the ways of the wild and didn't kill themselves or get killed. In 1932 Monroe had managed to save up enough money to purchase a flatbed truck. With that piece of machinery he picked up spare work, when it was to be had, by hauling wood and then butane for the locals and for the many mining companies that owned land in the area. He'd been doing that for over ten years now though it seemed like twenty. He was growing tired and was close to sixty years of age himself. He wanted to retire, retire and settle in the Bend for good.

He'd owned some land in the area once, down on the Rio Grande near the Johnson Ranch. He'd raised his family there. After his wife died in '36, he'd moved to Marfa so he could be closer to other humans who had odd jobs to offer. Then the fire happened. His twin girls had died in the flames and Monroe had damaged his lungs attempting to save them. Only he and his son had survived and the two of them rebuilt with the help of their neighbors. Now the war had taken the son, too. Monroe Leaton was alone once more.

He took another lengthy puff on his cigarette and coughed. He'd tried to make it a good life for himself and his family and there were many things he'd done that he was proud of. And unlike most men who found themselves in a similar position, he didn't blame himself. Monroe Leaton believed deeply in the Will of God. He'd learned many years earlier to accept both the good and the bad equally.

Leaton finished the cigarette and snuffed it on the support post, then eased himself down the steps, crunching across the gravel to his truck. He checked the tie-downs on the empty butane containers and was satisfied with the job the Mexicans had done. He climbed into the cab and started the engine. It was a long drive back to Marfa and he wanted to get there before morning. He pulled the light switch and the headlamps threw their cockeyed pattern out over the graveyard that stood several feet away. Yes, sir, he thought. That's where I gonna' be shortly, that's where I gonna' be. The words reminded him of an old spiritual from his youth and he began to hum the tune as he pulled away from the town. After he'd gone a few hundred yards, the words came back to him. He began to sing.

It was almost half past nine by the time Josh had put away the horse and wiped down the leathers. He walked across the rutted yard between the stable and his small house with the dog at his side, decidedly aware of the several pieces of metal still imbedded in his thigh. He stopped for a moment on the porch, sitting down on the steps to remove his spurs. He stroked the dog lovingly, then stood and entered the house.

One of the reasons Josh McComb had been able to purchase the small ranch was due to the fact that electricity hadn't been strung to the tiny outpost, so he lit a match and found a lantern, adjusting the wick until a soft glow bounced off the rough wood walls. In time he planned to build a wind charger, or even string some lines himself from the main highway, but that was a long way off and still pretty much out of the financial question. Until better days came along, he would have to make do. And he did, with several lanterns; an old butane stove; and an old Philco radio that ran off of two Chevrolet batteries.

The dog curled up in her corner and Josh moved across the one room, falling into his favorite chair opposite the still-incomplete stone fireplace. He thought about how much longer it might take him to finish the project that had already consumed six months of his life–in Sundays alone.

The bottle still sat on the hearth where he'd left it the night before; where he and Graylin had put it before falling asleep together on the mountain-lion rug that he'd had since his early days down in the Bend. He leaned forward and picked up the jug, holding it out in front of him, slowly swirling the remaining brown liquid around in the container, watching the flame from the lantern twist and distort through the flaws in the glass. After a long moment, he put the bottle to his lips and let the brown liquid slide down his throat.

Quiet nights brought back memories for Josh McComb, remembrances of times past when he'd explored the many paths that led to where he was now. He raised the bottle and let a couple more unmeasured jiggers coast under his palate then focused beyond the lantern's flicker to places and feelings of long ago. Reminiscing helped relieve the pain–both in his leg and deep down inside where a man felt his life.

He'd come back from Europe at the end of 1917 a defeated man. Actually still a boy, just nineteen years old. Because of his wound he was considered a cripple and was passed by when it came to the good flying jobs. He worked his way back to West Texas where he signed on with the U.S. government to fly border watch. They took him even though he was crippled because they desperately needed a pilot. He stayed with that job for a few years, always remembering the earlier days when he flew for Pershing's forces, hoping that maybe he could recapture something, which of course, was not there. He had met a few people while flying the river, one in particular–a woman. The two of them had fallen in love briefly until she had told him she had no interest in marriage. Josh McComb desperately wanted a family, so he moved to Marfa where he was able to pick up a job in Eden's Hardware, checking stock and clerking. He found he was welcome in the little town and because of his war record, respected. He was eventually able to fulfill his dream and settled down to marry a young thing, a local rancher's daughter by the name of Linda. The two had made their plans, as all young couples do, and McComb flew along on a continuous high until 1926 when both Linda and the baby died during childbirth.

Shortly after that he met two Kentuckians with the names of Grady and Williams and the three of them set out for the Big Bend where they had plans for a farm project. They tried to raise tobacco and opened a small trading post. The tobacco crop failed, but the store kept growing. In 1928, the partners sold out to Elmo Johnson, and Williams and Grady headed north looking for other adventures. Josh stayed on and continued to work the store for Johnson while his interests spread to other things like fur trapping, where he'd bagged his share of fox, coyote and cougar.

On July sixth, 1928, a small miracle happened for McComb. The United States Army had some years earlier dedicated a landing field on the Johnson Ranch and Josh was hired to train the young aviators. The ranch became a lookout and checkpoint on the international border and even had a radio station that made daily contact with El Paso and the nearby Fort D.A. Russell.

The Johnson ranch was an oasis in the rugged country for more than the young pilots. While there, McComb met the likes of Lieutenant Nathan Twining, who would later become General Twining, Commander of the 15th Army Air Corps, and John Dillinger. Another man he met who had become a close friend over the years was an ex-cavalry man from the Fort. His name was Monroe Leaton.

Around 1930, Josh moved back to Marfa where some friends ran him for sheriff. It was a close race but he lost. The move did him good though. He met and married his second wife. Their happiness only lasted one year. She died in 1934.

McComb lifted the bottle once again, this time with the professional ease of a man familiar with John Barleycorn. He rubbed his game leg and felt, even heard, the lead as it chafed the bone. He thought about the days following his second wife's death, those other days blurred by liquor. The endless months after he moved back to the Bend, living in an abandoned adobe near Terlingua. Half the time spent cutting wood in the Chisos with Monroe Leaton and the other half dazed and drunk in his stink-hole of a shack.

It was Monroe Leaton who finally straightened him out; starting when the big Negro kicked in the door to the adobe that cold January day. "C'mon, get up," Monroe had ordered him. "We gots a lot of trees ta' cut."

McComb had rolled over in a coughing fit, trying to shield his eyes from the blinding sun that etched the large black man's figure into the frame of the door. "Lea'me alone, damnit," he'd shot back in his stupor. "Just get the hell out, OK?"

Leaton hadn't budged. He carried a large ax over one muscled shoulder and the sunlight kicked even brighter from the steel blade. "Goddamnit, Monroe, I said get out!" screamed the drunken McComb, grasping for a bottle that rested on a nail keg next to the cot. His fingers never reached it. There was a swoosh of the ax and the razor-sharp blade sent splinters of glass and splattering droplets of whiskey flying through the vinegarish atmosphere, causing the already anxious man to jump.

"Jeezes, Monroe, that was my—"

"Shut up! Jest' shut up an' listen to me," the big man said through gritted teeth. Leaton's voice had a chill to it that made the outside seem like summer. "You a no-good bum, you know that, Missa' McComb?"

"Yeah, sure," Josh mumbled then he rolled over. A fist as big as a bowling ball rolled him back; and fingers the size of sausages clamped around his neck.

"Now you gonna' listen to me, damnit," said Monroe firmly, "even if I gotta' flap those ears of yours open an' pin 'em back myself."

McComb tried to focus but all he could see were two flared nostrils that seemed to be made of soft leather. He blinked then nodded.

Leaton relaxed his grip and McComb flopped back on the sweat-stained pillow. Then Monroe Leaton leaned in as close as he could until the smell of stale alcohol and urine stopped him. "No one's gonna' help ya' 'cept yo'sef. You understand that, Missa' McComb? Ain't no one gonna' help ya'."

There was a moment that seemed to Josh to take days to pass. Then Leaton stood to his full height, looking down on him. "There's no human power can help you," he said. "You understand that? Ain't no human power left."

"Why don't you just leave me alone," blubbered Josh.

"What an' let you die?" answered Monroe. "No, sir; I might beat you black as me, but I sho' ain't gonna' let you die."

Leaton used his foot, pulling the keg over next to the cot. He took in a deep breath and then sat down. Josh blinked again, his vision cleared some and he saw that there were several tears seeping from the large man's eyes. He felt Monroe's hands again, only this time they took his own trembling hands between them gently. Josh could vaguely remember asking him what he was doing. Leaton's reply still hung in his ears as clear as that day they were spoken. "We gonna' pray, Missa' McComb," the black man had said softly. "We gonna' pray that you get well."

It had taken Josh a full week to get rid of the shakes. A whole month before the whiskey had drained from his brain completely. He didn't pick up a drink for the next ten years, hadn't even had an urge. Not until last night. He always kept a bottle in his house for those that did drink and he knew that it was there if he ever wanted it. Last night, before Graylin had arrived, he'd even gone out and bought two more. It was like he'd known he was ready to start again.

The dog came across the room to where McComb was sitting, nuzzling his arm to get his attention. "It's OK, girl," he assured her. "I'm OK."

The dog went back to her corner, circled several times and curled up. Josh stood up. He had finished off the bottle and now he moved across the room and found a full one in the small cupboard he'd made from an old orange crate. He unscrewed the cap and downed another shot, then crossed to the Philco and turned the knob. The radio's tubes began to glow, making strange silhouettes against the wall through the backing. After a moment or two with some delicate tuning, he was able to pick up the Del Rio station that could only be found at night. Dick Powell was singing, "Ride Cowboy, Ride," backed by Benny Goodman and his Swing Band. McComb listened to the ballad for several moments, then moved back to the chair and plopped himself again into the stuffed pillows. The dog looked up; then she put her chin down, closing her eyes again. This time Josh kept the bottle close by, clutched securely in his left hand. He glanced at an old newspaper that lay on the floor beside him–an El Paso weekly that he subscribed to by mail. He let his eyes wander over the picture of a Texas version of Rosie the Riveter–some young girl dressed in blue jeans and a straw hat but still holding the torch and wearing the goggles– presenting a war bond to a local government official. McComb shook his head at the glossiness of the photograph and wondered if they'd ever print a picture showing a soldier with his balls shot off.

Josh chuckled to himself, trying to keep from choking up then he took another slug of whiskey. He should be thinking of Graylin and he wasn't. Their relationship was a little rocky and he should be thinking up reasons to keep it together. *Fuck it,* he thought, *I don't want to get married again, so if it is supposed to end, I'll let it end. Besides, when she popped the question last evening–that's right, she popped the question–asking me if I didn't think it was about time that we settled down together. Hadn't I avoided an answer like it was a prairie fire?* He'd changed the subject like he had always done only this time she hadn't let it rest. She'd even become angry, in the pouty little girl way that usually brought him to his knees. But the thought of another marriage was just too much for McComb. Something deep inside told him that to be that close again with someone would only end as the others had–in tragedy.

Finally she'd begun to cry and he'd taken her into his arms trying to lend comfort as best he could. Then, as they lay there on the rug by the hearth, she'd told him that she would be going away for a while. "I need some time to myself," she had whispered through the tears. "I've made reservations down at Hot Springs near Boquillas. Call it a vacation, or whatever," she'd told him. "I just need time to think."

She buried her face into the soft fur of the animal skin and Josh realized that he had no reassuring words this time. He could only lay there beside her, staring up into the nothingness while a thousand empty emotions spun in his mind, not one of them making any sense. The truth was, he was afraid– deathly afraid of making another commitment with a human being in this same lifetime.

When he awoke the next morning, she was gone. She hadn't left a note. There wasn't any need to. They knew each other that well. He knew she'd gone to The Springs. Right now Josh didn't know if he'd ever see her again. *Fuck it,* he thought. He lifted the bottle for another swallow. He wouldn't remember when the tears came. He'd consumed far too much whiskey. But they came. Just like they'd come those other times in his life.

CHAPTER FOUR

"Es ist eine grosse Ehre in gegenwart eines so beruhmten Kriegshelden zu sein, Herr Raller. Willkommen in Camp Russell."

The words punctured Erich Raller's gut like a dagger dipped in poison. He turned from where he sat smoking outside the barracks and saw the full pack of cigarettes offered him by a well-manicured hand. "A Chesterfield, Oberstleutnant? A humble offering for such a fine soldier."

Raller's look drifted up to the puffy, sweating face and the light-blue eyes set deep between pink folds. It was Spengler. Raller had been expecting him. "Here," the man said. "It is my gift to you." Spengler held the packet even closer.

"Thank you, no," answered Raller, refusing. "The Americans were kind enough to give me some of my own."

Spengler laughed and bent to his haunches, pulling the cellophane off the cigarettes and carefully tearing the pack open. He took a bone holder from one of his top pockets and delicately inserted the cigarette, sliding the mouthpiece between yellow teeth. "You should take cigarettes when they are offered, Herr Raller," he chuckled. "In this place, they are as good as Reichmarks." He lit his cigarette with a gold lighter, making sure that Raller had seen it before putting it away. Then he settled down fully on his flabby buttocks, leaning against the building as Raller did.

"Is there something I can do for you, Herr Spengler?" Raller probed.

The plump German answered: "Maybe it is what *I* can do for you, Oberstleutnant."

Raller shook his head. "I do not think so."

Spengler chuckled. "You are new here. Soon you will learn to accept what is offered. The others–" He swept his hand toward the yard between the rows of barracks where quite a few prisoners were lining up for exercise; then he continued: "The others have discovered there are only two ways in which to spend time in this place, and as you can see, most of them have chosen the correct path."

Raller sucked on his butt until the fire burnt his fingers, then he ground out the stub against a cement block that supported the building. "And that path is one that you have cleared yourself, I am sure," he said, raising his eyebrows.

"Most certainly, Herr Raller," smiled Spengler. "The path of the Third Reich."

Raller got slowly to his feet, working his shoulders until he heard several vertebrae snap into place. He looked off across the compound, not at Spengler. "I am not a member of the Party," he said bluntly. "Of course you already knew that."

"Of course," answered the fat Nazi.

Raller went on: "By the rules of Geneva I take my orders from the highest-ranking officer."

Spengler nodded. "That is correct, Herr Raller."

"And that is you, I suppose," added Raller, "regardless of any rank on your sleeve."

Spengler puffed himself to his feet and rolled his body around Raller until they were facing each other. Spengler's lips slid into a tightly pressed smile as a playful tick fluttered beneath the bag below his left eye. "Let us just say that I once served with Reinhard Heydrich. I am not your typical Lagergestapo," he winked.

Indeed you are not, thought Raller. Not if he had worked side-by-side with Heydrich. Reinhard Tristam Eugen Heydrich: The Butcher of Prague—Adolf Hitler's chief executioner. Master of Terror—Heydrich had been Hitler's personal choice as his successor until an assassin's bomb shattered any further dreams of unquenchable power. His untimely death brought immediate orders from the enraged Fuhrer: A Czechoslovakian bloodbath followed with the total annihilation of the village of Lidice, northwest of Prague. Now Raller was finding out that Spengler had worked with Heydrich. No, he was definitely not your typical Camp Gestapo. Dankwart Spengler was Waffen Schutzstaffeln to the maggot-infested core.

"What would you have me do while I am here?" Raller asked with mock humility.

The fat man chuckled again, ignoring his defiance. "There are plans made already for you, Herr Raller. In time you shall know of them." He pulled the smoldering cigarette from the bone holder and dropped it limply to the ground. Raller watched as he shook the spittle from the passage and pocketed the piece. Spengler smiled once again and the tick quivered. He clicked his heels from habit and made a slight bow, then turned and moved away toward the center of the yard.

Raller looked down at the cigarette. There was more than half of the butt left and he was down to his last Lucky Strike. His eyes remained motionless for several moments then he set his boot down on the cigarette and mashed it into the gravel.

Cecil Sitters slapped the last of the whitewash from a five-gallon bucket onto the near-finished barn door. He dropped the brush into a pail of water and turned to Clete Callahan, who was still slopping the other door, and yelled, "Gotta' drain the lizard." The older man nodded, so Cecil circled around and found a place inside the corral where no one in the main house could see him and he peed.

He watched the steady stream hit dry dirt and splatter and he moved his foot back to avoid the glancing spray. It was then that he noticed the sticky substance wedged between the sole and the heel of his left boot. Sitters threw his eyes to heaven and muttered, "Lord, please don't let me find that hound." He stepped back carefully and walked on the side of the foot toward the rear of the barn until he spotted a small stick and began to dig out the gob that had already begun to draw flies. He shooed with one hand while he scraped with the other, all the while cursing the absent animal under his breath.

When he had finished, he threw the stick as far as he could, then turned to chisel the remainder of the stuff off the heel by scraping it against a fence rail. He turned and stopped dead in his tracks. Marcy's old mongrel was sitting just two feet away, its eyes dripping from the heat and its mangy tail thumping the dirt, stirring up the dry mixture of manure and dust on the corral floor. In the dog's mouth–gripped firmly between the few good teeth that still remained– was the stick.

"Damnit ta' hell anyways," shouted Cecil, and he kicked out with all he had, catching his spur rowel on a scrap of barbed wire and almost falling. The hound dog dropped the stick, skittered under the opposite fence and disappeared into the chicken pen.

Cecil shook his head and closed the gate behind him, moving down the fence to the watering trough where he knelt to wash his hands in the mosscovered reservoir. He pulled off his bandanna and sloshed it around in the water, then wrung it out and wiped the perspiration from his face. About that time he heard the approaching plane.

He stood up and turned to the south, squinting into the glare, still wiping the back of his neck with the damp cloth. He pulled out his pocket-watch and checked the time. It was 2:54. McComb was back right on schedule.

Cecil retied the bandanna and walked back to the barn where Clete was still painting. He spoke loud and clear, as Callahan was a wee bit hard of hearing. "May as well put it up, Clete, here comes McComb."

The old cowboy nodded, tossed his brush into the pail then began gathering the other buckets and implements that were strewn around. Sitters moved out into the center of the yard and looked off toward the road where he could see the plane circle gently then straighten out and ease down, making an almost perfect landing. *Pretty good,* thought Cecil. *Not bad at all, considering the condition Josh was in when he'd arrived that morning.*

McComb had looked like death warmed over to Cecil when he'd ridden up on the roan–not the cheerful sort he usually was when the two men met. *Something must be bothering him,* Cecil had thought then he'd let it pass. Cecil Sitters was not one to pry into another man's business. Even when Josh had asked for a belt from Cecil's hideaway bottle as he changed in the tack room, Cecil hadn't said a word. McComb was over twenty-one. He knew what he doing.

Now Cecil watched as Josh McComb brought the plane through the ranchyard gate and taxied it into a final circle, planting the tail directly in front of the barn doors before shutting her down. He waited until the dust settled then moved in closer to give McComb a hand with the dog.

With Clete's help, the three of them pulled the plane inside. Callahan went back to his chores and the dog ran off chasing a lizard while Cecil followed Josh into the tack room. It was the coolest place on the spread at that time of the day so Cecil left the lights off. But there was still enough illumination coming through the several windows to see that McComb's hands shook slightly as he removed his leather cap and goggles and hung them on a nail. Cecil slid in behind his desk as Josh took off his jacket. Cecil's hand automatically went to the bottom drawer and he brought his bottle out, placing it on the desk. "Care fer' a belly-warmer, son?" Cecil asked. "Little hair of the dog?"

Josh turned as if he'd been waiting for the very words, his expression showing a somewhat embarrassed smile. He moved over to where Cecil was sitting and stopped. His eyes fell to the bottle. "You know I got troubles," he slowly said to the older man.

Cecil nodded casually and found two cups. He blew out the dust and poured four even fingers in both. Josh nodded back and took the nearest mug, lifting it into a toast. "Thanks," Josh said humbly.

Cecil held up his drink. "Any time."

The two men clinked cups.

Both of them poured the whiskey down. Cecil motioned for McComb to pull up a chair and he did while the cups were filled again.

Josh finally blurted out: "It's a woman, Ceese."

"Figgered," replied Sitters in a gentle way. "A man don't get hisself liquored up over no horse."

Josh had to chuckle. "No–a man sure don't."

"Nope," said Cecil, as he took a sip and watched as Josh drained his cup in one gulp. He poured some more. "Better slow down or you'll end up sleepin' with the livestock," he warned.

McComb nodded then reached into his shirt-pocket and took out a cigarette. Cecil found a match and scratched it on the desktop. Josh leaned in and puffed. "Thanks again," he said.

Cecil shook out the fire and settled back in the chair. "You wanna' tell me about it, Josh?"

McComb took a long draw then blew out the smoke. "It's Graylin," he said with some hesitation. "We had a little spat – a misunderstanding. She's gone to Boquillas, she's stayin' at the Hot Springs."

Cecil took his nose between his fingers and thumb then wiggled it back and forth slowly–a habit he had when he was thinking. "Do ya' reckon she's gone fer' good?" he asked.

Josh shook his head slowly. "No," he answered. "She just needs time to think. That's what she said. But I–"

"You want to be with her," cut in Cecil. "Ya' found out that ya' can't live without her. Ain't that so?" he added.

"You might put it like that, Ceese," said Josh. "I bin' drinkin' too damn much, I know that."

"Then it's simple," shrugged the older man.

McComb perked up. "It's what?"

"Simple as all get-out," Cecil continued. "Tomorrow's Sunday, ain't it?"

"Yeah," answered McComb.

"Well, jest ask Mr. Marcy if ya' can borrow the D.H.4. Then fly on down there an' get her."

"You mean–?"

"I mean, if ya' love the girl, then go get her. Fly on down ta' the Johnson Ranch, you know 'em there, they'll lend ya' a horse an' you can ride on over to the Springs. She's probably cryin' her eyes out right now this minute."

Josh reached for his cup, thought about it, then pulled his hand away.

"She wants to get married, Cecil."

"So?" Cecil wiped out his mug and put it back in the drawer. "Yer' the marryin' kind, ain't ya? Tried it twice before, didn't ya'? Liked it, too; if I recollect right, I've heard you tell me that a thousand times. Hell, I know ya' well enough to see that livin' without one of them lacy little critters is killin' ya'." Cecil glanced at the bottle and Josh received his silent message.

"Yeah," Josh said agreeing. "I reckon it is killin' me."

"Sure it is," Cecil went on. "Now you run on over an' talk ta' Mr. Marcy. I'll gas up the deHavilland for ya'."

A small grin broke across McComb's face. He shook his head. "You know something, Cecil? For someone who acts like a dumb old brush-buster most of the time, you sure have a way with words."

"I reckon I jest' watched my share of humans in my day, son," said Cecil. "Somehow the Lord gimme' a little inside look inta' human nature, I 'spect."

"Whatever it is, Cecil, I thank you," said Josh. "You said just what I needed to hear."

McComb stood up and shook Cecil's hand. He turned and moved out of the room, heading for the main house.

Cecil got to his feet and watched after his friend, mumbling to himself: "That's the secret, jest tell 'em what they wanna' hear." He picked up Josh's full cup and downed it with one long swallow.

"The pony run–He jump, he pitch–Heeee threw my master in a ditch– Heeee died an' the jury wondered whyyyyy–The victim of the Blue Tail Flyyyyyy." No one could hear McComb as he sang. He couldn't even hear himself. His off-key warbling was drowned out completely by the vociferous drone of the Eagle III engine. He was feeling better, much better than he had before his talk with Cecil. Now he was on his way down to the Bend. In the morning he would be with Graylin and by then maybe he'd know what he wanted to say to her.

With the dog at his side, tethered, as usual, to the cockpit next to him, Josh followed the Southern Pacific tracks out of Marfa about halfway to the town of Alpine where he made a sweeping turn and headed south. From that point on he followed the gravel road that wound its way lazily across the desert floor below. Staying within sight of the only road into the Big Bend from the west had become common practice for any aviator who flew the area. If one did happen to have a mechanical difficulty, or, God forbid, crash, the road was the only way rescuers could possibly reach you.

Josh remembered the days back in the early twenties when he and his partner flew the border watch, flying the river in search of marauding Mexicans. He recalled an incident in which two of his friends, two experienced pilots, Lieutenants Hank Peterson and Pat Davis, mistook the Rio Conchos for the Rio Grande and had put down near Boyame, Chihuahua by mistake. They had thought they were in the United States, having landed on the northern side of the river. So, thinking that they were still in Texas, the twosome wandered downriver, hoping to find the village of Candelaria and some assistance from the soldiers at a small post there.

Instead, they were captured by Chico Cano's gang and held for $15,000 ransom. A lanky, red-haired Texas Ranger had rescued the two after having paid the bandits only half the amount being asked. Both flyers had been decorated.

McComb glanced off to his right and watched the orange sun settle closer to the horizon. He could feel the heat waves shimmer past him at the low altitude. To the south he could see the distant etchings of the Chisos peaks against the cloudless sky, though they were still fifty miles away. Below, he could watch as the rugged terrain slipped by, becoming more hazardous and desolate with every mile.

It had been a while since Josh had flown into the "despoblado," as the Mexicans called the Big Bend, but it wasn't long before he was picking out familiar landmarks and rock formations.

At first he hardly noticed the truck below him, angled off the road with its nose in a ravine. He had to slow the plane and circle, dropping lower and making another pass before he recognized it as a disabled vehicle. It was on the third and even lower pass that he was able to make out the shapes of the butane tanks secured to the flatbed. It was Monroe Leaton's old truck, but there was no sign of Monroe.

McComb thought about landing then changed his mind. There was no way Leaton would have stayed with the vehicle. The road was traveled too little and Monroe himself was the most frequent user anyway. More than likely, the man had set out back toward Terlingua. There were more watering holes in that direction and besides, Josh was sure that he would have spotted a lone man walking in the desert deathbed that he had just flown over. He swung the plane parallel to the road once more and kept a constant watch.

Leaton spotted the plane before Josh saw *him* and as the wheels touched down, it was one tired but happy man that ran over to meet McComb as he climbed out of the cockpit with his canteen in hand.

"Missa' McComb," huffed Monroe with a tired smile. "I prayed to the Lord ta' send me an angel from heaven an' here you be–right out of the blue. Praise the Lord," Monroe added humbly. "Praise Jesus."

McComb handed him the canteen and Monroe nodded a grateful thank you before drinking. Monroe looked dusty and hot, but none for the worse. McComb climbed up on the wing, unfastened the dog and the two of them hopped down from the plane. Josh led Leaton and the dog into the shade of a wing and they sat down.

"My steerin' rod broke on that ol' truck o' mine, Missa' McComb. Run me inna' the ditch." Monroe wiped the sweat from his brow. "I thought I better try fo' Terlingua fo' I got baked alive. I prayed, Missa' McComb, an' Glory to Jesus—"

He took another swallow, then handed the canteen back to Josh who sloshed down some of the warm liquid himself and palmed a little for the dog before recapping the top. "I reckon it was a lucky coincidence that I happened along like I did," said McComb.

"Oh, no. No sir-reee," chuckled Monroe. "There ain't no coincidences, Missa' McComb. You know that. I done my prayin' an' it was God that sent you. That's who it was."

Josh smiled and got to his feet holding out his hand and helping the older man get up. "I'm headed down to the Johnson Ranch, Monroe," he said, "I'll drop you there. You can probably find the part you need for your truck out in that junk pile they got. I won't be comin' back 'til tomorrow. You're welcome to go with me, if you want."

Leaton's face widened into a half-grin, "That's jest fine with me, suh. Jest fine an' dandy. I did have me somethin' ta' do back at Marfa, but my truck breakin' down was God's will, an' I always follow the Lord. Besides," he added, "I reckon I could use a little rest."

"OK," said McComb, standing and nodding to the dog. "You climb in the back cockpit there, Monroe. Strap yourself in good an' tight."

McComb glimpsed a slight look of fright creeping across Leaton's face as the older man hesitated before he climbed up on the wing. "Monroe," Josh smiled, "have you ever flown in an airplane before?"

The black man shook his head. "No, suh," he said humbly. "My son was always sendin' me letters sayin' how he was gonna' take me up in a airplane when the war was over." Then his head dropped. "But that ain't gonna' happen now, is it?"

Josh shook his head, "I'm sorry about your son, Monroe. I only heard the news a couple of weeks ago. He was a good boy. I'm sorry."

"Well," said Monroe, changing the subject, "if I'm gonna' finally fly in a airplane, I reckon I better get used to it. I'll be an angel myself one of these days shortly, an' I sho' wouldn't wanna' *not* know how ta' fly."

The take-off from the rock-strewn road seemed smoother than the landing and within minutes, McComb, the dog and Monroe Leaton were moving deeper into the Big Bend at about five hundred feet and climbing.

After a half an hour or so, McComb could see the smoke from the smelter at Study Butte and he pointed it out to Monroe. The black man nodded with excitement as Josh took the plane down lower and several of the mineworkers on the ground waved at them. Monroe waved back.

The dog stood at the end of her harness with her front paws on the edge of the windscreen, the wind blasting in her face. The dog loved flying. Josh made a slight left rudder, turning the plane in the direction of the Chisos Mountains. He looked back and mouthed the word "Chisos" to Leaton, pointing toward the majestic peaks that jutted up from the sloping desert floor, all decked out with the fading afternoon light in pastel oranges and pinks. Leaton sucked in the tremendous vista. In all his years in the area, he had never seen the Big Bend from such a vantage.

As the plane drew closer to the Chisos, Josh climbed to a higher altitude just in case a hidden thermal lurked somewhere. He trimmed and settled back beside the dog for the next few minutes, pointing out some of the landmarks that he was sure Monroe would recognize.

Josh had begun to make a slow sweep south toward the Rio Grande when he happened to look back and see Monroe pointing off at something over near the mountains. He let his eyes follow Monroe's finger, and for just a moment, he caught a quick glimpse of what looked like another airplane. He glanced back at Monroe and the man was still smiling. Then Monroe's eyes widened and he pointed again. Josh swung back and sure enough, there it was–about a mile away–now much closer to the sheer southwestern face of the mountain range.

What McComb saw next, he didn't quite believe. The mysterious plane flew directly toward the towering wall of rock. Josh was sure it was going to crash and when the plane finally did disappear behind an outcropping, he knew that there would be an explosion following. There wasn't. The plane had just vanished. McComb looked back at Leaton and the older man shrugged. Josh motioned that he was going to fly over in the direction they'd last seen the plane to check it out. Monroe nodded that he understood.

What the outcropping had hidden was what the locals called "The Window." It was something that Josh had almost forgotten was there. The Window was a large V cut into the mountainside by thousands of years of erosion. It was the only water run-off for the basin–a large valley at the top of the Chisos, filled with wild game and ample vegetation, where at one time the Mescalero Apaches had secreted themselves successfully from the United States Army during one of their many escapes into Mexico.

Josh circled several times and when the angle was right, he could see the abandoned C.C.C. camp that marked the only sign of human existence in the basin. There was no airfield in the basin, only a dirt road that gave access to the camp. And there was absolutely no sign of the other plane.

The sun was about to dip below the western horizon. Shadows in the Chisos had been known to play tricks in the past on even the best of aviators. McComb kicked a hard right rudder then leveled out and aimed the nose toward the horseshoe bend in the river that he'd used for a landmark those many times long ago when he taught the young pilots out of the Johnson Ranch.

As the D.H.4 began to drop lower and lower, and the faint markings of the airfield came into view, McComb made a mental note to ask someone about the other plane that he and Monroe had seen. Josh knew that his eyes were not as good as they had been in his youth, but he was pretty sure that the plane had been painted solid black. And the more he thought about it the more he was sure that he had seen no markings–no identification numbers on the wings, whatsoever.

The wheels of the deHavilland touched ground with two almost-silent squeaks, and when Josh finally shut the engine down the ringing he thought was in his ears turned out to be the familiar sound of the Johnson Ranch dinner bell.

When their feet were finally on the ground, the dog spotted a covey of quail and gave chase. "Will that dog be all right?" asked Monroe. "This is pretty wild country down here."

"She'll be back in time fer' supper," answered Josh. "You can bet on that."

CHAPTER FIVE

"Josh McComb, you ol' peltflogger, what in hell's tarnation brings you down to the Bend?" Elmo Johnson shouted these words from the porch before Josh and Monroe had even cleared the small dirt parking area. "I took it fer' granted you'd be flyin' fer' the Yankees again this war," the old man added.

Josh shook his head as he and Leaton climbed the flagstone steps and were welcomed by the raw-boned Johnson who owned the place. "I still got that game leg, Elmo," said Josh. "You remember Monroe Leaton, don't ya'?"

"Certainly I do," said Johnson, shaking the black man's hand vigorously. "You used ta' live on the Starkey place over yonder. I remember ya' well, Monroe. Come on in, you two." He turned and yelled back through the open door, "Dos amigos fer' cena, Alice, por favor."

Josh put his hand up. "That's all right, Elmo." He nodded toward the two cars parked side-by-side in front of the main house, "You already got company, I see. We don't want ta' interrupt nothin'."

Johnson chortled, "Hell, you ain't interruptin' anything, my friend. Them ain't payin' guests anyways. C'mon." He ushered them into the main room of the Lodge and right out the back door to the courtyard where several tables had been pulled from the dining room and covered with red checkerboard cloths. The scent of barbecued venison wafted over the area and torchlight danced across the row of bottles set up on a makeshift bar.

Two older gentlemen stood near the table with complexions that matched the surrounding country. They looked up and smiled. "You remember Colonel Hattersby and Major Townsend don't ya', Josh?" asked Elmo. "They were down here in '32. Both retired now. They jest came back fer' a visit."

McComb shook hands all around and introduced Monroe. Then Johnson poured several drinks. "Y'all make yer'selves at home. Ha!" he choked back a laugh: "I reckon you could say that this was still yer' home, Josh. You built it."

"That's right kind of you, Elmo," McComb nodded.

Johnson turned to the others, "McComb an' a couple other fellers' staked this spread some twenty-ought-years-ago. I was jest lucky enough ta' be the better horse trader, I 'spect." He threw a large wink at McComb while the others chuckled.

A large man, dressed in white ducks and a loud Hawaiian shirt, stepped out onto the patio from one of the rear bedrooms. He sported a crisp Panama hat atop his balding pate and a green Havana dangled from his thick lips. Johnson turned at the man's arrival and shooed his other guests over to meet him. "Gentlemen, I'd like ya' all ta' say howdy to my most honored guest, Senator Gilmore Dobbs. He drove all the way down from Austin by hisself, savin' the taxpayers money, of course." Elmo winked, adding, "You know what I mean."

Dobbs seemed to bow ever so slightly with every handshake and Josh noted that it took some special courage on the Senator's part to place his hand in Monroe Leaton's, but he did. Monroe said, "Pleased ta' meet ya', suh."

Dobbs answered with a remote, "Yeah," then turned back to the others.

Johnson continued, "The Senator come all the way down here ta' welcome–"

Dobbs cut Elmo off. "I'm down here to unofficially represent the Great State of Texas on behalf of our beloved Governor, Coke Stevenson as sort of a prelude to the turning over of this land to the Federal Government come November."

Josh and Monroe nodded. A seductive woman's voice interrupted from behind. "I don't suppose that old deHavilland parked out there belongs to one of you gentlemen, does it?" the voice asked.

The senator excused himself, moving over to talk to another guest as McComb and Monroe turned to face a very attractive dark-haired woman with gray wisps who was dressed in whipcord jodhpurs and high laced boots. Josh appeared to be slightly uneasy by the woman's presence.

She smiled coyly. "Hello, McComb. Welcome back to the Bend."

There was an awkward moment as Josh fumbled for the right words. He obviously knew the woman and felt some embarrassment. "Uh, Katy," he mumbled. "Uh, this is my friend, Monroe Leaton. Monroe, may I introduce you to Miss Katherine Faver."

She laughed gracefully. Josh, though, was still uncomfortable. Katherine, in total control of herself, reached out and shook Monroe's hand.

"And, McComb," Katherine said without missing a beat, "you know Don Miguel Maldonado from Ojinaga."

McComb dipped his head to the distinguished, white-haired Mexican man who stood beside her.

"Sure," Josh said, and with a slight bow, "Mucho gusto, Don Miguel."

Maldonado removed his sombrero. His bow was sweeping. "Señor McComb. It has been many years, my old amigo," replied the Don with true humility. "Your friend, Mr. Leaton, and I already know one another. Buenos noches, Senor Monroe." The men shook hands and Maldonado continued: "And this is my friend from Mexico City, Señor Jose Sandaval."

The man called Sandoval stepped in closer. He was a slick looking man wearing a cotton business suit. He smiled, bowing to Josh and the others. "Con mucho gusto," he said politely.

Maldonado immediately took over the conversation. "We have just been showing off the despoblado to Senor Sandoval and his guests from the air. With Señorita Favor's assistance, of course."

Katherine chuckled. "I took them for a couple of loop-de-loops around the Bend, that's all," she said.

McComb perked. "That must have been you we saw, then, over near the south face of the Chisos."

"Not unless the Bravo changed its course," laughed Katherine. "No, we were down by Santa Elena then we circled over Lajitas once or twice for the view."

Josh scratched his head. "Me an' Monroe spotted a plane up near the basin: a black one. Couldn't see any numbers. Thought maybe it was someone from here."

Katherine shook her head. "No. It wasn't us. Heck, there're more airfields than this one down here now, McComb. The Big Bend has grown some since you were here last."

"Yeah, I reckon things have changed," said Josh. "Used to be a time when there wasn't anyplace to put an airplane down between here an' Marfa, that's fer' sure."

Katherine threw McComb a look. "I remember," she reminisced. "You ought to consider coming back down here, McComb. The Army's taken all the competition overseas. There's money to be made. I can't handle half my workload. I have crops to dust, I shuttle supplies for the big mines, and I still run an occasional border watch for the government."

"Oh," said McComb, humbly scratching his chin, "I've got my work cut out for me, too. I put in a regular week for C.D. Marcy. Then I run herd on the Germans they're keepin' over at old Fort Russell. I got my hands full, Katy."

"I noticed your plane was sporting some heavy armor," she said then turned to Johnson nearby. "Elmo's still got his deHavilland-VI, too, don't you, Elmo?"

"Sure do," responded Johnson. He directed his next words to Josh. "Sittin' right over yonder in the barn. Twin to the one yer' flyin' that Marcy owns, if I reckon correctly. Jim-Bob Pelliteer keeps her in flyin' condition for me. You both flew them two planes on border patrol fer' the Army back in the Twenties, didn't you? An' you both saw some action, too, if I recollect correctly. 'Corse you know that," he added.

"How is Jim-Bob?" McComb asked Johnson.

"Just fine," answered Elmo. "The boy works on that plane all his free time. Kid's a real buff on them old planes, he is. Too bad he's the way he is, he'd a made a damn fine soldier-boy."

"Jim-Bob's a good kid, Elmo," said Josh. "Where's he off to tonight?"

"I had him run over to the Terlingua store; Don Miguel's other guests run outta' tobacco."

"Other guests?" said McComb.

Katherine stepped in closer. "A couple of Dutch fellows who came up from Mexico City with Mr. Sandoval. They're the ones I took flying today."

The senator had been listening. He stepped back over to the others.

"Freedom Fighters might be a better word, Mr. McComb. The Nazis put a price on both of them. They're on a death list I'm told. Regular heroes in their own right. I met them this afternoon and gave them both my personal welcome to America."

Elmo piped in. "They're both washin' up right now, they'll be joinin' us fer' supper; a couple of real interesting fellas."

"If you say so, Elmo," said Josh. "I look forward to meeting 'em." He turned his attention to Katherine. "Say Katy, why don't you show us Elmo's D.H.4, that all right with you, Elmo?"

"Sure, go ahead," said Johnson. "That venison's got at least another twenty minutes ta' cook. Oh, an' Miss Faver, show 'im what we done with that south runway, why don't ya'."

Katherine, Josh and Monroe moved on through the house as the others began to re-cluster and continue the chatter. All, that is, except Senator Gilmore Dobbs. He watched after the three until their figures disappeared through the house and into the darkness of the night. Then he glanced toward Joseph Sandoval. As their eyes met, a subtle look passed between them, unseen by anyone else.

Raller lay on the top cover of his bunk dressed, like most of the others, only in his United States G.I. issue shorts. He listened to the strange sounds that spewed from the radio–American music, cowboy music, he guessed– though he'd never heard the style anywhere in Europe before. He drew some smoke from his last Lucky Strike and stared at a mud wasp that still chewed and packed at the walls of her home in the corner of the bed-frame above him. His thoughts were somewhere in the past, settled in behind the simple instrument panel of a triwing Fokker, back in the days when making war was a gentleman's game. He smiled to himself. It really hadn't been that enjoyable, had it? Not really. It was just that men seemed to forget the bad times while only remembering the good.

There was hushed conversation trickling from the far end of the room and Raller's eyes were drawn to where several of the officers–led by Spengler–were gathered around a small table going over some papers that he assumed were maps of some kind. Raller knew that these men were up to something. He'd seen them together before. He took another long puff on the cigarette then ground it out in a tin can on the floor next to the bed.

A fresh pack of Camels bounced across the wool blanket, landing near Raller's shoulder. He turned to see where they came from and found himself looking across to the next bunk where a young officer, whom he'd thought asleep, was indeed not. The man raised himself up on one elbow then whispered. "They are planning an escape, do you know that?"

Raller nodded. "I figured it was something like that."

"Some U-Waffe officers tried to make an escape from Arizona several months ago," the young man said. "They were caught. Herr Spengler seems to think we will have a better chance from this camp."

"What are the chances from here, my friend?" Raller questioned. "Have you not seen the country we are in?" Raller settled back, opening the cellophane on the cigarette pack.

"We are Afrika Korps," answered the younger man proudly. "We can survive the desert."

Raller raised his eyebrows. "You are planning to go with them?"

"If I am asked, yes," the man shot back, appearing to be offended.

Raller pulled a cigarette from the pack, lighting it, nodding a thank you. "I wish you success," he said, meaning it.

The young man rolled around, sitting upright, a smile on his face. "You will be with them too, Herr Raller."

Raller's eyes questioned the young man. "You know who I am?"

"Certainly Oberstleutnant," the young man said with a smile. "Everyone here knows who you are."

Raller turned away, his attention on the wasp once again. The younger man continued: "I have heard some of them talk about you, even before you arrived here. Have you not noticed that you are the only Luftwaffe officer in the camp?"

"Surely there are others," Raller said, puffing.

The young man shook his head. "No," he said. "You are the only one, believe me. I know this from what I have overheard." He leaned in closer. "They will ask you to go with them because you are a famous war hero. It will be good for the propaganda machine."

Raller was still puzzled. "Why am I the *only* Luftwaffe officer?" he prodded.

The young man found a cigarette of his own and Raller leaned across the open floor, lighting it for him. The man took a long draw before continuing. "I have heard that your being sent here was controlled entirely from Berlin," he whispered. "I have heard that to have a most famous war hero like yourself escape from an American camp would be very good news for our soldiers still fighting."

Raller shook his head. "I cannot believe that I am as important as that," he mumbled.

"Oh, but you are, Herr Raller," the young man continued. "You must realize how it will look to the world if a famous German war hero like yourself makes good an escape from an American prisoner-of-war camp."

Raller pondered. "But why this camp? There must be others that would offer a better opportunity–"

The young man cut in with: "That is *precisely* the reason why you have been sent here, I believe. Camp Russell is the most remote prisoner-of-war compound the Americans have; therefore, the most difficult to escape from, would you not think?"

Raller nodded. Things were beginning to come clearer for him. "Yes. For the Party it would prove a considerable achievement, no doubt."

"And with you, Herr Raller, safely back in the Fatherland," the young man continued, "it would certainly give the people something to cheer about ... a hero–of *two* wars."

Raller watched the young man's expression. He was not much older than Raller had been in the last war. *So full of pride*, Raller thought, *so full of honor. The direct opposite of men like Spengler who are such realities in this present baptism of fire.*

"Herr Raller," the younger man said, interrupting his thought. "You must go with them when they ask. It will mean so much to our country."

Raller nodded. "I will give it some thought. *If* they ask."

"God bless you, Herr Raller," the young man whispered.

Raller took another drag on the cigarette. "It will take many blessings, my friend. This is the Devil's country, for sure."

"I have been here six months," the young man offered. "It is no different from the Sahara. I will teach you how to survive, if you wish."

"Thank you," said Raller, nodding. "I will let you know."

The younger man smiled wide. "My grandchildren will be very proud of me for having known you, Herr Raller."

Raller returned the smile, speaking softly, "I will let the proper authorities know of the assistance you have been to me."

The young man shook his head. "No," he said. "You must promise that you will not tell anyone where you heard this … certain people would not like it."

Raller nodded, understanding. His eyes were still on the wasp as it tucked and folded the mud as the nest began to take shape. "I will say nothing," he told the man. "My word is good."

"I know that, Oberstleutnant," said the man. "The history books have told me that you are not only courageous, but also honorable."

Raller rolled his head toward the young man, "What is your name, please?"

The young man smiled again. "I am Ignaz Drescher. My friends call me Iggy."

Raller smiled back. "Thank you, Iggy. I am sure that I do not have to ask if you are a Party member."

Drescher started to laugh out loud and had to stifle himself. "There are many of us who are not, as you must know. But sometimes it is very difficult to recognize who you are talking to."

"I understand," nodded Raller.

Both men turned toward the other end of the barracks where the small group seemed to be breaking up. Several of the officers stood in the dim light and bid their farewells. Drescher turned back to Raller and spoke very softly. "To them we shall continue to be only bunk-mates, but I will let you know everything I hear."

Raller nodded. The shuffling of feet grew louder and he felt the presence of someone stop near the end of his bed. He glanced up and could make out the shape of Spengler through the bunk supports. He could see the fat jowls smile as the man studied young Drescher's body with what Raller knew were sadistic, lustful eyes. For once Raller felt comfortable being the age that he was and he felt sorry for the younger officers, still in their twenties, for he knew the sexual preferences of most S.S. officers–and Spengler, most certainly, had those fancies. Raller took a last drag on the butt and crushed it out, his look never wavering from Spengler. Raller could almost feel Spengler's stimulation spill into the tranquility; though the fat man said nothing. He just stood there for another long moment; then he turned and walked quietly to the end of the barracks and on out of the building.

"How much do you know about these Dutch friends of Don Miguel?" asked Josh as he ran his fingers over the wing of Elmo Johnson's D.H.4.

"Oh, come on now, McComb," said Katherine as she stood beside him and the plane. "They're on the level. I'm sure of that. I was with them all afternoon, they seemed like two of the nicest fellows you'd ever want to know."

"Are you sure that they're Dutch?" Josh continued. "I mean, did ya' see papers on em? Somethin' official?"

Katherine stammered, "Well, yeah, I– say, what are you, some kind of Federal official or something?"

"Of course not, Katy," Josh answered. "You just have ta' remember that there's a war on, that's all. Couple of foreigners comin' inta' the U.S. through the back door just don't seem right somehow."

Katherine laughed. "Ah hell, McComb, you worry too damn much. Don Miguel Maldonado's a Texican just like we are. If he says a man's OK, then he's OK by me."

Josh twanged one of the guide wires and nodded. "Reckon I'm gettin' a mite suspicious in my old age. Must come from watchin' over them German prisoners; or workin' part-time for the Army, whatever. I'm sorry, Katy, sorry."

"That's OK, McComb," she went on. "I know you didn't come all the way down here to play detective. So, why not cheer up some. Maybe tomorrow, if we have time, we can load up with some live ammo. I'll ride gunner and we'll take in some target practice over at Mule Ear Peaks, like in the good ol' days. What do you say?"

McComb's eyes dropped for a moment. "I'm afraid I can't, Katy," he stumbled. "I have ta' head down to Hot Springs in the morning; got me somethin' I have ta' do."

Wally Bowman leaned against the wall of the enlisted mess and sipped on a bottle of warm beer. There were Army regulations forbidding liquor on post, but Colonel Purrington was known to turn his head most of the time. That was due to the fact that the fort was so isolated and that the type of operation they were involved in–the supervision of dangerous war criminals–might cause undue stress to the men and "a few beers," now and then, never hurt anyone.

They were showing a movie inside the mess hall–John Wayne and Johnny Mack Brown in *Born to the West*–one that Bowman had seen several times before and had particularly enjoyed. But right now, because of the ninety-five degree heat, and a *special* appointment, Wally Bowman preferred to stand outside and just listen to the echoing gunshots and thundering hoofbeats.

While his ears continued to intercept the optical soundtrack that drifted through the open windows, his eyes kept a steady gaze toward the deserted building that was the stockade office and tool-house; situated about 20 yards from the perimeter of the garrison echelon. It was one of the only buildings in the camp that stood in complete darkness. The tool-house was also stationed less than ten feet from the double woven-wire fence that separated the Americans from their German captives.

Bowman took another sip of the beer then set the bottle on a railing and began to roll up his sleeves. He always kept them buttoned in the presence of the other soldiers because of the tattoo he carried on his left forearm. He had put it there himself when he was fifteen years old with a sewing needle and some thread wound around the point then dipped in India ink. He'd been in love then, and it had taken him two hours to prick the name "Peggy" into the skin of the trembling arm.

The tattoo had become an embarrassment to him almost before the blood had dried. Two days after he'd done it, Peggy had called him a shit-hole-cocksucker and run off with Oliver Hallinan. Bowman had immediately scraped away the scabs with his penknife and poured everything from alcohol to turpentine and even bleach on the wound, but the India ink had set and he realized then and there that he would carry "Peggy" with him for the rest of his life.

The tattoo had been a constant irritant for Wally Bowman until his mother had suggested that he try wearing long-sleeve shirts. They'd saved him one hell of a lot of ribbing since he'd been in the Army, except, of course, when he had to take one of his few showers with other men present.

When he'd finished rolling up his sleeves, he picked up the beer and glanced down at the tattoo. God, he wished he had never stuck that needle in his arm. Sometimes he wished it had been a knife instead–and that he'd stuck it in Peggy.

Bowman listened to the catcalls and jeers from inside as the film broke somewhere near the end of the final reel and he chuckled to himself. *Fuck those bastards,* he thought. *I'll teach 'em to put bugs in the shit-house. I'll teach 'em to play tricks on Wallace Bowman.*

His eyes narrowed as he saw the movement on the other side of the fence; the rotund figure as it crept from between the prisoners' barracks and to the deadline, where it stopped for a moment, then tossed something over the fence that landed behind the tool shed. Bowman continued to watch, not moving, as the figure stood there for another moment or two. He could feel the shadowed eyes staring at him in the dark. He finished the bottle and tossed it off the side of the porch. It landed with a dull thud.

Bowman stood in silence on the porch for several minutes after the figure disappeared back among the prisoners' barracks. He waited until the gunshots and hoofbeats swirled from within the mess hall again before he made his short walk to the tool-house.

Once there, he easily found the small waterproof match container and he quickly pocketed it. He whistled all the way back to the mess-hall and took a rear seat just in time to see Wayne and Mack Brown rear their horses and split up, going off on their separate trails, with the setting sun silhouetting them both in the billowing dust. He was also able to get the match container open and pull the two twenty-dollar-bills out, putting them securely in his wallet before the lights came up.

A single Mexican guitarist softly serenaded the remaining Johnson guests as they sat around the several tables on the tiled patio, carrying on their discrete conversations.

Josh and Katherine, dancing nearby, swayed slowly to the lone musician's winsome lover's ballad. Katherine's cheek rested easily on McComb's shoulder. She'd been there before and liked it. Her eyes were closed, her lips forming a soft smile, her mind reminiscing. She whispered in his ear. "What's the matter, McComb, am I bringing back too many old memories?"

Somewhat edgy, Josh answered, "Of course you bring back old memories, Katy. We were in love once."

After a moment Katherine asked him: "Are they *good* memories,

McComb?"

Josh hesitated. He smiled then nodded, saying nothing.

Katherine went on. "Mine are too," she told him. "We had a good thing going, McComb, you and me. Do you know that?"

McComb closed his eyes in thought. "Yeah," he answered quietly. "Yeah, I know."

Then Katherine spoke lightly. "Too bad it didn't work out. I just couldn't see myself as a happily married woman. That's all." She looked him directly in the eyes. "But I've always been sorry it didn't work out," she added truthfully.

McComb hesitated for a moment, then he said, "I've found someone else, Katy. Her name is–"

Katherine's quick finger to his lips stopped Josh from saying anything more. Then she said gently: "But, you're not married to her yet. Am I right?"

"No, Katy," answered Josh after a moment, "not yet."

"Good," she smiled. "Then we can have one last night together, can't we?"

Like most of the Texans Josh knew, he, too, was wary of outsiders. At first the two Dutchmen had brought with them a deep-set fear of foreigners that dated back to the Alamo. Then, after drinks, rare venison and some good conversation, Josh McComb had begun to warm up to the men. By the time Elmo Johnson brought out the tequila and everyone began drinking "Mes'can style," his previous hostilities had all but faded.

The big one was called Martin Leek, and the first time he had tried drinkin' "Mes'can," he ate the whole lime, peel and all. Katherine Faver had burst out laughing, slapping her thighs and almost choking. Then the smaller Dutchman had tried it. To everyone's delight, he hadn't missed a beat. Lime, salt and liquor: one, two, three. Everyone had applauded him and he stood with a grin from ear-to-ear, taking a small bow.

"Very good, Axel; very good," Martin Leek had said as he got up, clapping his friend on the back. "We must take this quaint custom with us to our own country once it is liberated."

"Yes, I am sure," the smaller man had commented. "It would make a most amusing diversion from the peace and tranquillity I so look forward to once we rid our beloved country of the Nazi invaders."

Senator Dobbs stood up, holding the tequila bottle high. He was just a little tipsy, and Elmo had to help steady him. "Here's to the war," he began, "and here's to life." He was slurring the words. "Here's to the men, and here's to their strife. Here's to the aeroplanes that circle in the sky, and to the gallant men who fly them, and to the flames in which they die." He expelled a silent belch and continued. "Shall we drink down from this bottle, while we pray to God on high–that He'll erase all war forever, now let us drink the bottle dry!"

The others broke into laughter and there was more applause as the senator did his best to drain the bottle. When he'd finished, he sat down beside Don Miguel and handed him the container.

It was the Texican custom for Maldonado to continue with a toast of his own. He waited until the laughter quieted down, and when he had everyone's attention, he got to his feet and held the bottle out. "I only wish to salute all of the free men in the world," he toasted.

He held the bottle toward Leek and made a small bow then he turned smoothly and made the same gracious gesture toward Axel. "To our amigos from across the sea: May God be with you."

CHAPTER SIX

McComb's dog barked good-naturedly and Jim-Bob Pelliteer grinned lopsidedly as the boy patiently held the saddle while Josh currycombed the dust and thistles from the horse's coat and mane. Monroe's mount was already saddled and the black man hummed a tune as he cinched up and adjusted the stirrups to fit his legs. Finally McComb turned to the young man: "OK, Jim-Bob," he said to the boy. "You go ahead and finish up here; I wanna' say g'bye to Don Miguel and his friends." He patted the boy on the shoulder then nodded to Monroe and the two of them headed over toward the house.

When they'd gone about twenty yards, Josh glanced back toward the corral, turning to Monroe. "Give the kid a little more time," he said, "an' he'll know as much about horses as he does about airplanes."

Monroe chuckled. "Come in handy don't he?"

Josh nodded. "You bet," he said with a wink. "I'm real glad he's found a home here with Ida an' Elmo. There are still some folks that'd like ta' send 'im to that institution up in Terrell County, you know."

Monroe glanced back at the boy who was trying to pet the dog at the same time he was fumbling with the cinch as he tried to straighten the saddle on McComb's horse's back. "I know," he chuckled softly. "It's funny how God works, ain't it? Makin' that boy slow in some ways then givin' him a gift when it come to mechanics. You know, Missa' McComb, that boy found me the part I needed to fix my truck outa' that junk pile in the barn, an' I'd gone through it at least a hunnert' times myself."

Josh smiled to himself. "He knows what he's doin'," he said. "It's just too bad some of the other folks 'round here can't see it."

"Yes suh, it's a real shame," said Monroe, shaking his head, "a real shame."

As their long shadows reached the porch, scribbled into the dry dust by the early morning sun, Elmo Johnson stepped out, followed by Maldonado, Sandoval and the two Dutchmen. Monroe and McComb stopped at the foot of the steps. "We just wanted ta' say that it was a real pleasure meeting you all," said Josh with a pleasant smile.

Maldonado returned the smile and Sandoval made a short bow; the Dutchmen stepped down and shook hands. "We all had a very charming evening, Mr. McComb," said Leek, his eyes scanning the ranch yard. "Miss Faver had promised to take us for a sunrise flight this morning but I'm afraid she never showed up. And alas, now it's too late, I suspect. You walked her to her bungalow last night, Mr. McComb. Was she perhaps, feeling ill?"

Josh smiled again, "I'm sure she's fine, Mr. Leek. She prob'ly overslept, that's all."

The two men laughed. "Give her our best, if you will," said the Dutchman. "Tell her it was our pleasure. I'm sorry, but we must be off now. We shall be staying with Señor Maldonaldo for another week at his rancho in Ojinaga. Maybe we shall meet again before we must depart."

They shook hands all around then the visitors climbed into their car. Don Miguel started the engine and shifted into gear. Leek stuck his head out of the rear window. "Please tell the gracious senator goodbye for us," he said, "if you would be so kind."

"We will," said Elmo. "Y'all come back an' see us now, ya' hear?"

The clutch was engaged and the car boiled away into the vastness of the desert.

McComb turned to Johnson. "Two nice gents," he said. "Hope everything works out for 'em. I mean the war, an' all."

Monroe added: "Yes suh. An' I'll keep sayin' a little prayer for all the other Dutchfolks those Nazis are holdin' hostage."

"You do that, Monroe," said Elmo, winking at the black man. Leaton knew that it came from his heart.

Within five minutes, both McComb and Monroe were in the saddle and watching the Johnson ranch disappear over their shoulders. "You take good care of my dog, now will ya'?" Josh called back to Jim-Bob. The boy grinned proudly and nodded as he held the dog and watched the two riders move off into the desert. The day was cooler than usual. It would be a good ride to Boquillas. Josh looked forward to the time he'd have to think while they trekked through the southeastern Bend. He figured that they'd be at the Hot Springs in less than four hours.

Wally Bowman stepped out onto the porch of the enlisted mess and stopped for a moment to pick at some sausage lodged between his molars. He could see the parallel rows of glistening bodies through the chain-link and barbed wire, lined up like chessmen as they went through their calisthenics while a booming foreign voice counted cadence. Bowman paid them little attention as he checked his watch then headed out past the garrison echelon to his barracks. It was 0658. His next watch began at 0700.

Several things turned in Bowman's mind as he crunched his way across the gravel. One of the abstractions, one that stood out from the rest most of the time, was a daydream he'd had since childhood. In his fantasy, Wally Bowman was a king–a monarch who sat upon a throne made of rubies and pearls, with a footstool of crimson velvet and solid silver legs. His crown was pure gold, unbroken in its perfection with an array of sparkling jewels that encrusted the entire surface. His one duty, the only piece of work Bowman performed as king, was sentencing people to execution. "To death!" his royal voice would echo whenever the face of a resented person was brought before his mind's eye.

The first person he had ever sentenced and sent to the chopping block had been his mother. He had been five. Her crime: his birth. The second person, of course, was his father. There had been no face for this dastardly offender, no visible neck for the guillotine blade to fall on. In retribution for his father's non-existence, the make-believe monarch had sent what seemed like hundreds of others to the gallows in his place. They had been people he knew, both men and women, and some of them his close friends. Their collective sin had been: making fun of Wallace Bowman–fucking with the king. "Lop off their heads," the king had commanded.

And it had gone that way, this recurring reverie, through his childhood and teenage years. This obsessive dream of absolute power; this ability to instantly dismiss any problem from his life by merely creating the court in his mind in which he alone was the final judge. Whenever he came face to face with a dilemma, all he would have to do was close his eyes and there he would be, sitting high up on the throne, snapping his fingers and pounding the floor with his sceptre. Making decisions, judging the defendants of crimes committed against he–the king–then sentencing them to immediate extinction.

As Bowman grew older and finally into a young man, he sat back one day and tried to count the number of offenders he'd sent to damnation. There'd been teachers; a scoutmaster or two; his fourth-grade sweetheart; the storekeeper who had caught him stealing gum-balls; two of his friends who'd snitched on him; a lifeguard at Coney Island; 17 cops; three social workers; six judges; one recruiting sergeant; nine corporals; five sergeants; three lieutenants; a captain; and one major. A pretty good record, he thought. All of them as guilty as hell; every one of them had made the grave mistake of trying to fuck over Wallace Bowman. He'd run down the list and had to chuckle to himself. He'd left out a bunch of the most important felons–the regular soldiers who'd tried to screw with him. Hell, there were too many of them to count. When he'd joined the Army, he'd had to start lining up the bastards and blowing them away with an imaginary machine gun, there'd been so many. But even with all the chimerical blood he had spilled, Wally Bowman felt justified. Being the king in his daydreams seemed to do the trick. It had helped him to grow up well adjusted and free from guilt, he thought, unlike most of the others around him. Bowman was quite proud of himself. And even when he held back the angry tears, late at night when he was as alone as he could get under the blanket in his bunk, Wally Bowman could comfort himself. For in his heart, he really knew that he was the king.

The barracks were empty as Bowman entered through the double screen-doors. All the windows were open, their shadeless frames casting stark sunprints across the orderly ranks of bunks and onto the spotless, highly polished floor. It took a moment for his eyes to adjust to the contrast and he could hear a solitary fly as it snap-rolled against the top of a windowpane–too dumb to escape out the open bottom. *Just like them krauts,* he thought, *so many ways to break out of this joint, and too dumb to see them.* He chuckled to himself. Hell, one of them had even given him forty smackers to send a postcard for him. Dumb suckers these Germans. A postcard; one lousy postcard that he'd paid a penny for at the P.X. The guy had actually given him forty fucking dollars, and all he had done for it was copy the guy's message onto the card, scribble the address and get it mailed. The German didn't want a Marfa postmark on it so he'd given the postcard to a truck driver who was headed for Del Rio, given the guy a quarter to mail it. Forty bucks! Shit. If that kind of thing got to be a regular deal, he might just get rich off of this damned war.

Bowman moved down the row of bunks until he came to his own. He stripped off his blouse and soiled T-shirt and opened his footlocker for a fresh change. That was when Wally Bowman damn near shit his pants. Someone had put a Mexican-red tarantula on top of his shaving kit.

The steam billowing from the stainless steel showerhead reminded Raller of the baths the flyers in the Great War used to take upon completion of a mission. Back then, there were smiles on the men's faces, laughter in the tiled rooms; champagne would flow in celebration of their many victories–a different war, a different time, a different place. Echoing now like the flushing toilet outside the shower stall.

Iggy's fresh young face stood up and he stepped into the shower area, turning on the showerhead beside Raller's. "I will scrub your back, if you like, Herr Raller," he offered childlike.

"That is kind of you, Iggy, but no," said Raller. "I am doing all right by myself."

The young man smiled again then scooped up a soap bar and began to lather up. "You know," he went on, "it was hard, at first, getting used to all the American luxuries."

Raller nodded, "I know."

"In the Fatherland we travel in boxcars," continued Iggy. "In Afrika, we walk. Then we are captured and they care for us like we are newborn babes."

"What rank do you hold, Iggy?" Raller asked.

"Oberleutnant, Herr Raller."

"So young for such a big job," said Raller, rinsing his arms.

"A field commission, I must confess," the young man went on. "Most of my group was killed at Tobruck. I must admit I was not the best choice."

Raller rinsed the suds from his hair, letting the warm soapy water cascade down his shoulders and to the cement beneath his feet. He closed his eyes. "I'll wager you made a fine officer, Iggy."

The young man laughed, "I commanded in the field for exactly fifteen minutes. A mortar knocked me unconscious. I awoke behind British barbed wire."

Raller shook his head. "And that was that, I suppose?"

Iggy did not answer. Even with the sound of the spraying water, Raller sensed the presence of someone else. He rinsed the soap from his eyes and opened them. Spengler had just stepped into the stall. The fat Nazi stood facing the young man with a half-cocked smile on his lips, his eyes lapping at Iggy's nakedness. Then he slapped the boy lightly on the buttocks and nodded toward the door. "I would like to be alone with Herr Raller."

Iggy's eyes never went back to Raller. He stood to attention and shot Spengler the Nazi salute. "Heil Hitler," he snapped.

"Heil Hitler," Spengler's bare heels clicked back.

Spengler waited until the young man left the area then the pelting water would cover what he had to say. Raller felt a burning bile creep into his gullet; his eyes could not help but fall on Spengler's grotesque belly. Not a firm paunch, like so many older, well-fed officers, but a large, flabby pouch, like the rippled blobs made when raw cake batter is poured into the pan. Rolls of opaque, loose flesh that all but obscured Spengler's dwarfish penis–with its puckered head peeking out below as if gasping for air.

"I have orders for you from Berlin, Herr Raller," Spengler said as he stepped under the showerhead vacated by Drescher. "Putting all personal animosities aside, you are to join us." Then he added: "When the time is right."

Raller made direct eye contact with the man. "Am I to assume you are speaking of escape, Herr Spengler?" he asked.

The blue eyes flashed. Sepulchral bulbs, laced with cerebration deeply connected to evil, Raller thought. "Escape?" said Spengler. "Of course, escape, Herr Raller. Is that not our first priority?"

Raller cocked his head. "It might be that I find where I am, agreeable," he told Spengler.

The Nazi found the soap bar and began slowly to work up suds on his arm. "Do not be the fool, Herr Raller. You are wise enough to know of our ways."

"I am somewhat familiar, yes," said Raller.

Spengler went on. "Then you realize that we can involve your family."

Raller nodded. He knew the Waffen S.S. and their ways quite well.

"Then I should say no more," Spengler continued. "Except to say that it has been decreed, by the powers higher than both of us, that you join us. It is expected that you will comply."

Raller took in a mouthful of the showerhead's volley then spat it against the wall.

Spengler smiled. "Then you do consent," he said with a sneer. "I would hate to see anything happen to your loved ones when you have been placed in such a position."

Raller's vise-like grip on Spengler's testicles caught the fat man completely by surprise. A nauseating cramp jolted the Nazi's knees while two sharp pangs bolted deep inside his stomach. His body made a defensive attempt to pull away but the vise tightened. Beads of perspiration popped through several pores on his forehead as the excruciating torment increased. His eyes found Raller's, inches away. "You, too, are in a position, Herr Spengler," said Raller through gritted teeth. "A position from which, with one small twist, you will lose your manhood–what there is left of it. I will warn you only once," he continued, "if any harm comes to my family–you will die. And I say this and you remember it well–all the people of Lidice combined did not suffer as you will."

Spengler nodded slowly. The cords from his testicles were stretched taut, jerking sharply at every nerve throughout his body, causing his tongue to spasmodically compress against the roof of his mouth, his eyes to well with tears.

Raller continued speaking slow and even. "Then you must understand that when I say I will go with you, it is only because of the position you have put me in."

Spengler gasped, attempting to acquiesce, his lungs shocked into temporary inutility.

"I will cooperate," Raller went on, "only because I know that my family's safety is *not* in your hands–for no other reason. If you *were* directly responsible, Herr Spengler, I would not hesitate to castrate you this very minute."

Raller released his grip and Spengler dropped to the floor, writhing on the saturated concrete in a swirl of suds like a floundering sea lion.

Raller stared down at him, watching for a moment as Spengler huffed, trying to avoid drowning in the torrent of water that still cascaded down, his knees pulled up as far as they would, attempting to stem the pain pounding his intestines.

Raller turned and went to get dressed. It would be twenty minutes before Spengler could do the same.

The first Sunday morning service of the Marfa Cavalry Missionary Baptist Church let out at exactly ten o'clock. After church it was a customary Sabbath--day ritual for Captain Red Collinson to take the old Ford out for a Sunday drive and then stop by the cemetery near the Mexican section and spend a half-hour or so with his Juanita.

This particular day of rest presented something a little different for Collinson. As one of the church deacons, he'd been stationed at the front doors throughout the service. About halfway through, he'd heard what he'd thought had been a late arrival drive up. He had taken a peek through the crack in the doors and seen that the car wasn't a familiar local at all, but an Army staff car, either from Fort Russell or Fort Davis. He wasn't sure until he recognized the soldier behind the wheel as Colonel Purrington's regular driver.

Several days earlier, after the big council meeting–the one where Collinson had spoken and quieted his neighbors nerves on the German camp situation– the very same man, this Army driver who now sat out front in the olive-drab Dodge smoking like a chimney, had delivered an envelope to the ranger office. An envelope marked "Personal"– addressed, quite officially, to Collinson.

The letter had stated, quite simply, that if the Commander of Fort Russell–Purrington–ever needed to confer confidentially with the Texas Ranger Captain, and it appeared that the subject matter might require complete privacy–meaning the Marfa phone system would be out of the question–then the colonel would send his personal driver into town to track down the ranger's whereabouts. And when and if that happened, in a very casual way, the driver would honk three times and continue on his way so as not to attract any attention. Then Collinson would slip out of town and drive the back way to the Fort where the two men could converse in complete privacy.

But when the Army driver blasted away three times right at the moment The Reverend Fred Hayes was about to lead the flock in prayer, causing everyone to turn around and the good minister to call out, "Hey, Red. Go an' see who in the hell that is makin' all that noise, will ya'?" Collinson decided just to climb on into the staff car and let the Army pay for the ride out to Russell–seeing's how the whole cover was blown anyway. Not to mention the fact that the state's allotment of gas rationing stamps for the last month hadn't come in yet.

So that was how Red Collinson found himself face-to-face over a couple of stiff ones with a very distraught Colonel Purrington later on that Sunday morning; instead of making his regular sojourn out to the cemeterio Mexicano with his customary wildflower bouquet and pint of whiskey, where he usually sat for a spell beside his dead wife's grave.

"You and I, Captain Collinson," began Purrington, "appear to have been handed a top-secret priority. One, I am sorry to say, that has been covered in political excrement."

The colonel slugged down the entire contents of his glass while Collinson sipped and listened. His eyes wandered around the room as the officer poured some more from a crystal container. The room hadn't changed one slight bit since the turn of the century when it had served as headquarters for the cavalry post. Purrington, in his antiquated way, appeared to fit in perfectly.

The colonel fell back into the overstuffed, red leather chair, crossing his highly polished boots on the desktop. He began slapping the boot-tops rhythmically with his ever-present quirt. He took another long draw on the whiskey before he spoke again. "A postcard was intercepted by the O.S.S. in Austin," he continued. "It was on its way, apparently, to a very high-ranking Nazi spy in D.C."

Collinson nodded, taking out his pipe and casually preparing a load, completely unaware of the distasteful look from Purrington.

"What I'm about to tell you, Captain," said Purrington in a loud whisper, "is strictly confidential."

"It'll go no further, Colonel," said Collinson. "You can rest assured."

Purrington got to his feet and began to pace. "A postcard, Captain, a picture postcard with a snapshot of the Rio Grande on it, believe it or not; sent from this camp by one of my own goddamned prisoners. From right under my nose."

"That's possible, I 'spect," said Collinson, thumbing tobacco into the pipe's bowl.

Purrington picked up an official-looking folder from his desk, found a piece of paper and handed it to Collinson. "Here's the message that was written on it. Go ahead, read it."

Collinson found his wire-rimmed reading glasses and slipped them on. Then he looked at the paper. He read:

Sid

Texas is great. Saw a real stampede the other day. Too bad you didn't go with us. We have seen beaver, cougar and an eagle. I will be seeing you soon. We'll be back by Friday. Drank something the other night called Aguila. Got drunk.

Your friend,

Jack Ballena and family

Collinson wiped at his nose and removed the glasses, putting them back in his pocket. He handed the paper back to Purrington and continued preparing his pipe. "Looks all right ta' me," he said. "Lotta' things like that're sent back home by the tourists that come through here. All the time," he added.

"Yes," Purrington said anxiously. "Yes. That is just what they wanted it to look like. A simple postcard sent off by some vacationing vagabond. So simple, in fact, that if it hadn't been for the address, the O.S.S. boys would have missed it."

Collinson struck a Blue Diamond and puffed. Purrington winced at the smoke then continued, "Now look, look at this." He handed the ranger another piece of paper. On it was the same message; only now, certain words had been officially underlined and stamped by the O.S.S.:

Sid,

Texas is great. Saw a real <u>stampede</u> the other day. Too bad you didn't <u>go</u> with us. We have seen beaver, cougar and an <u>eagle.</u> I will be seeing you soon. We'll be back by Friday. Drank something the other night called <u>Aguila.</u> Got drunk.

Your friend,

Jack <u>Ballena,</u> and family

"You see, it's a secret message." Said the colonel. "'Texas stampede go. Eagle will soon be Aguila.' And it's signed, Ballena."

Collinson shrugged, handed back the second piece of paper and took his seventh puff. He found another match and re-lit the pipe.

Purrington stopped pacing and faced the ranger captain. "Yes, sir, we've definitely got a problem on our hands, you and I, captain. A very *large* problem."

Collinson waved the flame out and casually replied, "They're gonna' try an' escape, are they?"

The colonel cleared his throat in an embarrassed flutter, "Uh, yes, Captain. Exactly." He took the second piece of paper and scanned it again. "'Texas stampede go' obviously means us, Fort Russell. At least that's what our code-breakers tell us. But due to certain circumstances, we're officially not supposed to know about this."

Collinson raised an eyebrow, "How's that?" he asked curiously.

Purrington re-sat himself and began hammering with the quirt again, "This, agent, spy, whoever that postcard was sent to. He's just too big of a fish, I'm afraid. The O.S.S. and my superiors would rather not interrupt any correspondence, so they sent the original postcard on. I guess I should feel grateful they even informed me."

"Sounds like he's bait for a bigger catch," muttered Collinson.

Purrington slapped his quirt hard, "On the nose, Captain. But, in the meantime, it looks a pretty good chance that they're planning an escape. And damnit, I'm under direct orders to ignore it. I'm to be on my own, Captain. The damn Army won't help me one bit."

"And that's why I'm here, I suppose," said the ranger.

"And that's why *you're* here, Captain Collinson," echoed Purrington. "It appears that I may be needing your help."

Collinson cleared his throat. "I'm understaffed; you know that," he said softly.

Purrington nodded, "Yes, I know. And so am I, but I'm afraid that's where it stands. Just you and I, Captain, and our small staffs; joining together in pursuit of those Third Reich ragamuffins should this jailbreak turn out to be a reality."

Collinson picked up his glass and drained the last of the warm liquid. Purrington refilled both receptacles.

"So, what you're saying, Colonel," Collinson went on, "is that the American Government knows all about what's going on, only they can't admit to it, or they might miss their chance on uncovering something much bigger. Is that it?"

Purrington nodded, "In a nutshell."

"Then if it happens," said Collinson, "we'll jest' have ta' do our best, won't we?"

Purrington shook his head. For the first time since he had received the priority message, he felt some of the load lift. "That's right, Captain," he said. "And what makes it somewhat amusing is that we can't even prepare for it."

Collinson shrugged, "We'll catch 'em, Colonel. This is Texas, not a European battlefield."

"I understand that, Captain," said the colonel. "I realize that you are a professional in these matters, but–"

"I'm a Texas Ranger, Colonel," Collinson cut in, "an' I bin' trackin' Mes'cans and border weasels down in the Bend damn near all my grown life. Between you an' me," he went on, "I don't think them cabbage-suckers'll have a Chinese chance crossin' that hard country."

"They are Afrika Korps, Captain," said Purrington bluntly. "They've been nursed on the desert."

Collinson got to his feet, draining the glass once more. "They only fight in the desert, mister. We Texicans *survive* here."

Purrington couldn't help smiling, as he got up, moving around the desk. "You know, Captain," he chuckled, "even with our hands tied behind our backs, I feel this little exercise might prove somewhat enlightening for us both."

"I 'spect it could," said Collinson, setting down the glass. "You jest' let me know when, an' I'll be there. I'm always ready to do what I can ta' help Uncle Sam."

Purrington agreed, and the two men moved toward the door. "The rest of the message, we think, has something to do with the route they plan on taking. Maybe you can figure it out."

Collinson stopped for a moment and thought. "Well, aguila means eagle in Mes'can lingo, I do know that. Let's see, 'Eagle will soon be Eagle.' Maybe they plan on sproutin' wings an' flyin' 'cross the border," he joked.

"I doubt that seriously, Captain," said Purrington, "but see what you can come up with if you can. I'll be in touch. Just remember, this is all top-secret, whatever that means."

Collinson nodded, reassuring the officer. "I bin' through it all before, during the Big War," he said. "It's all part of the game, Colonel. But that don't keep it from bein' a deadly one."

"Thank you, Captain," said Purrington, as he pulled open the door.

The ranger stopped once more, still pondering on something. Finally, he looked Purrington directly in the eye and said: "That message was signed, Ballena. That means 'whale' in Mes'can. Now you don't suppose them krauts plan on crossin' the Rio Grande in a submarine, do ya'?"

CHAPTER SEVEN

Josh had wanted to circle around and stop by Boquillas first to find out if Graylin might be visiting with friends there. The two of them had made a few acquaintances in the small Mexican border town when they'd stayed together at Hot Springs before, sharing one of the intimate rock-walled rooms. But by noon, when he and Monroe crossed the Tornillo Creek bridge, there was undeniable evidence that the swirling black clouds they'd been watching form for the past few hours had let go somewhere nearby. The usually dry creek bed was now alive in a wash of twisted mesquite, greasewood and shifting desert detritus that had chanced to be in the path of the snapping ophidian of brown murk that now gushed down the small gorge toward the Rio Grande.

Quivering flares of heat-lightning fluttered silently deep within the Sierra del Carmen mountain range, mostly on the Mexican side, illuminating the expanding skyswells and slapping intermittent silhouettes of the two riders alongside the clip-clopping hooves of their mounts as they turned south toward the river.

A ghostly wind picked up from nowhere and by the time they spurred the horses into the small Hot Springs compound comprised of a post-office/general store beside a line of stone cabins, the rain pellets had begun to fall. The large drops crashed into the dry dust in a staccato of minute explosions that made the earth appear to bubble in anger.

"Take the horses over to the barn," Josh shouted over a sharp clap of thunder as he dismounted. "I'll go check an' see if she's here."

The black man nodded, dismounting also, then gripping the reins and yanking the two trembling animals along behind him. The rain was now coming down in angular sheets. Josh watched for a moment as Monroe and the horses disappeared into the deluge, then he turned and headed toward the main structure.

The cool damp from outside crept in through the double doors, accompanying McComb, melding with the smells of stale whiskey and the years of human occupation that hung heavily between the thick walls. The furnishings were a general everything–rotting pelts and mildewed blankets sagged from the drooping beams, separating the one room into several sections: The post office, with its warped card-table desk and sorting area; the general store, with hand-made shelves loaded to capacity with the ample staples required by those who traded there; the cabin rental desk, created many years earlier by turning two peeling steam-trunks on end and placing a splinter-prickled board across them both; and the bar, another level surface, with its back-bar hewn from rough wood and yucca staves, cluttered and piled with hand-made trinkets and half-empty bottles.

Josh stood for a moment, letting his eyes harmonize with the room's eerie glow: a strange light produced by the already-gray illumination filtering through the two grime-encrusted windows that provided the only link to daylight. The rain pounded the galvanized roof with horrific applause, all but drowning the slow, hollow ring made when McComb's spurs followed him across the scuffed and battered floor to the bar. Josh measured the contents of each bottle with unslaked eyes. The thought of Graylin's presence tickled at the skin of his scrotum and at the same time made his stomach turn sour. His brain sent two messages in unison–the first, to search and find his woman as quick as he could; and the second, to stop for one moment and guzzle as much of the brown liquid as possible to calm his nerves.

His hand reached mechanically for the closest bottle, clammy fingers closed around the neck. As he raised it slowly, bright lightning flashed again from outside, firing a flickering blaze through the room for a stark second– bouncing a blurred reflection in the glass of the bottle: A face, a woman's face.

"Thank you for coming," the reflection said.

McComb didn't reply. He just turned around and stared at her for a long time. He eventually set the bottle down so he could take her into his arms.

Monroe Leaton stood under the lean-to across from the general store and tried to roll a soggy cigarette. He had seen the woman enter the building and he knew his place was not to interfere. He recognized his friend's need to be alone with his woman and he understood McComb's love for her just as he perceived the uncertainty that churned within the man. *If it's the Lord's Will,* he thought, *everything'll work out fine.* That was the way Monroe Leaton believed–*always* in the Lord's Will–because for Monroe Leaton, The Lord had the final say on everything.

Leaton settled into an old rocker that had only three legs and propped himself against the side of the barn for a spell. He lit his cigarette and closed his eyes, listening to the rain. He didn't see the two figures as they ran from the building toward the cabins. Monroe Leaton just settled back and spent some time communicating with his Higher Power–his Lord. As it had been with him for a long time, Monroe Leaton was at total peace with himself.

By two o'clock that afternoon when they came out of the cabin, Graylin had agreed she would go back to Marfa with him. They had decided that the two of them would return on horseback to the Johnson Ranch and they would ask Monroe if he would drive her car back and meet them there. Then the two of them would fly home while Jim-Bob Pelliteer took Monroe to his truck. They would come back down to Elmo's for Graylin's car later.

What they hadn't planned on was the Tornillo Creek Bridge. It was no more. A flash flood had unearthed the structure, sending it to the Rio Grande. Now it was somewhere in Mexico where its planks and concrete would more than likely end up as a beam ceiling and corner stones for some lucky estanciero's jacal.

A new resolution had to be improvised and it was decided that Monroe and Josh would ride over to Boquillas and negotiate for a horse for Graylin. Mexican horses came cheap and Boquillas was only a half-hour away. McComb assured Graylin that they would be gone no longer than a few hours. He also promised her that the two of them would spend a couple of days at the springs at another time, *if* he could talk Marcy into another short vacation. Maybe when the roads dried up and they came back down to the Bend to retrieve her car.

Graylin watched the two men as they spurred the horses across the shallow Bravo and melted into the Mexican artemisa. It never crossed her mind that she would not see either one of them for at least several days.

Boquillas, Mexico sat atop a small bluff overlooking the Rio Bravo and seemed to drip sorrow from its adobe bricks. The two horses left sharp crescent impressions in the soft, slippery clay as Monroe and McComb rode slowly into the tiny village. It was siesta time and the streets were vacant and deserted as the animals' hooves sent their hollow rebound between the drying buildings. Josh knew that one establishment would cater to them at that hour and they reined up in front of the local cantina. They tied off and entered the building through a low portico.

The belly of the cantina was ten degrees cooler and smelled of lye, pungent sweat and rosewater. The several empty tables and raw wood benches served as landing strips for the squadron of horse flies that appeared to be practicing touch-and-goes until Josh and Monroe interrupted them. The flies dispersed and, as if on command, stuck themselves to the greasy walls between the scattered bullet-holes and the wasp nests that sealed the corners like dried peanut butter.

A stringy man was slouched behind the once-expensive, but now gone to paint-peeled bar. He was reading a month-old Chihuahua newspaper and working at the wax in his ear with the dull end of a bent safety pin. He didn't look up when the men entered through the sagging bat-wing doors that slap-slapped behind them. It was only after McComb cleared his throat and took several steps across the dirt floor that the bartender finally acknowledged the two. The man folded the newspaper and stuck both it and the rusty pin under the bar out of sight. He wiped his hands on his scurf-crusted apron and flashed a plaque-fringed golden smile in their direction.

"Buenos tardes, hombres," he said, before switching to broken English. "Is there something I, for you, can do?"

McComb nodded, moving up to the bar. "Si, Señor, he answered, "I would like to know where there might be a good horse for sale."

The man's eyes lit up. "Oh, si. Caballos. Yes, I think I know where there is one. It–" His voice trailed off, his eyes re-focusing on someone behind McComb and Leaton who had just come in.

Josh turned slightly and saw the silhouette of the Zapata sombreros standing just inside the door. The distinct, mechanical click of a Mauser bolt-action whipped his attention to another door in the rear. He felt the strong black hand of Leaton's lock around his own right wrist, stopping his automatic reflex as it grasped for the gun at his waist that wasn't there–a habit he hadn't kicked since the war, twenty-six years earlier.

A familiar heavily accented voice spoke from the doorway: "You will come with me, Señor McComb. Mr. Leaton will stay here with my hombres. Please cooperate and no harm will come to either of you."

A small warm breeze sent a tattered curtain fluttering, letting a ray of damp sunlight slip in across the speaker's face. It was Don Miguel Maldonado.

Josh went with Maldonado and two of his men down a small incline behind the cantina to an adobe back-house that was pressed against the flagstone bluff, its fourth wall actually the boquillas itself. The inside was musty and dark and though it was closer to noon than night, several lanterns lit the room. Maldonado asked that Josh seat himself, and when he did, his host poured some mescal into a clay cup and set it in front of him.

McComb took a steady sip. The sound of a car driving up turned everyone's attention toward the door. Several pairs of boots crunched across the shale then the door was slung open. Four men entered: Sandoval, another Mexican carrying a rifle–and the two Dutchmen. The one Josh had known as Leek now appeared to be directing the group as he nodded for the others to be seated. The man drew up a dusty nail-keg across from Josh and poured some of the mescal for himself. He downed a heavy swig and spoke. "It's quite nice to see you so soon, Mr. McComb. I'm terribly sorry that the circumstances could not have been a bit more agreeable." The accent was no longer that of a Hollander. It was very British, indeed. "I suppose you must find it quite sinister," Leek went on, "the way in which we were brought together again. I must apologize." He reached for the bottle and topped off both cups, "You see, Mr. McComb, my friends and I happen to be on a very important mission. One which, I'm afraid requires the utmost secrecy."

McComb nodded toward the Mexicans with the Mausers. "I kinda' figgered' that one out when I saw these gentlemen with their Chihuahua snake-shooters."

"You have a sense of humor about this all; I'm pleased," chuckled Leek.

"Ain't nothin' funny about havin' a gun pointed at you, mister," said Josh in all seriousness. "An' if I was a gambling man, I'd bet yer' name ain't Leek, neither."

The man dipped his eyes. "You're right, Mr. McComb," he said. "The name is not Leek. You may call me Blakely – Edward Blakely. My friend over there is Dennis Fordham."

The one Josh had known as Axel nodded.

The big one continued: "We are with British Intelligence, and I am afraid that we are going to require your assistance, Mr. McComb; both yours, and that of your friend, Mr. Leaton."

Josh took another sip, shaking his head, "I'm sorry amigo, but we're still not ridin' in the same wagon."

The Englishman smiled, "Then I must explain. But first I must ask for your solemn promise."

"Mister," McComb said, "like most folks around here, my promise means a little something more to me than just words. You're gonna' have ta' tell me a whole bunch more before I'll agree to anything."

"Again, I apologize," said Blakely. "I forget I am dealing with a different breed of men in this border country, as I so humbly found out with Señor Maldonado here. I will try and be more specific." He took out a cigarette case and pounded a butt against its gold-plated skin. "My colleague and I had been assigned to keep several high-ranking Germans under close surveillance–follow them wherever they went, you know the scenario." Josh nodded. Blakely lit the cigarette and continued. "They were posing as Portuguese citizens and two weeks ago they suddenly picked up and flew to Mexico City. As puzzled as we were, Dennis and I trumped up the Dutch Patriot cover and followed them. We contacted our Latin American office and Señor Sandoval was assigned to help us. We picked up their trail and it led us all the way to Tanque. Then we lost them. Poof! They just disappeared." He settled back, taking another drink from the mug. "That was three days ago," he said. "We're assuming they have entered the States. Señor Maldonado was kind enough to bring us into your country for a brief look-around. That's when we became somewhat suspicious of your friend, Katherine Faver."

"Katy Faver?" said Josh. "What's she got to do with all this?"

Blakely took a long draw on the cigarette and blew smoke to one side, "We have reason to suspect that Katherine Faver is responsible for flying the Nazis across your border."

Josh took a long drink of the mescal, draining the cup. "Katy Faver in cahoots with the enemy? You've got to be off yer' rocker."

"No, Mr. McComb," said Blakely, shaking his head. "It's no joke. Señor Maldonado has told us of your past relationship with Miss Faver. That is why we would like for you to work with us. Katherine Faver trusts you."

"I think you're swimmin' up a steep creek," Josh went on. "Like you said, Katy Faver's a friend of mine. And if you think she trusts me, then you damn well better figure that I trust her, too."

The big man went on, "All we're asking is that you help us find out if she's involved in something as serious as we think she might be. It just may be that we're not positive about Miss Faver, but it is a fact that there are two dangerous enemy agents somewhere in the general vicinity and it's more than likely they've crossed into your country. Miss Faver's involvement appears quite feasible from where we stand and there are people we've talked to that can place her in Tanque this past week."

"I'd reckon that's part of Katy's job, don't you think?" said Josh in Katherine's defense. "She runs errands for lots of folks around here–on *both* sides of the Bravo."

Fordham stood and moved to the small table, injecting a thought of his own: "That is irrelevant, sir. It is most imperative we find if she's involved– immediately. If she is, she may be able to lead us to these Germans. On the other hand, if she's not, then you'll have our humble apology. I promise you that, sir."

McComb shook his head. "I don't know. That'd mean I'd have to lie to a friend. Katy knows me too well. She'd catch me up on some little thing in a New York minute."

"We're only asking you to try," said Blakely, pouring the last of the mescal into McComb's cup. "We need your assistance. And from what little we know about you, and from what Don Miguel has told us about your patriotism–your war record and all that–we feel you're a man we can depend on."

Josh shrugged, draining the cup once again, "That, and about four bits, might get ya' hung with a new rope if you were lucky."

Blakely frowned. "I'm afraid that some of your American epigrams slip by me, Mr. McComb, though I do find many of them amusing and would very much enjoy hearing more of them once this war is won. At the moment," he said, "we really *do* need your cooperation on the matter at hand. So if you–"

McComb leaned back, clearing his throat loudly and pulling at his ear. "Ya' know, amigo," he said bluntly, "I've always bin' a person that takes a man at his word. But you two come at me sayin' yer' Dutchmen without a country. Next thing ya' say, is that yer' really some kinda' secret undercover spies for the English government. Now I suppose you'll be tellin' me next that ol' senator what's-his-name is workin' for the F.B.I. or some hogwash like such."

The two Englishmen exchanged glances. "We must give you credit due, Mr. McComb. Mr. Dobbs is indeed with your Federal Bureau of Investigation. In fact, he comes to us with the personal recommendation of Mr. J. Edgar Hoover himself. Unfortunately, your government has implored that they not be asked to step foot on Mexican soil, otherwise, Agent Dobbs would surely be here with us in our attempt to convince you of our sincerity."

Maldonado stepped forward. "Excuse me, por favor."

Blakely nodded, giving him the floor.

Don Miguel spoke softly. "I wish to say something to my friend, Señor McComb." The Mexican gentleman sided up to Josh then took his hand between both of his own. "Señor McComb," he began. "These men speak the truth. They are indeed who they claim to be: British agents. As one Texican to another, you must believe me. For the sake of your beloved country; and my own." Josh caught a genuine concern in the man's eyes. Maldonado continued, "It has been explained to me that what these gentlemen do is just as important as those with rifles on the front lines. You must know, Señor

McComb, that war must be fought on all fronts and by all of the people that remain in the world, *if* we are to succeed in destroying this Nazi monster. And I am afraid, my amigo, that the war has come to our precious despoblado. I have committed myself, and those who claim their allegiance to me, to assisting our companeros Britanicas in any way we can. I only hope you will feel the same way as I do."

McComb took a minute to let all that Don Miguel had said mesh in his mind. All the time, he never took his eyes from Maldonaldo's and the Mexican never let go of his hands. It was almost as if the man's absolute veracity was being absorbed into McComb's soul. When he finally spoke, Josh McComb had made his final decision.

"OK, OK." The words came slow and even. "Just tell me what you want me to do."

CHAPTER EIGHT

Red Collinson drew in a deep breath of the wet air, letting the sweet smell of damp creosote and mesquite filter through a thick twist of gray hairs that curled from each nostril, blending smoothly into the full mustache that he had worn since 1900. *Big storm down near the Bravo, most likely,* he thought, as he wheeled the Ford down a side-alley that would bring him to a stop behind the ranger office where he always parked when he wasn't officially on duty.

As he stepped out of the car and closed the door, he could barely make out the distinct rumble of thunder. *Could be some rain might hit town by sundown,* he predicted to himself. Then he found the key to the rear door and went on into the building.

The back hallway of the Marfa Texas Rangers' Office led past the file room on one side with doors to a small toilet and a utility room, used sometimes for interrogation, on the other. As Collinson moved down the narrow passage, he could just make out a pair of socked feet propped on the edge of one of the two desks that faced each other in the main office at the front of the building. The socks would belong to Lester Suggs. Plunker Hancock, Collinson's second-in-command, was in charge of assigning "days to be worked" and Collinson knew that Hancock was courting a Mormom widow who lived out near the cottonwood grove, so he was certain that the fraying hosiery that rested on the desk-top belonged to Suggs. He also knew that Lester slept on duty. The deputy didn't do it on purpose. It was just that when a specified level of silence fell in Lester's vicinity, it was inevitable that the old fart would doze off.

Collinson never liked to embarrass a man, especially one like Suggs–a harmless gent, with a heart of pure gold–so before he entered the office, he stuck his hand into the small bathroom cubicle and chain-flushed the commode.

"Holy Judas," echoed the gravely voice from the other room; the flush had caused the overhead pipes to sing like a set of bad brakes on a diesel truck from the years of strain and rust. Collinson could see the socks slip from the desktop to the floor and a pair of stubby, liver-spotted hands groped for the boots that somehow weren't where they were supposed to be.

Collinson waited until he heard the old ranger's heels squeak into place inside the boots and the sound of the swivel chair as it was slid into an upright position before he cleared his throat audibly and continued on down the hall. When he entered the office, he found a very serious and alert Lester Suggs going through a stack of fliers and making imperceptible notes on a yellow pad with a leadless pencil stub.

"Looks like it might rain," Collinson remarked as he tossed his hat on the rack between the two vacant holding cells and plopped into his own chair behind the second desk.

A wheezing sigh whistled out of Suggs, then he turned around slowly and greeted Collinson with a gnarled but sheepish grin slapped across a two-day growth of white stubble and said, "Thank God it's you, Captain Red. I thought it was that dern Plunker spyin' on me again."

Collinson chuckled, "Not on the Sabbath, Lester. Plunker Hancock's got more important things on his mind, come Sunday." He winked. "Mormon widow out on the other side of town, remember?"

"Yeah, reckon I do," said Suggs. "Say, Captain, now that yer' here, would you mind watchin' the post so I can get my can of Walter Raleigh? It's in the glove box out in my pick-up. I plumb forgot it this mornin'. I won't be but a minute."

"Take yer' time, Lester," answered Collinson, easing back in the chair and finding his own pipe and pouch. "I'll go ahead an' pack my briar, then we can sit an' have a smoke together, talk some, if yer' a mind ta'."

"Sounds fine ta' me, Captain. Thanks," he said as he moved to the thick oak front door, removing the two-by-four security bar from the iron brackets. He noticed Collinson's curious stare and said, "Oh, I, uh, always lock it on Sundays, Captain. Just in case. You know what I mean?"

Collinson winked and continued thumbing the light brown Kentucky Burley fibers into the pipe bowl, smoothing them down after each measured pinch. He had to hold back the chuckle until Suggs' footsteps cleared the sidewalk. He knew the security bar was for Suggs' protection, all right; protection against his getting caught sleeping on the job.

He finished packing the pipe and planed the top of the tobacco gently with his thumb until it lay flat. Then he took out a Blue Diamond and hesitated. He'd wait until Suggs returned before lighting up, he didn't want the ol' boy to go thinkin' he'd got a head start on him. He set the pipe down on the desk and removed his tie, unbuttoning the collar button for comfort. Then he took in a deep breath and let his mind wander, thinking about the meeting he'd had with Colonel Purrington and the unruffled way with which he'd dealt with the situation. *Hell,* he thought, *what else could I have done, the son-ofa-buck told it like it is. A man's gotta' face up ta' what has to be done, don't he?* Collinson leaned back further and put his boots up on the desk, closing his eyes.

For an instant, he saw the faces of the men he'd killed during his lifetime. Not the usual flash of blurred sombreros and drooping mustaches hidden behind an assemblage of cocked pistols, but a series of detailed studies, the actual photographic frames taken by his brain the moment before hard lead had stopped heartbeats and closed eyes forever. Collinson blinked. The room was in front of him again and he was still alone. The old clock ticked from the opposite wall, his pipe still lay on the desk where he'd put it just seconds before. He was having those memories again. The same memories that woke him from sound sleeps on cold nights drenched in July sweats; the same memories that bounced between his temples like gunshots from dark alleys– echoes from his forgotten past. Only what was once forgotten was now beginning to creep back, and Captain Red Collinson didn't care for it at all. He reached for the pipe and noticed that his hand was trembling slightly. He passed it off to age. It sure enough wasn't fear. Fear came *before* the trigger was pulled, not after. No. Nothing was wrong with Red Collinson; just memories, that was all. Nothing was supposed to bother Texas Ranger Red Collinson. Certainly not the Red Collinson who'd turned the dreaded Cano brothers into three harmless jars of mountain oysters. Damn, he wished Juanita were still around. He'd never had the memories as long as she was part of his life. Juanita. Now that was some woman. Never talked, just listened–listened and made mucho coito. No. There had been none of those memories when Juanita was around. No sir-eee. He lit the pipe.

When Lester Suggs returned not more than three minutes later, Red Collinson was gone. Lester could hear the Ford drive off down the alley. By the sound, Suggs could tell it had turned south on the farm road. *Funny,* the deputy thought, *nothin' out that way but the Mexican cemetery.*

Wallace Bowman had never seen a German until three months earlier. Up until he arrived at Fort Russell, the closest Bowman had even been to a resemblance of one was the distance between the first row balcony and the torn screen in the Brooklyn Loews Theater–Bowman pronounced it "Lowees."

He had met Peggy in the Brooklyn "Low-ees" balcony where he'd met so many of the others. But Peggy was different. She'd actually let him feel her tits that first time. The others had always stopped him long before he got any tit. Hell, he'd been lucky if any of the others had even let him put his arm around their shoulders. "Swoosh, Chop," went the guillotine. But Peggy had been different. His arm went to her shoulder right away. No problem. Then a finger was allowed to creep down her neck and under the collar of her blouse– easy as pie. Then the soft, pudding-like flesh of upper breast, rising and falling with her every tense breath–piece of cake. Finally, his fingers sensing the tightened skin–the difference in its consistency–as he neared the nipple. He stopped there for a second, to catch his breath, and then to try a for a quick nibble at her ear like Vince Vitello had told him to do if he ever got a girl in that kind of situation. That's all it took with Peggy. He'd found out that just one quick tongue-tap to the ear-hole was all it took. His fingers never got all the way to her nipple that afternoon in the Brooklyn Loews. As soon as his tongue had made the initial contact, Peggy had let out a deep sigh and buried her entire head into his erect lap. That was Peggy. What a girl. Gawd damn Bitch! "Swoosh, Chop, Thump!" And Peggy's entire head landed in the guillotine's basket.

Bowman fingered the tightness of his necktie as he waited behind the tool shed. He'd brought a paper sack full of beer bottles with him and he was chug-a-lugging the third one already. He sat on the ground, using an old newspaper to keep his dress slacks clean. Also, to put a protective layer between himself and any poisonous ground creature that might happen by looking for some New York meat. He'd picked the position himself. Just out of sight of either guard tower on that particular perimeter, yet still as close to the woven-wire fence as he could get without being seen from the enlisted men's mess or the barracks. All he had to do was wait. No one would miss him. It was Sunday. He usually got drunk on Sunday and the others were used to him disappearing for a few hours or so when he got drunk. No one would come looking for him anyway, that was for sure. No one liked him that much to be concerned. So he just waited. Waited and sucked down the beer. The last waterproof match container had held fifty dollars, and there had been a note, too. It had said: "sunday/tool shack/9 p.m." and it was signed "Ballena." *Fifty bucks is a lot of dough,* he thought. Vince Vitello had always said money talks and bullshit walks hadn't he? Well, enough for the bullshit, Wally Bowman was ready for some talking.

He reached for the sack and took out another beer. He found the opener and popped the cap as silently as he could. The long shadows slithered across the German compound faster now. It would be dark in half an hour–and nine o'clock was not far after that. Wally Bowman was ready to meet this Ballena, whoever he was. Maybe he had another postcard for him to mail. Just maybe there would be another fifty smackers attached to that.

The dull staccato of the rough-shod hooves traversed the blood of McComb's inner ear as he and Monroe Leaton backtracked toward the Johnson Ranch, inching their way along the storm-torn Indian trails, through ancient gullies and across mud-plugged creek-beds.

Pendulous thoughts of earlier days trickled in. Those days with that salty sweat-sting biting the raw corners of parched eyes, sandwiching the cool nights. The balmy border evenings filled with corn whiskey and Mexican body smells. These things swirled through McComb's mind. The distant laughter echoing from crusty, thick-walled cantinas. A warm twang–silently quivering deep within testicles, faintly recalling the many tequila-soaked carnal escapades he'd had in those numerous dirt-floored rooms tucked away somewhere in forgotton back streets. All of those things happening before he'd met Katherine Faver, of course. All of those things coming to an abrupt halt when he'd fallen in love with her.

Their relationship had been sewn all the way back to those fight and fuck border days following the first war. The young Josh had been taken totally by surprise with her assignment to join him on border-watch duty–they had called it liquor patrol–because she was the only other qualified aviator in the area. And the two of them had swept the skies over the Bravo in the government's twin deHavillands, looking for illegal rumrunners during that period of the prohibition.

Most evenings back then, the two flyers had been able to land the tired planes near the U.S. Army troop encampments, wherever they might be, and that had remained their habit until the one time they found the terrain too rough near a certain night's bivouac. So, the two pilots had just flown on, hedgehopping into the Texican twilight until they spotted a small rio villa with a wide, dusty street where, upon landing, they were greeted like Cortezes conquering army.

To hear Katy Faver tell the story, it sounded as if villagers had brought out all of the church's valuable possessions for the twosome. That was damn near close to what happened. Josh still remembered that night like it was yesterday. The two of them had just climbed out of their planes and were surrounded by the cheering townspeople who then literally lifted them to their shoulders and carried them to a small adobe church where a fiesta was already in progress. Both were immediately handed jars of Sotol, a home brewed liquor made from the fermented juices of the woody plants of the same name that grew in abundance in the surrounding area, and a favorite among the natives. As guitars began to play and trumpets sounded, they watched and sipped in stunned silence while the food placed on the tables before them began to grow into volcanic piles. The Mexican delicacies eventually spilled over to the dirt floors where the wide-eyed children would battle over the grapes and other fruits in mock warfare. Though the young Katherine and Josh neither spoke nor understood a word of Spanish at the time, it didn't take them too long to "comprende" what was going on.

It appeared that between the Cano gang's adventurous attraction and the Federales' frequently forced recruitments, virtually all of the young men from the village had gone off to join either one side or the other. The villagers had not had a young couple around to overindulge for a long time and they just assumed that Josh and Katy were a pair. They gave them a small hut of their own to share that night, assuming that they had slept together before. By the time the night had passed, the twosome had proven the villagers correct, *and* they had fallen in love.

From that time on, the two young aviators had made damn sure that when they were making other aerial surveys that they always picked out the rockiest place they could find for certain, allowing them to bounce around from village to village indulging in many nights of lovemaking.

Many stories sprang from those prohibition days, giving birth to yarns and ballads on both sides of the border; allowing the two Americano flyers to become somewhat infamous around the Big Bend. Word of their affair spread like wildfire from outpost to tiny outpost along the winding Bravo– the beginning of a Texican legend.

"What's that you smilin' 'bout to yoursef' fo', Missa' Josh?" Monroe's dry voice sliced into McComb's reminiscence, bringing him back to the present and he turned to locate the puzzled face beside him.

"Oh, just the good ol' days, I reckon, Monroe," said Josh. "Just the old days."

"Mussa' bin' a good thing that happened back then, Missa'," chuckled Monroe. "You was almos' laughin' out loud."

Josh nodded and smiled to himself just as the horses reached the top of a rise and the Johnson Ranch and the horseshoe curve of the Bravo came into view almost hidden in the deep shadows of the sloping valley below.

McComb reined up and looked down toward the cluster of adobe buildings that stood on the river's bank where he remembered once there was nothing. He blinked as he saw a soft glow illuminate a window in one of the adobe cottages near the bunkhouse. Katherine was there.

A familiar emptiness filled his stomach for a moment. A skeletal hand reached up his dry gullet and clawed at his throat with raking nails, scratching the word "whiskey" into the tender membrane of his palate. He knew that he wanted a drink–needed just one swallow–more than anything in the world at that moment. Just one drink–one diminutive suck on a bottle until all of his thoughts would piss themselves away. Then maybe, just maybe, when he woke up afterwards, all that had happened on this day would turn out to have been nothing more than a dream.

"We best be getting' on," Missa' Josh," said Monroe. "Sun's 'bout ta' go down. Gonna' be dark by the time we get there anyhow."

McComb stuck a spur to his animal's responsive flank and edged silently on down the soft side of the shale rise. Monroe followed. In moments, the feeling in his stomach had faded completely. What he had to do now seemed much more important. Katy Faver had been his best friend, his lover, a woman he could wholly trust. His partner. And now Katy was suspected of being a partner to espionage. McComb was growing tired of weighing the possibilities. The return from Boquillas had taken three hours longer than the ride there and his brain was pounding with overuse. He'd do what he had to do even though deep down he knew that he might have to face the reality that his friend was a traitor. The final decision would not be his, though. McComb knew that. Monroe had taught him long ago that it would all be in God's hands. But if it did turn out that Katy Faver was indeed in trouble, and in fact, needed his help, Josh McComb would make sure that he would be there to provide all the support for his friend that he could muster.

CHAPTER NINE

The King stood in vainglorious rapture as he reviewed his latest accomplishment. In his hands he held the Elixirs of Life and Everlasting Happiness, precious gifts bestowed upon His Majesty in return for royal favors to be provided. The King smiled softly to himself as the quiet evening breeze tickled the back of his neck, for he felt secure in this moment, knowing that besides the gift of the Elixirs, his royal treasury would soon be filled and he would then live happily ever after. And he chuckled, assured that the covenant he had made would eventually prove to the others–show those who were still non-believers in his Divine Power–that he was indeed royalty, and that his sovereign hand ruled supreme.

"Well, kiss ol' lady Mitchell," declared Leroy Skuggins as he took his eye off the cue-ball just long enough to look up and see Wally Bowman enter the rec-room carrying the two bottles of whiskey. Several other off-duty gaolers of the Military Police Escort Guard Detachment assigned to Fort Russell were there too, and they stopped what they were doing to watch as Skuggins devoted his full attention to the tipsy soldier.

"I'll be hog-tied an' butter-greased if the ol' fairy-queen ain't got herself some real cuttin' piss," laughed Leroy. "Lookie there, boys."

The others chided in with a few catcalls and whistles, laughing anxiously behind Skuggins as he set down his pool cue and slid around to where he could block Bowman's path when he passed by the pool table.

Skuggins folded his arms, setting his heels. Wally Bowman had to stop himself awkwardly to avoid bumping into the much larger man. Bowman's eyes held tight to the floor in front of him, he took a better grip on the bottles that he carried. Skuggins was not going to move out of his way. Bowman knew that he wouldn't budge. This had happened before, more than once.

"Hey, you little turd-bird," Skuggins chortled. "Are you gonna' just stand there like a lead fart stuck in a parrot's ass, or are you gonna' share some of that Loosiana'-lay-me-back with yer' comrades in arms here?"

Some of the others coughed and tittered quietly in the background. Bowman slowly shook his head as Skuggins' eyes narrowed. "What's that supposed ta' mean, piss-puff?" said Leroy. "I asked you if you was gonna' share them bottles with yer' buddies."

Bowman's head jerked slightly, his eyes began to slowly climb the buttons on the other man's uniform shirt one-by-one. Up past the knot in Skuggins's tie, on up and over the big man's polished chin, then to his lips, pausing for a moment at the pock-marked nose and moving on still further until the two men's eyes met dead on. Skuggins felt the immediate chill; his words fell off as if they had been hacked with a cold cleaver.

When speech finally came for him, Bowman spoke slow, deliberate. His words echoed with tremendous care, an effort to obscure any slurring that might be caused by his alcoholic tongue. "Before me, thou shalt kneel," he bade them all. "Then, and only then, wilt the Elixir of Life be offered to thee."

For a moment there was complete silence. Then, little by little, Skuggins's mouth twisted into a ghoulish sneer as he turned to the others, "The little buggar-butt's gone bats again, boys," Leroy sniggered. "Maybe we ought ta' give his Royal Highnee' sumthin' ta' think about."

Bowman's eyebrows dropped, his lids tightened, "To thy knees, blackguard!" he shouted at Skuggins. "Speak not before your master until permission has been granted!"

Skuggins' return was slow and guttural. "Oh, you little prick," he said angrily. "Just who in the hell do you think yer' talkin' to?"

Bowman ignored him, continuing: "I have ordered you to your knees, commoner!" he proclaimed. "Bow before me and all that you wish shall be yours."

"I'll show you knees, punk," muttered Skuggins, bringing up his own knee, connecting precisely with the point of khaki that targeted Bowman's testicles.

Two of the other soldiers caught the bottles of whiskey in flight as Wallace Bowman's face arced abruptly through the air and smashed into the rough wood floor. In the last seconds before unconsciousness obliterated all–just before the final head-kick was administered by the steel-toe of Skuggins's boot–someone heard Bowman spit out a raspy commination: "Off–with– their– heads!"

Monroe had offered to unsaddle and feed both horses long before he and Josh rode through the Johnson Ranch gate with McComb's dog barking her greeting. Leaton knew that his compadre had something personal on his mind that he had to get off as soon as possible. Monroe said he would take the dog with him and make sure it got fed with the horses. McComb dismounted near Katy's cabana while Leaton rode on. Now McComb stood alone in front of the cottage, the faint sounds of the horses' hooves echoing into the nothing behind him as Monroe led the animals to the barn on the other side of the ranch yard.

The air around him had grown fair to dark by that time as the fading sun's lingering grasp slowly let go and slipped off behind the western hills, leaving a final trickle to fold itself and eventually blend into the early West-Texas moonglow. Prickly bursts of glittering star-points began to silently explode onto the velvet evening and the hushed hint of a soft wind bounced delicately between the adobes that were scattered around the Johnson Ranch. Vague voices filtered over from the main house, carried on a current of warm air and McComb could recognize Elmo's laugh above several others. There were more visitors tonight–not an unusual occurrence for the Johnsons. Both Elmo and his wife, Ada, were well known as genial hosts in the Big Bend. There might not be a week of days in a given year when the couple would have the big, tin-roofed adobe to themselves.

Josh re-fixed his eyes on Katherine's bungalow, focusing in on the lighted window. He could see movement behind the soiled oilcloth shade that had been drawn as a woman's silhouette sometimes peeked through the several snags in the faded material. It was Katy Faver all right. Josh knew her every move, her every gesture. The way she rolled her cigarettes, pouring the dark tobacco in two separate rows from the bag of Lobo Negro she always carried; wetting her index finger and lightly dampening the thin brown paper instead of outright licking it, as a man would do; and that final twist, pinching each end with the same pressure until the perfect cigarillo was somehow formed. Yes, that was Katy Faver on the other side of that blind all right. Nothing Josh could do would change that.

Thoughts whizzed between McComb's ears like Fourth-of-July skyrockets, exploding and showering his brain with fragments of anticipated answers that would only fade and vanish before ever becoming clear. He was about to confront an old friend and accuse her of treason. He needed to know more facts. Facts! The British had facts. Hadn't they said that they knew Katy was up to something no good? Wasn't she supposed to be ferrying Nazi spies across the border? So, how was McComb to handle this meeting? Would he just walk in and ask Katy outright? Say something like: "Katy, ol' friend, I heard tell that you're a Nazi agent," or something like that? God, wouldn't that be a cold thing to do–especially if she were innocent. And what if the

Brits were wrong? What if their eyewitnesses had lied? Jeeze! There were just too many "what ifs."

Again, that clutching urge to swallow a bottle bit into McComb's gut like a snapping steel trap. What was he thinking? He was pre-judging his friend and onetime lover before he really had any concrete facts, wasn't he? Those Limeys could be damn wrong. They just didn't have anything positive, did they? Or else, why would they have gone to so much trouble to enlist his help in finding out more? He'd just have to find more evidence. That was all there was to it. More information - period. Right now, all he could do would be to act as normal as possible in front of Katy. He'd just have to hope that his real intentions would go undetected for the time being. He would just listen. Listen and watch. Keep his eye on Katy without her knowing it. Hang around and–

The door opened with a high-pitched creak. McComb's tumbling thoughts stopped abruptly. Katherine Faver took a step out into the evening, hedging for a moment, squinting quizzically down the backlight that slanted from the open door to the man who stood in her path. The song of a single cricket scratched the air from somewhere close by. Then Katherine spoke, "Is that you, McComb? Is that you lurking out there in the night?"

The outline of McComb's hat was seen to nod. Then Katy fumbled in her pocket, finally looking up with a girlish grin. "You wouldn't happen to have a match now, would you?" she said. "I was just about to walk all the way over to the big house looking for one. I have a fresh-rolled cigarette I want to smoke, plus that old butane stove of mine keeps going out."

Several long seconds passed as McComb felt his tension uncoil. Then he reached into his pocket and found a Blue Diamond, snapping it into a blaze with his thumbnail, holding it out toward his friend. He knew he couldn't lie to Katherine if it ever came down to "get off or buck," so he just said: "Uh, I just wanted to tell ya' that me an' Monroe are gonna' be stayin' on here for another few days."

And Katherine Faver, being the kind of person that Josh knew she was, just puffed, nodded and said simply: "That's nice, McComb. It'll be good to have you around again. I really mean that."

Raller knew that he would be going. He now understood fully the intent of the escape plan and he knew that its success or failure would depend on him alone. If Spengler were not involved, he thought, it just might be a good idea. It was one of the few half-intelligent stratagems ever to emerge from the menagerie of egos that comprised the corrupt Ministry of Propaganda. They wanted him back. Back in the Fatherland, alive and in one piece. It had nothing to do with his personal welfare. It would be only to show the German people that nothing was impossible for the Nazi Party. A prison breakout; an escape from the furthermost German P.O.W. outpost in the United States; a getaway that would defy all previous attempts; a feat of derring-do that would certainly, were it a success, help rally the citizens of Germany into one last unified stand behind Hitler's lunacy.

Raller felt a tug on his sleeve and he eased over so he could hear what Iggy had to whisper. "They are not going to include me," said the young man. "I can feel it in my bones."

The two of them had been invited, as had all ranking officers, to a clandestine meeting in which all of the chosen names were being read. Thirty or so men were gathered quietly at the north end of the barracks room to listen as Spengler read from a list that had been hastily scribbled on a halfused roll of American toilet-paper. As expected, Raller's name had been first–and of course, Spengler's had followed second. Now he was reading off the final name. It was not Iggy's. Raller could see perspiration from the young officer's palm drip to the floor as Dreshler consumed the inevitable. Dreshler leaned in once more, this time with a grating fear to his voice. "I am nothing to these men–nothing."

Raller patted his trembling hand with a tender reassurance. "You must consider yourself fortunate, my friend," he told him.

The meeting broke up as quietly as it had begun and the two walked slowly back to their bunks. "But I must go with you," the young man begged, ignoring Raller's earlier remark. "It is my duty. Not only to the Fatherland, but to my own conscience, as well."

Raller stopped near their bunks and waited a moment as some other officers passed them by, moving out of earshot. He placed both of his hands on Dreshler's shoulders, looking him straight in the eye. "Your duty, young one, is to stay alive," he cautioned. "That should be your utmost priority. How can a man of your age expect to achieve anything on this earth if he is not living?"

Iggy shook his head. "No," he seemed to whine. "To die, to fight, that is to achieve. There are already too many among the living who are, in reality, the dead ones."

Raller had to chuckle, a small laugh to himself as he looked into the youngster's helpless eyes and saw his own innocent reflection staring back from those many years before. "Here," he said quietly, "sit down." He took out his cigarette packet and lit two, handing one to Iggy through his confusion. They sat themselves across from one another and both fell silent for the next few puffs. Finally Raller went on. "Iggy," he began. "You can only be dead in life when you yourself deliver the obituary. You have yet to do that and I feel that you never will. But, for you to wish for death? You have not yet begun to live, my friend. So please, take my advice. As long as one precious breath lingers within, the struggle is to live. Never to die."

Dreshler's eyes teared up, "But I must have the chance to be a hero like you, Herr Raller. That is all I desire."

"I am a *living* hero, Iggy," said Raller. "But only by fortune, remember that. Your fate may not be as mine. There are many men who have thought like you and who would now gladly change to your shoes if they but could. For they sit not on a comfortable prison bunk, but instead remain strapped, for eternity, in their burning planes, dying their valiant deaths a thousand times over in the hapless minds of their souls." Raller took a long puff, inhaling and letting the smoke trickle back through both nostrils. He leaned in closer, putting his hand again, on the boy's shoulder. "Think it over, my young friend," he went on. "Listen to my years. I have seen death come too easy. Please believe me. It is a much greater challenge to strive for life. I know this. The war will end. Only the living will have gained."

"But, if I do not go with you," Dreshler protested, "I will be called a coward by my own soul. Please, Herr Raller. Let me make my own choice; let my heart tell me what I must do."

"You will do what you have to, young Dreshler," said Raller. "You will always have that option. My words are merely suggestions. Just remember: you will only be what you think you are. To the ones who will die, you will be the only true hero—because you will still be alive."

Iggy let the words digest for a long moment then he looked over to Raller once again. The fear seemed to have faded some. "Maybe one day I will understand, Oberstleutnant. Maybe one day I will see beyond my own selfishness."

"It takes many years for some, my friend," Raller continued. "But, I am sure that you will, one day, grasp my meaning. Maybe when you have, like you say, captured some more wisdom."

Dreshler nodded, "As you have, Herr Raller?"

Once again Raller chuckled softly to himself. "I, too, am still learning, Iggy," he told the younger man. "Every day I find knowledge of something I have never known. No one will ever know everything. But we can continue to learn, to search, and then to accept what we find. We will never know all the answers because they simply do not exist. They just do not. The final truth," Raller went on, "comes not in the form of answers."

Dreshler asked, "Then, how is one supposed to know when it arrives?"

Raller answered, "Keep on living my young friend and find out for yourself. Now go to sleep. Understanding sometimes comes to us while we sleep."

Raller lay back on his bunk and finished his cigarette. After several minutes, the lights dimmed. There was nothing more for him to say at that time, for no matter what he did say he knew that the final volition would still be left up to Dreshler. Raller knew from experience that most men made up their own minds to their own way of thinking anyway, regardless of what other information was offered.

"A Colt .45 has no feelings. Which means: it has no brain of its own. It hasn't any reasoning, nor can it choose the target at which it is sighted. Yet, a Colt can remove a colored man's ear with the same ease that it castrates a Mes'can. It can de-gut an Injun, or remove a white man's heart. A Colt .45 is a piece of unique cold steel, designed to tear apart warm flesh, nothing more. A man says any different, that man's a damn liar. Now you got just two choices, mister: thin an' none. I've made up my mind ta' close yer' windows; put out yer' lights. So, you got just one minute ta' get things right with yer' Maker, 'cause this is truly the moment. This is yer' judgment day, amigo an' that simply means that it's all over. So, you better start countin' yer' blessins'."

Those words echoed through Red Collinson's brain as he tried carefully to aim the neck of the bottle in the direction of the hole beneath his mustache. When the connection was made, he gulped down some more of the soothing liquid and settled back again. His eyes were gone–out of commission. He'd found that he could no longer just sit and stare at Juanita's flagstone grave marker like he used to and reminisce about the good old times. As of late–after a given amount of whiskey–Red Collinson's eyes would blur up and seal themselves shut from the combination of the hard liquor and the tears. Then he'd have to take his seat in the theater of his mind once again while the old two-reelers were threaded into that broken down projector encased beneath his skull where he would be forced to watch his life repeat itself with perfect recollection in both picture and sound.

His mind's movie always began with the same speech, the exact words, spoken the same way and by the same voice. Red Collinson knew the voice well. It was his voice. The words had been what he'd called his "Death Sermon." A monologue, of sorts, that he had always delivered before each of his "justified" shootings. The words never varied. In his younger years he'd delivered them too many times. It had never mattered whether the victim understood English either; for most had not. But, they'd understood the Colt in his hand, all right. The gun always helped men comprehend the sounds of reckoning that spilled from Red Collinson's icy lips. They could always spot the complete sincerity in his eyes, too, every single one of them, just before they'd felt the lead's impact. Collinson had made sure that they had.

Now he cringed at the memories of his bloodlust as the screen in his mind began to brighten. Soon, the faces would return. He lifted the bottle once again and settled back. There was nothing more he could do. There was just no way to close the curtain.

CHAPTER TEN

The high-pitched whine of the Stearman's engine sliced through the morning air. The sound ricocheted between the walls of the ranch buildings with piercing indifference until it found its way to the breakfast table in the nook near the rear porch of the main house where Monroe Leaton and Josh McComb were finishing up their breakfast. Neither man said anything as they scraped their plates and mopped at gravy stains with the remains of Alice the cook's buttermilk biscuits. As the sound of the Stearman's engine revved to the proper pitch then roared off to begin fading away, McComb nodded to Monroe and the two of them stood up, thanked Alice, and went out the back door.

They stopped on the porch to shield their eyes and to watch Katherine Faver's plane's outline shrink to a pinpoint as she flew directly into the early morning sun. After several minutes, the diminishing dot above the horizon made an abrupt right turn, heading south toward Mexico. Josh brushed Monroe's arm and moved off briskly toward the airfield, "C'mon," he urged, "I don't want ta' give her too much of a head start."

"She mighta' got too big of a jump on ya', Missa' Josh," shouted Monroe, as he stood by with both hands on one of the four blades of the deHavilland's prop, waiting for McComb to get the magneto sparking.

Josh had asked that Monroe stay behind. It would be up to the big man to hang around the bunkhouse then search through Katherine's belongings when no one was around. McComb, in the D.H.4, would follow Katy to wherever she was going, keeping a safe distance behind and below the Stearman.

"Don't you bet on it, Monroe," yelled back Josh, "Katy had ta' go a mite out of her way, I expect, so we'd think she was headin' east. I figger' ta' head due south then cut over. Figger' ta' head her off at the pass, so to speak. Contact!" he yelled.

Monroe nodded, giving the blades a whirl. The engine chirped and chugged, surprising both men when it exploded into life on the first attempt. McComb eased the throttle forward, upping the R.P.M.s. He lowered his goggles and tightened the strap on his leather cap. Monroe stepped back, shielding his eyes from the dust storm kicked up by the turbulent backwash while McComb waited a few moments, listening for anything that might be wrong with the engine. He let off the brakes and pedaled a right rudder so the plane swung around. He gave her a full throttle and the plane began moving off down the rough-graded runway.

Jim-Bob heard the plane taking off from his room. He had been sleeping while holding McComb's dog in his arms. Now the two of them moved to the window to watch as the deHavilland's wheels left the dirt of the runway and took to the sky. The dog recognized Josh's plane immediately and made an attempt to get away from the boy. Jim-Bob grabbed her, holding her tight by her collar, shaking his head and finger to tell her she would have to stay with him for the time being.

Within minutes, McComb was circling and climbing over the Rio Grande, watching as the black man on the ground below turned into a dot. Off in the distance, to the north, he could see the twin-monuments known as Mule-Ear Peaks standing at attention like two sentries, guarding the towering Chisos on the horizon. These two identical geographic formations had played a large part in the days when he helped train the pilots at the Johnson Ranch. The airmen used the peaks for more than just landmarks. They would actually fly their planes between the two pinnacles, firing their guns. Some of the real daredevils performed rollovers and other acrobatics with unruffled ease while passing between the two giant outcroppings, much to McComb's discomfort.

To the west, Josh could make out the giant wall of rock that ran along the Mexican side of the Rio Grande from where the river emerged through what appeared to be a colossal gash. That would be Santa Elena Canyon. The morning sun was hitting the sheer rock wall head on at the early hour and the seventeen-hundred-foot ramparts that paralleled the river at the mouth of Santa Elena reflected the Bravo's dancing surface all the way up to the canyon's rim.

At twenty-five-hundred-feet, McComb banked and turned south, leveling off and trimming for the next hour or so of flight. He figured it would take about that long before he would have to begin searching the horizon for signs of the Stearman. For the time being, he would just settle back and relax, take in the scenery and keep an eye out for "Fiscales"– those Mexican Law Officers along the Bravo who had never taken kindly to American planes invading their air space.

About fifty miles or so into the Chihuahuain wilderness, a warm thermal sucked the floor-boards right out from under McComb, abruptly snapping him out of a semi-snooze, instantly gluing his stomach to the roof of his skull. Instinct won over consternation and in less than a trice, the deHavilland was cruising along again as if nothing had happened. Later, McComb would tell Monroe that the thermal must have been God's hand shoving him down for a closer look because he'd never have seen the Stearman on the far horizon from the altitude he'd been the several seconds before the rapid plunge. But, there it was–Katy's Stearman–soaring along almost parallel to the deHavilland, about a mile off to the east.

McComb glanced over his right shoulder from habit, drawing in an easy breath when he saw a seven-hundred-foot rocky ridge to his other side. The deHavilland's profile would not be so readily observed from Katherine's plane with the dark outcropping behind him. He felt that he would be safe from detection for a while, as long as he stayed low–and as long as Katy was in the air too, with her engine noise drowning out the D.H.4's own monotonous modulation.

The two planes flew along for the next few miles of desert and McComb was about ready to settle back once again when he suddenly noticed that the Stearman was quickly losing altitude. Katy was going to land the damn thing.

It took some fast thinking and some luck on McComb's part, because he knew he had to land and shut down before Katherine did, or his own presence would surely be discovered from the sound of his engine booming out over the shimmering solitude. By sheer chance, a small mesa appeared to pop up out of the desert floor, rising quickly between the two planes and it looked like Katy was going to touch down on its far side. In an instant, McComb raked the throttle, blindly kicking a left rudder, sending the plane half-sliding, half-diving for the rim of the mesa. As the deHavilland's structure shuddered from the unexpected lurch, a quick pilot's prayer helped Josh locate the flattest spot. He aimed to put down just inches from the brink, cutting the engine and deploying full flaps while bringing the plane in on the small table-top like a talons-out hawk diving on a liberty dime. McComb pumped the brakes to the maximum and the D.H.4 whipped and slid across the short stretch of gravel and greasewood. Before the aircraft could nose in, it careened tail-around and skidded to a dead stop less than fifteen feet of the opposite edge, coming to a silent rest within an ace of exposure to the other plane below.

McComb gathered himself and cocked an ear as he heard Katherine Faver shut down the Stearman's engine a fraction of a beat later. The dying sound of her plane's pistons rang loud and clear. Katy Faver was just over the mesa's lip.

His years in the Big Bend had taught McComb that as much as a fluttering breath or even a quiet breeze whipping at a person's hair could be heard at a great distance in the spiritless quiescence of the vast desert; where there was absolutely no other sound, a single sound could carry forever. It pleased him to no end that he had removed his leather-flying jacket and tucked it away early in the flight. He knew that had he still been wearing the damn thing, just one slight move of his arm would have resounded like the entire Eighth Cavalry mounting up in full battle gear. So he just sat: motionless—listening. He would not attempt a move until Katy Faver did.

The truck first made its presence known as a small suppuration on the unblemished horizon, discharging a boiling dust-cloud against the pellucid sky that fanned out into a brown haze, like a plague expanding across Biblical badlands.

Knowing that Katy would have seen it too, McComb utilized the momentary distraction to unbuckle his seat belt and climb down from the plane. Before his heels kissed sand, the truck's engine noise had grown loud enough to cover any other moves he would have to make. Dropping to his elbows, Josh slid himself along on his stomach to the edge of the mesa where he took up a position behind a lone Sotol shoot. He carefully parted the sharp leaves and peered down the rugged incline.

Katy had planted the Stearman on good ground. It sat in a small alcove at the base of the mesa, like a crouching cougar, positioned for immediate takeoff. Katherine paced silently in front of the propeller, anxiously rolling a cigarillo and glancing up, every now and then, to check on the truck's progress.

The several minutes it took for the truck to reach the slope of the mesa ticked by in magnified seconds, allowing McComb to dig in tighter behind his cover. He had no way of knowing whether the vehicle's occupants could see the deHavilland from their vantage. All he could hope for was that they were too intent in searching at ground level for sight of the Stearman.

As the vehicle grew larger, making its way up from the desert floor, Katherine began to signal them, waving her aviator's cap and her scarf in a conspicuous semaphore. The people in the truck saw her and the vehicle angled around then headed directly toward the plane. Josh flattened out even further as the truck crunched its way in beside the Stearman and two men climbed out. The first man, the driver, was dressed in peon whites and a straw hat. He moved around to the bed of the truck and threw back a canvas tarpaulin, revealing an oblong box that was nailed tight and secured with heavy binding. The second man got out of the passenger side and was met by Katherine Faver. A large Mexican straw hat shaded his face and concealed his features from McComb's angle, but the three-piece wool suit and the polished patent leather footwear he wore told a European story all their own.

There was a brief conversation and a quick exchange of what appeared to be a roll of bills; while the peon unloaded the box from the truck, then reloaded it into the cargo cockpit of the Stearman. The transaction had taken all of three minutes and McComb continued to watch as Katy climbed into the plane and sparked her magneto.

Josh didn't wait for the peon to crank the blades. He was already sparking his own magneto when Katy's engine shattered the desert's silence. Three whips of his own prop got it spinning and he was just strapping in when he threw a quick glance over his shoulder and saw the Stearman's back-wash surging up side of the mesa behind him like a small hurricane. McComb knew that he must get airborne before Katherine did, or he'd be spotted for certain. He jammed the throttle wide open and released the brakes. There was no time now to worry about being seen by the departing truck. He could only pray for acceleration.

The deHavilland lumbered back across the mesa, picking up some speed, but not nearly enough. The plane shot over the rim and arced out over the edge in a tilted swan dive. McComb pushed a full throttle, jerking the stick back as hard as he could, feeling the strain on the extended cables as he watched the desert come up at him. He thought for sure that he'd bought it–then, the heavy plane's four blades finally bit into ethereal stability and the D.H.4 nosed up gently, but not before bouncing down twice and almost blowing both tires. McComb managed some control and the plane began to gain a little altitude. Then he swung a low right turn and leveled out, paralleling the same rocky out-cropping, using it for cover as he had earlier. He glanced over and spotted the Stearman off in the distance and he could see the festering wake of the truck as it headed back to from wherever it came.

"Son of a bitch," he found himself saying aloud. They hadn't seen him. Now all he had to do was hightail it back to the Johnson Ranch before Katy got there–and he would only be able to do that if Katy was headed back by the same round-about route that she had come.

As soon as he could, McComb kicked a slight left rudder, bringing the deHavilland's nose around and he headed for the Texas border like a horse to the barn. Maybe Monroe had come up with something. Josh hoped that he hadn't. Then all there would be was the box, the oblong box he'd seen being loaded into the Stearman's cargo cockpit. Did it contain secret enemy contraband? Or, was it just ordinary border booty Katy was transporting for a local rancher who was trying to avoid paying duty. The guy in the white suit sure hadn't looked like a local, though. He had appeared to be one hundred percent European–probably German. Well, McComb would find out soon enough. If he were able to get back before Katy Faver did, he would just confront his friend right out front and the question would be answered once and for all.

"Herr Spengler, there is a young officer outside who is demanding to see you," said the young blond-haired man. "He prefers not to give his name."

It was ten minutes past one P.M., the beginning of the unofficial rest period for the prisoners at Fort D.A. Russell. That hour of the day when every man scrambled for his own intimate scrap of shade to hide from the brutal overhead sun for that sixty-minutes of peak incalescence.

Ignaz Dreshler had made his decision. It had taken him a full night of sleepless deliberation, weighing–on his unbalanced scale–the top priorities of his young life. Intrepidity had won out. Dreshler was still certain that to perform heroic held his destiny. At this precise moment, it seemed not to matter that a young woman waited for him back in the Fatherland. And that his love for the earth, the dirt and growing things, were taking a waxen rear seat while his thoughts dripped of bronze medals and cheering crowds advancing at a double-time goose-step.

"Dreshler? Dreshler," muttered the fat Nazi. "Ah, yes, I remember you now. What is it you want? I am a very busy man, as you know. Please make your request as brief as possible."

The young Iggy was taking his one-time dreams for the future and dashing them aside for this chance to hear his name proudly spoken from the lips of others. In all that double-talk last night with Herr Raller, he knew that he had lied. It was much more than just a fight with his conscience. It never really had been that. For his sense of self? There would be only one thing to feed that, wouldn't there. His inner-person hungered for parades and dinner parties, history books that contained his name. Was that not his real purpose in life? And just what would the life of a farmer gain him anyway? His woman would grow fat, for sure, and turn to sassing as his mother had. And his children would run off when they were barely old enough, leaving him a sour old man with nothing– just like his father. Not that life for Ignaz Dreshler. Even if he were to die, history would not let them bury him; let them fail to remember. History would never let them forget who he was. No. Raller was wrong. He had to be. Nothing could ever outweigh the life of a hero. Not even death itself.

"Am I to understand that you are willing to do anything?" said the smiling Spengler; "anything, to be a part of our plan, Herr Dreshler?"

Iggy's brain was spinning: *A man must sacrifice in order to gain; must do unthinkable things in order to obtain his future state; the mills of the Gods turn only for those who grind them; a man must create his own destiny*—words spoken by the Fuehrer himself.

"If what you say is indeed the truth, Herr Dreshler," the Nazi continued, "there just might possibly be some way of including you in our small group. Do you understand what it is I am saying to you?"

To be a hero; a mortal man above all others; loved by all; loathed by none. The ability to bestow one's presence on all humanity; to be worshipped and bowed down to by Presidents and Kings; to be known by every schoolchild from now until forever; to be—

"Herr Dreshler." Spengler's sharp snap sucked him back to the peppery stickiness of the small room. "Herr Dreshler, we haven't much time." The over-sweet words rolled from the Gestapo's mouth like soured milk from a scum-crusted ladle. "Come over to me, please."

Dreshler hesitated for only a brief moment as Raller's words from the night before echoed again: "Do what you have to, young Dreshler, that will always be your option."

He took a first slow step toward Spengler, then another. He would now do what he had to do.

Spengler said to him, "That is fine, my young pretty. Now come even closer. That's right. Good, good."

Dreshler stopped, facing the man. He closed his eyes slowly and stood, almost at attention. He could feel Spengler's vapid breath intruding, penetrating his nostrils. Then he felt a hand rest on his shoulder and begin to push him gently to his knees. "It should not take too long to find if you are worthy of joining us," said Spengler as he kissed him.

Dreshler did not resist.

CHAPTER ELEVEN

Jim-Bob Pelliteer's father came to the Big Bend somewhere around 1915 to work as a civilian blacksmith with the Army pack trains that made the sixday round-trips between Fort D.A. Russell–called Camp Marfa in those days–and the outpost at Lajitas. Jeptha Pelliteer had not been a young man. When he'd put in just under seven years working for the Army, he up and quit–retired, some say– and moved into the Bend permanently to take up with a Mexican-Zapotec Indian widow-woman he'd come to know over the years–a woman who was somewhere around the old man's age.

Something not too common happened to the couple within the next few months–she gave birth to twin boys. The children were healthy and brown from the moment of birth and both took to a horse's back like wood ticks to a hound dog. That came from the father's side of the family. Their mother would teach them other things. Before the youngsters could form words with their mouths, she had taught them the ancient language of the Avisadors: the secret code of the Mexican-Indians that was sent across the vast and desolate land with the use of mirrors or polished rocks. A tradition going back to the Aztecs at the time of Cortez, when the Spanish conqueror, upon landing, had been amazed at the short time it had taken for the news of his arrival to reach Moctezuma–some four days away by horseback–in the country's capital.

The woman would also teach the two boys the secrets of the Curanderos– *The Healers*. They were to learn all the necessary information from her on how to use and prepare the local plants and their roots and barks. Grinding and simmering the correct combinations until the preparations, along with the special healing skills and methods–secrets handed down through the generations–would be used for the curing of sickness and saving lives.

Jeptha Pelliteer and his Indian woman taught the twin boys everything they knew, and when the children turned six years old, Jeptha said it was time for the boys to go to a proper school and there was such a school at the Johnson Ranch.

No one quite knows how it happened–whether it was Jeptha's mule that had slipped, or if it had been one of the boys' animals. The father had tied them all together, saddle-to-saddle, while fording the Bravo at one of its deeper crossings. It was to be a short cut to the Johnson's; and either one of the animals had lost it's footing on a smooth rock pulling the other two mules down with it, or a log or drifting branch had tangled the line.

What the mother had found a day later—when her family had failed to return home and she'd spent all night tracking them, searching the river's banks—were the bloated remains of two of the animals, one of Jeptha's boots, and only *one* of the twins—just barely alive.

She carried the boy back to their jacal and with her secret potions—her knowledge as a Curandera—she'd brought him back to health within a week's time. She refused to recognize the child as a single entity and had bestowed upon him his dead brother's name, calling him Jim-Bob from then on. She took him to the school at the Johnson Ranch and left him with Ada Johnson, telling her the story of what happened and that it had been her husband's last wish that his two sons would have proper schooling.

She never returned for the boy. Whether she had been killed by some wild animal, or just gone back to her people, no one ever knew. But something had happened. When she failed to come back for her son that evening, the boy stopped speaking.

Jim-Bob Pelliteer. Was he James or Robert? It didn't really matter to Elmo and Ada. The boy was alone, so the Johnsons took him in to rear as their own.

Over the years, the Johnsons were to have to fight on several occasions to keep the boy. There were those in the area—some do-gooders down from Alpine—who thought that they knew what was best for the boy. "A child who cannot speak needs special training," they would say. And it took three separate trips to the Brewster County courthouse to eventually prove them wrong.

At first Ada could communicate with Jim-Bob better than Elmo. The boy had an understanding of English and Spanish that he'd learned from his parents. So when Ada spoke to him, or tried to teach him something new, the boy listened intently, and most times picked up whatever it was right off. He would return her conversation with variations on nods, smiles and frowns, and in no time, they had developed a simple form of sign language between them to which Elmo easily caught on.

Mechanical things intrigued the boy and the airplanes at the ranch became his toys. By the time he turned twelve, Jim-Bob Pelliteer could take apart any engine on the place and put it back together in less than three days—all by himself. Jim-Bob Pelliteer fit in perfectly at the Johnson Ranch. He just didn't talk, that's all.

Since just after sunrise, the low hills on the Mexican side of the Bravo had been alive with signs of the Avisadores. Flashing pin-pricks of coded communication bounced across the river in punctilious progression, reporting only to those who knew how to decipher them the progress of the two aeroplanes that had left from the Johnson ranch earlier that day.

Jim-Bob Pelliteer had been reading the avisos from the moment they had begun. The boy had been awakened several times that morning by the sounds of airplane engines; he was able to watch both Katherine Faver and McComb when they had taken off; and had seen the messages being flashed in the south shortly after. Later on that day when he first heard the sound of Josh McComb's returning deHavilland's engine break the silence, and then saw its outline on the low horizon preparing to land at the Johnson airstrip, he already knew about the meeting between Katherine and the man in the shiny shoes. And how McComb had followed and watched the transaction from hiding, even though it had taken place several hundred miles inside Mexico.

"I need your help," McComb said as he jumped down from the cockpit, "can you understand what I'm saying, Jim-Bob?"

The boy nodded. He had put the dog on a rope leash and it wiggled happily as McComb knelt to stroke its coat.

Josh continued as he petted the dog. "Block the wheels and tie her down. When Miss Faver gets here, you act like I've been here all day, OK?"

Jim-Bob nodded again, this time with a smile. He picked up two wooden wedges and started to block the plane's wheels. McComb told the dog to stay then headed off toward the bunkhouse. While he worked, Jim-Bob kept his eyes on the mountains. From them he learned something that McComb did not know—the avisos told him that the Stearman was not on its way back to the ranch at that moment, as Josh thought; but instead Katherine had flown on through The Window, and into the basin of the Chisos Mountains.

"Missa' Josh, am I sho' glad ta' see you." Monroe met McComb at the door as he entered the bunkhouse, "I think I found sumthin' that might be what we lookin' fo', suh."

McComb erased the words before he'd even chalked them on his mind's blackboard. "Yeah, Monroe," he uttered impatiently, "but right now I gotta' look like I've been around here all day." He began to pull off his boots, untucking his shirt. "We gotta' act like nothin's happened." He tossed himself onto his bunk, ruffling the covers.

"But, Missa' Josh, suh," Monroe urged him, "I think you best take a look at this, right now."

McComb threw a glance toward the black man who stood in front of him. "Monroe," he said with some irritation in his voice, "Listen to me. She should be right behind me. Act like you've been napping. We don't want her ta' know we've bin' pryin', now do we?"

Monroe seemed not to be listening. He just reached down and lifted the bed cover on McComb's cot, pulling it up slightly and revealing a large metal object. Josh sat up. From what he could see of it, it looked to be painted olive drab. "What, what is it, Monroe?" he asked, puzzled.

"Well, suh'," the black man continued, "it done look to me as to be one of them short-wave radios. I found it in Miss Katherine's cabin."

McComb stood up slowly, his eyes locking into Monroe's. There was a long moment as the stark reality finally hit him. Katy was one of them. That crazy woman was working with the goddamn enemy. He sat down, then laid back on the cot. All he could do was stare at the ceiling, while his battered hopes slid to the floor. He tried to think, but his brain threw blank images. There was nothing left. He slowly closed his eyes and whispered, "What do I do now, Monroe?"

The black man's words came slowly. Josh McComb had heard them many times before. "Why don't ya' jes' turn it over, Missa' Josh. Jes' turn it over to the Lord. Let Him handle everything."

Oberstleutnant Erich Jurgen Raller was falling again. This time it was not from the cockpit of a shot up Messerschmitt, nor was it taking place over the English Channel. In actuality, he was not quite falling. He was rolling over and over down an incline, a small knoll, covered in dry mustard grass and dandelions, somewhere near the outskirts of his own village in the Fatherland. He held Anna in his arms and they tumbled, together, down the velvet slope, entwined in the echoes of their own laughter, entranced in their deep love for one another. Anna was Erich Raller's wife. And when they'd rolled down the hill together on that afternoon so long ago they had only recently become engaged to be married.

Sometimes Raller would have liked to dream of his Anna as she was now–in the present. A sturdy, silver streaked, mother of their three grown children; who waited, as she had many times before, on the porch of their home near Leipzig if–between the bombings and God's Grace–the house still stood. Instead, his subconscious seemed to always bound back to those earlier days when they were both much younger; to those oh so few quiet times, that short span of serenity–between the two wars–when they were forever together.

They had just come to a rest at the bottom of the hill and he was brushing some thorns from her hair when his attention was drawn away. Beyond her radiance he could see the figure of a soldier. The uniform he wore was so tattered Raller could not tell from which war he came, but the voice was familiar. So was his face. The soldier was Erich Raller himself.

He lay there silently, beside Anna, neither of them daring to breathe, as the young soldier began walking slowly toward them. It was apparent that the soldier had been mortally wounded, for his body gaped with huge, bleeding holes and his face had been partially ripped and blackened by exploding gasoline or gunpowder. His eyes were void of expression or direction and he was filled with fatigue. When the soldier stopped, just a few feet from the two of them, he did not look down. When he finally spoke, the words came tired and empty: "I will fight this war, Mein Herr. I will fight at your side. I have chosen it to be this way."

Though Raller knew he was dreaming, the words were too real. So real, in fact, that they caused Raller's eyes to roll half-open, arousing him from his fantasy. Young Iggy stood beside his bunk in the steaming barracks and spoke with the same cadence as the soldier in the dream. "I am going with you, Herr Raller." The statement spoke for itself. "I have now been accepted into the group."

His clothes were not torn; nor was his body battered. But Raller could tell by his look that he had been victim to something. "Spengler has had a part in this decision of yours. That is a sure bet," Raller found himself saying. "Here, let me help you." He rolled off his cot and to his feet; then took the boy's arm, easing him to his own bunk. There appeared to be no outward bruises, no blood, but it was apparent that Iggy had taken some kind of abuse. If Spengler *had* been involved–Raller placed his second bet–the involvement had to have been sexual. That was how the S.S. worked in these situations.

"Please, Herr Raller," Iggy whispered. "What has happened to me was of my own asking. My body will heal. My soul, I cannot be that sure of."

"What in God's name has he done to you?" asked Raller.

"I requested a favor of him," replied Iggy, "and he asked one in return. I guess I have, as they say, paid the piper." He chuckled quietly, a painful grimace altering his brow.

"The man is swine, Iggy," spat Raller. "If you would like for me to, I will–"

Dreshler's hand reached out to Raller's lips, covering his words. A silent smile crept into the young man's exhausted face; he shook his head slowly. "If you are truly my friend, Herr Raller, you will do nothing. I have made my own decision. My own selfishness drew me into something I was not ready to believe. But, what happened is now the past and from it I have discovered a great deal. I look now only to the future and that I will be going with you back to the Fatherland. That is all that matters, is it not?"

Raller had to nod in agreement, at the same time holding his emotions back. His instinct was to seek Spengler out at once and to put an end to his evil life. But the words flowing from Dreshler's mouth perked him. Iggy, though he had not done what Raller had suggested, had been listening. The thought made him smile.

Dreshler watched Raller's reaction; and because it was unexpected, he began to smile also, if only from curiosity. "What is it that you find so amusing, Herr Raller?" the younger man asked.

Raller substituted his smile with a low laugh, "Oh, Iggy, you beautiful fool. It is just that you remind me so of myself at your age that is all. Just let me say that it will be a pleasure to have you along."

Dreshler's smile faded some and he appeared to pull back, "Then, it does not bother you, what I did to make it all possible?"

"Iggy," Raller went on, "your conscience belongs only to you, no one else. It is your own to do with what only *you* want. Treasure that. What a man does in the name of what he thinks is right, makes that thing right whether it be wrong in the long run. Enough said?"

Iggy nodded.

"Then, it has all been said." Raller leaned across to younger man and took his hand in his own. "Welcome, Ignaz Dreshler. Welcome to life."

CHAPTER TWELVE

Fort D.A. Russell was situated in such a way that had it a back door it would have damn near opened directly into Mexico. At least it appeared that way. Mexico was eighty miles to the south and in between stood some of the most inaccessible territory ever to bubble up from the depths of prehistoric Northern America. For that very reason, the Army post had come into being in 1914. It was mainly utilized as a Quartermaster Depot for the pack and wagon-trains that traversed the Big Bend area supplying the twelve outposts in the immense district during the Mexican Revolution; the subsequent bandit raids; and on into the following years when prohibition brought the rumrunners in droves.

By the late 1920s, the Fort, known as Camp Marfa up until then, had all but served its purpose and came quite close to being abandoned. On January 30, 1930, its name was changed in honor of David Ashley Russell, a United States soldier who died a valiant death serving as a colonel with the Massachusetts Infantry while fighting the War with Mexico: 1846-1848. After a brief attempt to prolong the fort's survival, which didn't quite work out, the post was closed down in 1933. Fort D.A. Russell's 6,000 acres were to sleep peacefully for the next few years, remaining in government hands until she silently crept back into business with the onset of the present war. In November of 1943, the German Prisoner of War Camp was established on the grounds to help the British government with their overflow, making it one of the several hundred bases and branch camps in the nation to be utilized for such purpose. On a map, Fort D.A. Russell appeared to be the furthest most outpost of its kind in the United States. If one happened to be American, and stationed there; or if one were German and incarcerated behind its windblown barbed wire; one was continually, if not peremptorily, aware of the eternal solitude.

"Wake up, Iggy. It is time to go." Raller's whisper jerked the young officer from his restless slumber with the acuity of a booming command. "Roust yourself and be as quiet as you can," he continued. "We will be leaving soon. Make ready the best you are able."

Dreshler's eyes took a moment to adjust to the darkened barracks. Fuzzy configurations appeared to swim across the dim backlight that filtered in from the compound outside. Hushed hisses swirled silently around him: murky sounds of men moving; inaudible buffeting, as feet slid into trouser legs; the muffled buckling of brass to leather; and the stifled bumps of boots being pulled on and fastened. He found his own breeches and jerked them on. His boots were located beneath his bunk where he always left them. Across from him in the inklike darkness he could still sense Raller's presence and he blinked until a silhouette of sorts was faintly formed. "Herr Raller," he whispered, "I do not understand. We have not prepared. We have received no instructions. How can this be?"

He felt Raller's hand take a firm hold on his arm and he could detect the man's familiar scent as he drew closer. "Iggy," Raller whispered back, "in the Wehrmacht, there are no questions. You have not been here so long to forget that. Now stay quiet and continue dressing. I will find Herr Spengler and tell him that we are ready."

Earlier that afternoon, Josh McComb and Monroe Leaton had waited in the bunkhouse for the sound of Katherine Faver's Stearman. After an hour of expectant minutes had ticked by and there was still no sign of her, they decided to take a walk on over to the airfield to continue their vigil.

Jim-Bob was picking bugs off the deHavilland's windscreen and rubbing down the wooden struts. Josh's dog, sleeping nearby, awoke and looked up as the men crunched their way across the reflective gravel from the ranch yard. As they approached Jim-Bob, the boy continued with his chores. McComb moved up to one of the wings and leaned against it. He looked off toward the river while Leaton found a shady spot near the dog and sat down, reclining against a wheel. Neither man said a word for the first few minutes while the faint squeaking of Jim-Bob's polishing-cloth massaging the wood, and the late afternoon breeze fluttering through the windsock, cut pleasantly into the isolation.

Monroe took out his makin's and began his ritual of rollin' one. McComb watched as the big Negro tugged open the pouch with his teeth while his fingers creased the papers. He poured one neat row of tobacco and rolled, licked and lit in his usual way, waving out the match and breaking it in two as he always did. He took a long drag of the smoke, inhaled deeply, scratched his lower lip with his upper teeth and spit something dry and mysterious into the wind. Josh shook his head and chuckled softly.

"What's that you thinkin' this time, Missa' Josh?" Monroe chuckled back.

McComb pawed at the sand with his boot-toe and squinted off to the horizon once again, "Oh, I don't rightly know, Monroe. Just the way you roll them cigarettes, I reckon. No two men ever do it the same way, did ya' ever notice?"

Monroe nodded slowly, taking another long draw. "Reckon I have, Missa' Josh, reckon I have," he answered quietly. "Mos' peoples don't do nothin' the same way at all. They'd sho' 'nough die iffin' they did. It's as if the good Lord gave 'em that free will an' danged if they ain't gonna' use it–no matter what." He took a third drag and blew out the smoke slowly, twisting the butt in his long brown fingers. "I learnt' how ta' fix my makins' from my pappy, 'ceptin' along the times, I done changed a few of the 'gottas' an' 'just sos', so I could say that I was doin' it my own special way. Seems mens jus' have ta' do that, Missa' Josh. They jus' caint' be happy walkin' another man's path."

Josh agreed. "Yeah, just like Katy," he said nodding. "I'd a bet fer' sure she'd be on the straight an' narrow. I mean, the two of us used ta' do a few things just shy of shady when we were together, but I'd never thought she'd be in a mess like this. An' even now, where the hell is she? Probably off sellin' more secrets to the Nazis, or maybe even plannin' on–" His voice trailed off. There he was, pre-judging again. Only this time there were a few facts. "Jeeze, Monroe," he continued. "I'm still way up in the air about all this. I feel like a trapped coyote." His eyes searched the sky again. "An' damnit, she shoulda' been here by now. I know she couldn't a' been more than fifteen ta' twenty minutes behind me. More than two hours have already gone by since I got back."

Monroe's eyes had shifted from McComb to the boy. Josh followed his look and saw that Jim-Bob was shaking his head and making some kind of signs with his hands, gesturing toward the Chisos. Josh asked, "What's he saying, Monroe? What's the boy trying to tell us?"

Leaton got to his feet and moved past McComb, stopping next to the boy. He appeared to recognize some of the hand motions. After a few moments, he turned back to Josh. "Jim-Bob says that Miss Faver went to the mountains–that she flew her plane through The Window."

McComb thought for a moment. "The Window? Hey, that's the place I pointed out to you the other day," he said excitedly. "That's where we saw that black airplane disappear inta' the Chisos, remember?" Josh moved closer to the others. "Ask 'im if he's seen a black plane around here–ask him that, Monroe."

Leaton did not have to attempt any more sign language. Jim-Bob understood Josh's words perfectly. He sent back his answer with three simple hand movements. Monroe translated: "Jim-Bob says that the black plane belongs ta' Miss Faver, too."

Wallace Bowman had stolen the knife when he was ten years old. It had been on display on the faded green velvet in the dusty counter-top showcase in Mr. Rubin's sporting goods shop–between the replica of a Genuine Bowie Knife and the chrome B.B. pistol–for as long as the boy could remember. On the day he stole the knife, he had vowed to kill Tubby Brockman because the larger boy and two other neighborhood toughs had pantsed him on the playground while Becky Stein and Patsy McCorkindale looked on and laughed at him. The incident had caused him much embarrassment. And since there was nothing he could do to the two girls, after all, hadn't they also been victims? And because he didn't know where two of the boys lived–he'd seen them before but didn't know their names–the only one left to pay for the crime of holding him down and pulling off his knickers and underwear–exposing him to the greatest humiliation he had ever experienced in all of his ten years–was Tubby Brockman. So he stole the knife–a pearl handled switchblade–and when he got the chance, he would de-gut that fat-assed bastard Tubby Brockman and string his intestines all the way to Queens. Only he never got the chance. Tubby Brockman had either moved away, or transferred to another school or whatever. Bowman really didn't remember. But he had carried the knife with him ever since. It had stayed in his righthand pocket throughout his school years, on into basic training, and had traveled all the way to West Texas with him. But he had never used it. Not even to clean his fingernails. As a matter of fact, he'd almost forgotten that it was even there.

The final agreement he had made with the fat German he knew as Ballena was about to be consummated. For doing his part, Wallace Bowman would collect a cool thousand; not the twenty or fifty bucks like he'd been getting along the way, tossed to him, whenever they felt like it, in the waterproof match container. But, one thousand big ones: ten-hundred dollars. Enough to split to anywhere he wanted to after the war was over. Enough to get his New York ass as far away from Brooklyn–and the bitch called Peggy–as he ever wanted to get.

Even though it was night, from his vantage in his tower Bowman could look across the three compounds with an unobstructed view of every single barracks building in the entire fort. It was his job to watch them all with equal scrutiny. Except on this night he would only be interested in one. It was the third building in number two compound, the building from which the fat man would send his signal. When that happened, all Wallace Bowman had to do was to climb down from his guard tower and open the gate below. That was it. And one thousand smackers would be his. So damn simple–so damn easy. Just how dumb could these sourkrauts be? Shit, what a bunch of suckers.

That afternoon, when the Stearman finally appeared on the eastern horizon–looking at first like an orange fire-fly as it dropped out of the deep blue and into the twilight, angling down lower and lower in its approach to the Johnson airfield–Josh had turned to Monroe and said, "Lookie there. Here she comes. Just like a traitor to come back like nothin' has happened."

The black man had moved in beside his friend, resting his hand on McComb's shoulder in an effort to calm his anxiety. "Missa' Josh," he had said, "maybe you oughtn't be accusin' Miss Faver right off the stick. You don't really know– "

"Damnit, Monroe," said Josh cutting in, "she's makin' a fool out of me. Can't you see that?"

Monroe just shook his head and replied, "It's only you that see the fool, Missa' Josh. All I can see is a broken heart."

The Stearman touched down, its engine drowning out Leaton's last words. The two men stood at the side of the runway, neither saying any more, as Katherine taxied the plane around and finally stopped it a few feet away. "Howdy fellas," said Katy, as she climbed down from the cockpit.

The engine hadn't even chirped to a stop before Josh was on her.

"If you were a man, Katy Faver," he said angrily, "I'd knock you on your backside."

Katherine had already sensed his rage. "Geezes," she replied instinctively. "What's gotten into you? What the hell's the matter, McComb?"

Josh pushed his way past her, jumping up on the wing of the Stearman and leaning over to check into the cargo cockpit. When he was satisfied that it was empty, he dropped back to the ground. Moving back to the woman, he took her by both shoulders, forcing her up against the Stearman's fuselage. "Where is it, Katy?" he said, "What did you do with it?"

Katherine still acted quite innocent. "Where is what?" she asked, somewhat jumpy. "For heaven's sake, McComb, what in God's name are you talking about?"

Josh didn't miss a beat, "The box, Katy," he said angrily. "The damn box you picked up in Mexico this morning."

Katherine attempted a surprised reaction but realized McComb wasn't going to buy her story.

Josh continued. "Don't look at me like that, damnit," he said, speaking sharply. "You know exactly what I'm talking about. The wooden crate you got from that damn–Nazi."

The emotions involved in this altercation were working Katherine Faver toward tears. She realized that Josh hadn't forgotten; that he still knew her much too well for her to get away with lying to him. All she could do was look away.

McComb shook her slightly. "Why are you doing this, Katherine? What's making you do this?"

Katherine blinked away a tear. Was she angry? *No. Just relieved*, she thought. "I'm sorry, McComb," she finally said softly. "I'm truly sorry."

McComb released his grip on her shoulders. Stepping back he said to her, "Would you mind telling us why you did it?" His fury was beginning to fade.

Katherine avoided making direct eye contact with him. "Please forgive me, McComb. I'm sorry."

Josh shook his head. "Sorry don't cut it, Katy."

Katherine looked up, attempted to say something. "I guess I thought," she said faltering, "I guess," she hesitated again. "Damnit, McComb, I can't lie to you anymore."

McComb dropped his head, putting their eyes on the same level. He spoke in a dead serious tone. "Just tell us about the Germans, Katy. What are they up to? The box you were bringing back from Mexico isn't on your plane anymore. What were you hauling, Katy? What was in that damn box you brought across the Bravo for 'em?"

Katherine laughed softly. "You followed me, didn't you? I kind of thought you were on to me. I guess I should have come out and told you about everything last night when we– " She hesitated once again, then began anew. "McComb," she said solemnly, "I brought in some guns for them. I smuggled in a couple of high-ranking Nazis a week ago, brought in some gasoline for them, too. Then today, I brought in their weapons. That's what the big box had in it."

Josh could only shake his head. "In God's name, Katherine–why?"

"What else?" answered Katy. "Money … I was broke, McComb. I lied to you the other night, too. You were right, I was wrong. There never was enough business down here. You were oh so right to get out when you did. I bled myself to death financially trying to keep up the payments on the planes I bought."

She seemed to choke up momentarily. Josh handed her his bandanna. Katherine blew her nose, dabbing her eyes. Then she continued. "The Nazis showed up when I was at my lowest ebb, McComb. I was crying in my beer down in Tanque and they just squeezed up to me real friendly. They offered me some real good money if I'd take them and some other things across the border into the United States. I didn't know that they were Nazis until after I'd flown them here. That's the God's truth, McComb."

McComb interjected, "Then they blackmailed you after you found out who they really were?"

"I only wish it were that simple," said Katherine. "No. They just dangled more dinero in front of me. They needed a plane, and I had one I wanted to sell."

McComb's eyes widened, "The black plane Monroe and I saw the other day. That was yours?"

Katherine nodded. "That's the one I sold them. They were going to fly it out themselves but the engine blew up on them yesterday. They radioed me while you were down at Hot Springs and said that I was in too deep now not to continue cooperating with them. They sent me for the guns today. Tomorrow I'll be flying them out of the country. That is, if they can all get back down here by then."

"Wait a minute," said McComb, "I thought there were only two of them. You said 'all.' Are there more?"

Katherine nodded. "They're coming down from Fort Russell. They're breaking out some real important prisoner."

McComb turned to Leaton. "Monroe, you get on up to the house. Phone Marfa. We better notify someone up there."

Monroe nodded and started to move away. He stopped when he saw Katherine reach out for McComb's arm, gripping it tight. "McComb," she began, "it's too late. And this thing is too big. No phone call is going to stop anything. They're too smart for that. I'm willing to bet they've already cut the lines for sure."

McComb looked her directly in the eyes and said, "Katy, try to remember if they set any time limits. Can you recall if they ever said how long it was gonna' take 'em to get back down here to the Bend? And, where were you supposed to meet them?"

"They've been holed up at that abandoned C.C.C. camp in the Chisos basin," said Katherine. "They're using that old forest road in the basin for a landing strip. I'm supposed to fly in there at dawn tomorrow and wait for them, then fly this special guy out of the country."

Josh turned to Monroe. "Maybe we should fly up there right now and try an' catch 'em by surprise. There's gotta' be somethin' we can do to try an' stop 'em."

Katherine shook her head, "No, they've gone by now. They were getting ready to leave when I delivered the box of weapons this afternoon. They had two of those old Army quad trucks the government left up there, and a ton of gasoline. They were going to head on up to Marfa while there was still some daylight. The escape is set for midnight. They're going to meet the prisoners and bring them back cross-country to the Chisos by morning."

McComb had an idea. "Then, what if *both* of us were waitin' for 'em when they showed up back at the basin, instead of just you?"

Katherine shook her head. "We'd be outnumbered that's what. They're bringing out at least ten men, for protection. They'll all be armed to the teeth."

Josh thought for a moment. "Hey, didn't you say that Elmo still has the machine guns for his deHavilland around here somewhere?" "Stored in the barn, I'm sure," said Katy.

McComb's lips curled into a slight smile; then he said, "How long would it take us to remount those guns, get 'em in working order? Do you think we could get Elmo's deHavilland war-ready before the sun comes up?"

Katherine raised an eyebrow, "I really don't know, McComb." She turned to the silent Jim-Bob who had been listening intently all along. "Jim-Bob," she spoke slowly, "do you honestly think that's possible?"

The boy smiled softly. Then he nodded assuredly.

The signal had been nothing more than the flame from a cigarette lighter. Wally Bowman had expected a flashlight, or something larger, but instead it had just been a small, orange flame reflected in the German officers' barracks window. One, two. One, two. A long burn, then repeat again. That was it. That was Ballena's signal. Two long flashes meant that it was a "go." Bowman now had just three minutes to do his part and then he would collect his one thousand dollars.

Bowman was sure he knew at least two reasons why they had picked him and his tower. First was that it stood guard over one of the two gates that could lead them to complete freedom, and the second was that every other gate in the outer fence that surrounded all three compounds was watched over by at least two M.P.s at all times. Bowman's gate had the only twin towers, but because it stood so near the garrison echelon and the officers' quarters, and because Fort D.A. Russell was always short on staff, the brass had figured that only one man would be needed at that particular position.

Bowman felt in his pants pocket for the key. It sure had been easy to come by. He chuckled to himself as he thought of what people would say if they ever found out how he'd switched the locks on the tool shed with the ones on the gate. No one would ever know the difference anyway because no one ever opened the gate, and no one would ever be the wiser because he was in charge of the tool shed anyway. Oh, did he cackle to himself as he set aside his shotgun and climbed down the wooden ladder to the ground. From the base of the tower it was just fifteen feet. Fifteen small paces to the gate; a quick twist of the key in both locks; then back to the foot of the tower where he would wait for his pay off: one thousand smackers. The thought of the money flared in his mind as he moved out toward the gate. His hand was in his pocket, the key between his fingers. A thousand bucks. Just a few more steps and his troubles would be over for good.

"Hey, soldier!" echoed the voice from the dark. "What in the hell are you doing down here?"

Bowman stopped in his tracks. Who in the shit was that? He stood motionless and waited as he heard footsteps crunch up behind him. His hand remained in his pocket. He let go of the key.

"I asked you a question, soldier." The voice was closer now. "What are you doing in this area?"

A large hand fell on his shoulder and spun him around. He found himself looking past an Officer of the Day armband and up into the bulldog face of Leroy Skuggins. *Oh shit,* he thought.

"Why, if it ain't ol' Queen Cole, out fer' a stroll," Leroy grunted sarcastically, his grip on Bowman's shoulder tightening as a sneer replaced the smugness on his lips. "You really did it this time, punk," he continued. "This is court-martial stuff, asshole. Leavin' yer' post while on dut–"

Skuggins heard the rusty snap just a second too late. By the time the sound had registered in his mind, his upper intestine was spilling its halfdigested contents down his perfect military creases. Bowman didn't even wait for him to fall. He left Leroy standing there, attempting to scream, while he moved to the gate. But Skuggins' lungs refused to pump air. The blade of the switchknife had severed too many nerves.

Bowman slid the key into the first lock. Click–it opened. And the second one: click, click–on the button. He turned, re-pocketed the key. Skuggins still stood where he'd been left. His knees were refusing to buckle. The shock had set his knees stiff, frozen Skuggins' muscles, and he was slowly dying on his feet. Bowman moved back to him and stopped. The switchblade's pearl handle was protruding from the jellied wound that he'd made in the big man's stomach. Should he retrieve it, or just leave the knife there as a reminder to others? A gurgling hiss lifted his attention to Skuggins' face, the mouth already mute in an immobilized cry. Leroy's eyes were bugged out like overinflated balloons, ready to explode with horrific pain. The man's hands still pressed against his shirtfront in a last feeble attempt to retain what was left of his insides. Bowman just stood there, watching him die. Why had he waited so long to kill someone for real, he thought. Every damn one of them should have suffered like Leroy was suffering. Skuggins' head dropped with a startling jerk–just an inch or so. A knee had begun to give way. Bowman could wait no longer. He could hear the muffled footsteps of the Germans coming from between the barracks buildings. He raised his hand and shoved slightly. Skuggins's body crumpled into a heap at his feet. "Fuck you, sucker," said Wallace Bowman in a hushed tone. He moved back to the ladder.

"Oh my God, that man is dead," whispered Iggy. He and Raller were crouched beside a building with the seven other prisoners, huddled and waiting while Spengler went to deal with the American soldier whom Raller had figured was going to–or had already–assisted them. From their position, they could see the two men as they met and engaged in what appeared to be a heated argument. On the ground beside the American and Spengler, half hidden in the deep shadows, lay the dead body. "Something must have gone wrong, already," added Dreshler.

"In times of war, Iggy, *things* do not go wrong," whispered Raller, *"things* just get in the way. More than likely," he nodded toward the body, "that American soldier lying there is one of those *things."*

They continued to watch Spengler and the American soldier until the two finally appeared to agree on something. Then Spengler turned and motioned to the prisoners. They moved out quietly, one by one, until they were all gathered under the tower. "We will wait here until we receive a signal from the outside," whispered Spengler, "then we will move on through the gate. It has already been unlocked for us by our American friend here," he nodded toward Bowman, "who, I would like to add, will be joining us. He is, how should I say, defecting."

There were several cautious looks thrown around by the prisoners. Spengler continued, attempting to calm some fears, "Our American friend has killed one of his own, and because he fears the consequences of the act, he feels it best that he accompany us. Please make him feel welcome. His name is Bowman."

Wallace Bowman could feel every eye fall upon him–dark, shadowed eyes; the eyes of respect shown by fearful men; men who had seen bravery before; men who had tasted death. He knew that they were admiring him for his courage–something that his own peers had never done. He nodded slowly with the Germans nodding back. He felt glad that he had told Ballena that he would be going with them. He'd known that the fat man would argue, but being as smart as he was, he'd also known that Ballena would have no time to waste, and he'd finally agreed to let him go with them. Now, it was all set, and of course, he wouldn't be going all the way to Germany with them either. He'd just stick around until they crossed over into Mexico, then he'd thank them and be on his way. The one thousand dollars in his pocket that Ballena had given him warmed his thigh. In Mexico one thousand dollars was a king's ransom; and after all, he was The King.

"Stupid American idiot," spat Raller in a hoarse whisper from where he and Iggy were huddled near the rear of the group.

"Why do you say that, Herr Raller?" Dreshler asked quietly.

"Because Spengler will kill him, that is why," was Raller's answer. There was a hushed rustling of clothes as heads turned toward the gate.

Distant headlamps could be seen flickering on and off from a far plateau. They had blinked twice. Now there was darkness again.

"That was our signal, gentlemen," said Spengler in German. "Our Fatherland awaits our gallant return."

CHAPTER THIRTEEN

Red Collinson had only been eight years old when he'd witnessed a man's death for the first time. His father had taken him by buckboard up the road from Marfa twenty-three miles to the Army post at Fort Davis, where one Seth Culver was going to be hanged. The trip had taken them a full day. People came from as far away as El Paso and San Antonio to observe the moribund occasion. Many of the travelers had been allowed to use the fort's parade ground to camp overnight so they could all gather at sunrise for the execution.

The only other thing that Collinson remembered from that day in the last century–besides the blur of a thousand faces and the excitement that ran rampant through the crowd–was the ringing of the bells. Someone, either a guard or the hangman, himself, had tied a hame-strap around the condemned man's ankle. On that leather fastening had hung several harness bells. Because of the noise of the crowd, the sound of the bells had been muted as the prisoner was led to the gallows. But when he climbed the steps and the noose was placed around his neck and tightened, all the talking had ceased and it was then that the boy had been hoisted to his father's shoulders for a better look. And it had also been then that young Red Collinson first heard the bells play their death song. At the time, young Red hadn't the foggiest notion of where the faint ringing was coming. But when the trap was tripped and Seth Culver fell the few feet to the end of the taut rope and his feet began to jerk and kick, young Red would hear the bells ring clear, as did the rest of the gathering. All would listen in awed silence to the discordant tinkling until Culver's body was finally still.

Red Collinson was dreaming of that day from his past, dreaming of it in more complete detail than he had ever dreamed it before. And his subconscious eyes shut as the body dangled, just as they had shut on that warm morning in 1890. He could hear his father say, "Open your eyes, boy. Open your eyes." And the sound of the bells clanged in his head as the intensity built, and when Seth Culver's legs jerked and kicked, Red Collinson's legs jerked and kicked and he sat upright in the darkened room. From somewhere in the murky obscurity his phone was ringing. He wiped the perspiration from his face then flung back the covers. Throwing his feet over the side, he got out of bed.

"Collinson here," he mumbled into the mouthpiece, "wha'd'ya' want?" Red Collinson's vocal chords hummed rough and dry. He cleared his throat and tried again. "Texas Ranger Captain Collinson here, go ahead," he said into the phone.

"Captain," said the voice on the other end, "this is Colonel Purrington out at Russell. Sorry about being so late, but–" He paused. "What we talked about–" There was another hesitation and Collinson could hear a long, deliberate breath being taken in. "What we talked about. Well, it's happened," said the colonel, letting out the rest of the breath in a whoosh of air that made Collinson back off from the earpiece for a brief moment.

The ranger thought for an instant, picking his words, making them simple in case some busy-body or the Marfa Operator might still happen to be on the party-line. "When'd it happen?" he said in a monotone.

"About twenty-minutes ago," answered the colonel. "One of my men spotted them," he continued, "and, thank God, he reported to me and didn't start shooting. We found a body. They killed one of my soldiers, Captain."

"Now Colonel Purrington," said Collinson calmly, "you just take it easy. I'll go round up some men and be there as soon as I can. How many prisoners got out?"

"Ten or so, we think," said Purrington. "As far as we can gather; no more than that. We're taking a roll count right now."

"OK, you just–" Collinson damn near said, hold down the fort, then he thought better of it and continued: "You just do what you have to an' we'll be there before you know it."

Purrington sounded relieved. "Thank you, Captain. Thank you," he said. There was a quiet click. Collinson held the phone to his ear for another few seconds until he was sure that there had been no other listeners. He hung up and found the pull-chain for the kitchen light. *Damn*, he thought, *why did these things invariably have to happen at night?* He couldn't remember one chase in his entire career that hadn't started out at some God-forsaken predawn hour. Collinson stared at the phone for a few moments and decided not to use the damn thing. If someone did happen to chance on overhearing him calling in for a posse, why, the whole danged town might fly off the edge; and what he didn't need was a bunch of out of control vigilantes. No. What he'd best do was stop by and get Plunker on the way to the office. Then he could pick up Lester Suggs and some extra guns. The three of them could then stop off quick at the Marcy place on the way to Fort Russell. C.D. Marcy would surely furnish some horses and trailers and he knew that he could count on Cecil Sitters to join up. And if he were lucky, maybe he could deputize some of Marcy's hands to go along with them. That should be enough. And there was Josh McComb. Yeah, he'd get Cecil to send someone over to Josh McComb's place and get him, too. Use McComb and Marcy's plane to kind of scout ahead just like they used to do back in the bandit days. "Well, giddyup, Charley," he said out loud, "what're ya' waitin' fer'." He stood up and moved back into his bedroom and started to dress.

The Germans crept along–one behind the other–at uneven distances, using a shallow barranca that ran parallel to the fort's perimeter as cover. After several hundred yards, they found temporary safe harbor in a small cottonwood grove where they could regroup. From that position they could see both the fort from which they'd come, and the low mesa where they were going. At this point, Spengler took a count of the men as they clustered in around him.

"Janish?"

"Ya," came the hushed answer.

"Wilming?"

"Over here, Herr Spengler."

"Von Vaerst?"

"Ya."

"Schroer, Kozur?"

"Ya. Ya," came the replies.

"Raller?"

"Do not worry, Mein Herr. I will not go far."

There were some hushed chuckles. Spengler did not think it funny. He continued, "Dreshler, Rossmeisl, Hurferichter."

"Ya," "Ya," "Ya."

"And Bowman," he said, smiling; looking at the American beside him whose anxious eyes were still fixed on the Fort Russell gate they'd left behind. "Bowman, what about you?" Spengler said in English. "Are you still with us?"

"Oh. Yeah," Bowman answered while nodding. "I was just making sure that no one was following us; that's all."

"Good, good," said Spengler. "If that is your preference, maybe I should appoint you as our rear guard."

"I hope you ain't making fun of me, Ballena," hissed Bowman, "'cause if you are—"

Spengler shook his head, cutting him off. "No; no, of course not, Corporal. You are one of us now. I was just treating you as such."

Bowman nodded. For some reason he believed the German. He felt at ease around these men. In all his time as a military police guard, it was damn sure the first time he had ever been treated with such respect. Hell, this was the first time he'd ever even spoken to a German personally, and damned if they weren't all turning out to be some OK guys. Bowman began to let his second thoughts about his being accepted so easily fade away, and he started thinking about his future. Overseas, these same German soldiers would be blowing American brains out, and behind barbed wire, he had always thought of them as animals. But now he was beginning to see them in a different light. Maybe there would be a few of them who would follow him into Mexico. Follow him as their new leader—their new Füehrer—and settle with him in the kingdom he would build in the new land. He looked around at the faces in the small group and saw their fears seeping through. He could also see their warmth and their inner emotions showing. They didn't make fun of him and they didn't seem to consider him their inferior as his brother M.P.s always had. On the other hand, maybe he would go all the way to Germany with them after all, he thought. They might just treat a man of his intelligence with respect over there. With his knowledge, and his being from America and all, just maybe he could be of some value. And Hitler; when Hitler heard about his deeds, Hitler just might want to consult with him— one ruler to another.

"All right," said Spengler in a loud whisper, "we will move out now."

As they started off again, Bowman waited until the last man passed him, then he glanced back toward the fort for one final look. It was a good distance, but he was sure that he saw the figure of a man running from the gate toward the officers' quarters, and he was more than sure that he saw the lights in the old man's billet snap on. Ballena had said that the Army would not follow them, that something had been arranged by higher-ups to prevent a pursuit. But Bowman could not be sure of that. He'd served under Purrington just a little too long to bet on a sure thing like that.

Hein Pachter and Wolfgang Kuft were waiting atop a bluff a short distance from Fort Russell sucking calmly on American cigarettes, dressed in Union Made cotton and looking rather native themselves. Both men sat behind the steering wheels of twin quad trucks, the two ancient but well greased four-wheel drive vehicles they had acquired from the abandoned C.C.C. camp that rested securely in the basin atop the rugged Chisos range, some one-hundred miles southwest of where they were now. As of that moment, the two Nazis had reached what they believed to be the halfway mark in their present assignment– a mission that had begun many thousands of miles to the east, yet had commenced only two weeks earlier.

Pachter and Kuft were Waffen S.S. Cream of the crop. Both had been with the Schutsstaffeln pre-Himmler, back in the days when Maurice Schreichenheiden led the group; back when it had been considered by most to be just another band of toughs, rather than the elite clique of personal bodyguards to the Füehrer that it was now. Both men had donned the black cap with the silver death's head emblem and had worn it with sincere pride and efficiency throughout the growth years of the National Socialist Party. On direct orders from Hitler they had gone underground in 1936–during the Spanish Civil War.

Always working together, they had carried Hitler's private espionage war to every single country in Europe at one time or another and had been on assignment in Portugal when the special orders for this particular deputation reached them. Their instructions were to fly immediately to Mexico where a rather large Nazi network would assist them in getting as far north as Tanque. From then on the two would be on their own. Once they were in Tanque they would receive their final orders. And when they decoded that last dictum both were somewhat startled. They were to be personal envoys of the Füehrer; bodyguards, as in the old days. Only now they were to escort a famed war hero from a prisoner-of-war camp in Texas, all the way back to Berlin. An easy assignment for these two, as nearly all arrangements for the escape itself would be left up to others. All that would be required of them would be to cross into the enemy's territory and bring the prisoner out–unharmed.

The first thing they had needed was an airplane. They found that easily enough. A drunken Texas female aviator they encountered in a Tanque cantina turned out to be more than happy to fly the two into the U.S.–for the right price. An additional sum helped her to drop them exactly where they wanted to go: a deserted C.C.C. camp located in a desolate mountain range twentymiles inside the United States–the installation picked out for them by one of their undercover agents working in the area. From the same woman pilot who had brought them to the mountains, they purchased an airplane in which they would make their return trip to Mexico with their prize. But the plane developed some kind of engine trouble on their first test flight and they'd had to re-enlist the lady aviator's help; which wasn't too difficult because the woman was deeply in debt and running scared. Even the greatest plans sometimes go awry; so now this woman would be meeting them at the C.C.C. camp with another plane, and of course after that she would be eliminated. Then, the two of them would fly the war hero out themselves.

They had also brought with them automatic weapons and explosives for the escaping prisoners that would be breaking out with the war hero. These other men, unbeknownst to any one of them at the moment, would be left behind. But for the time being, they would be along as additional guard, just in case there might be any trouble along the way.

Red Collinson pulled his Ford into the Marcy ranch-yard at ten of two, exactly one hour and forty minutes after Purrington's phone call. Several things had caused the delay: the first being Plunker Hancock, Collinson's number one man. Collinson had not found him at home and was forced to drive all the way out to the Mormon widow's place to rouse him—a somewhat embarrassing situation for all involved. And secondly, Lester Suggs seemed to have been cursed with the diarrhea, either from something he'd eaten the night before, or from the abnormal intestinal excitement brought on when Collinson told him that some German prisoners were on the loose. When they were finally on their way out to the Marcy Ranch, Collinson had to stop the Ford what seemed like a hundred times while Suggs hopped out of his own vehicle, blasted the dogwood and filled a few chuckwalla holes.

Cecil Sitters was awake and sitting behind his desk in the tack-room when he heard grinding tires against the gravel out in the yard. He'd been up since midnight, could not sleep, so he'd gotten up and come out to the shed for a couple of belts. Whiskey had been known to gently close his eyes in a dire emergency.

As the vehicles crunched to an echoing stop and emergency brakes scratched their ratchets, Cecil gulped down a healthy slug then went out to see who it was making all the noise.

Tommy Biscoe, Gilbert Turpin and Leroy Huffaker, nickname Shorty, were the only cowboys sleeping base that night. The headlights and confusion out in the yard awakened all three of them. As soon as the first one stuck his tousled head out the bunkhouse door, Cecil's voice lassoed him: "Biscoe!" he yelled. "Round up them other two sad cases and pack yer' blue lightnin'. Captain Red Collinson's gonna' deputize you boys. Seems that some a' them Fort Russell sourkrauts done went among the willows."

The drowsy cowboy nodded and disappeared back inside. Cecil turned to Collinson and said, "C.D.'s gone ta' San Antone' fer' a few days, but I know he'd be more 'an happy ta' lend some horses to the law." He pointed over to the corral, "Have yer' men rope that claybank an' that coyote dun fer' themselves, you can have that big ol' blood bay, Captain Red."

Within ten minutes, seven horses were saddled and trailered, the trailers hitched and ready. Extra boxes of .30-30 shells and .45s and .44s were added to the soft-nosed Winchesters Collinson had brought along. The ammunition was packed into saddlebags and slung over shoulders, then dumped inside the horse trailers where they could be easily accessed. Cecil ran into the main house, sliced off a couple of pounds of jerked beef; grabbed a couple of loaves of bread, a pot, and a can of Arbuckle's coffee, throwing it all in an old gunnysack. When Cecil returned, Collinson asked him about McComb.

"He's still down in the Bend somewhere, Captain," said Cecil. "Had some woman trouble. I ain't worried, though," he continued, "Josh needed some time alone with her anyway."

"Been drinkin' again, has he?" asked Collinson.

Cecil nodded. "Some. But not too much, mind ya'. Ol' Josh just needed some time alone with his woman, that's all. He'll be all right."

Collinson shook his head. "McComb had gone ten years without touchin' the stuff. Too bad," he said; then added: "Sure wish he was around, though, we sure could use him an' C.D.'s plane."

"Yeah, well," mumbled Cecil. "That's the way it goes, I reckon."

"Yeah." Collinson drifted for a moment. Josh McComb was a good man. Maybe he was a goddamn drunk, but he was still a good man–to the core. Too bad he didn't know when not to drink, like, well–like most men. And a he was a darn good pilot, too. Damn shame that he wasn't around. *Could have used that son-of-a-buck for re-con. Oh well,* thought the ranger, *he must have needed the time to get his head straightened out, settle that hunger fer' the liquor, get rid of that cravin'. He musta' needed to get away from it all–needed some peace. Like, kinda' like–* He was about to say, *settin' out at Juanita's grave*, to himself, when:

"Captain Red."

Collinson snapped around, "Yeah Lester?"

"We're all set ta' go."

Collinson nodded and slid into the seat of the Ford, starting the engine. Cecil climbed in the other side and slammed the door. Just before they took off, Collinson turned to his passenger. "Ceece?" he asked straight out, "do you still keep that bottle in that drawer?"

Cecil winked and patted his pocket, "Don't you worry, Captain. I got it right here."

Raller and Iggy were assigned the same vehicle that Spengler chose. Pachter turned over the driving chores of the second truck to Carl Janish then came over to the first one, crowding into the rear, while Kuft continued to stay at the wheel. The two of them would need to be close, close to the prize–and that was Erich Jurgen Raller. In the cab, Kuft explained to Spengler that they had come by way of Presidio, using the gravel road all the way. For the return trip, they planned to head back in the same direction for a short distance then cut off on the road to Plata. From there, they would head across country, using the old Army pack-train trails, in a somewhat direct line to the Chisos Mountains. If they were seen by anyone, they hoped to be mistaken for a group of hunters. Spengler agreed to the plan, but only after studying the maps they'd brought along. He said that it appeared to be a good strategy, as long as there were no signs that they were being followed.

The automatic weapons and grenades had been distributed among the prisoners and the metallic sounds they made as the men checked them out and jammed home the full clips could not quite override the obstreperous cacophony of crickets that surrounded them. Pachter nodded and the engines were started. The two trucks rolled down from the mesa and onto the desert floor as quietly as possible, headed south, away from Fort Russell. In less than a half a minute, the darkness had covered all traces.

CHAPTER FOURTEEN

The small posse of deputized rangers being led by Red Collinson with Cecil Sitters in the Ford consisted of Plunker Hancock and Gil Turpin in Plunker's Model-A; Lester Suggs, alone in a borrowed pick-up; and Biscoe and Shorty in another C bar D vehicle–all of them pulling horse-trailers. They were all in for the surprise of their lives as they cleared a small rise on the road approaching the fort. Some wet-eared, R.O.T.C. dropout calling himself a lieutenant mistook the small caravan for what he thought to be the returning Germans and ordered a burst of .50-caliber machine gun fire sprayed across their path.

Collinson hadn't seen luminescent automatic gunfire since Pancho Villa had attacked Columbus, New Mexico and the intermittent glowing blue and white bolts took Cecil Sitters all the way back to the World War One trenches. "Holy buckets of petrified snake shit," Cecil bellowed. "Those crazy bastards are shootin' at us!" He ducked to the floor and spilled half the contents of his whiskey bottle down the bib of his Sanforized Roebucks.

Collinson stopped the car immediately, pulling the brake. He slid out, and using the door for cover, was in the process of tying his handkerchief to the barrel of his rifle, to be used as a truce flag, when a shaky voice came blasting over an unseen P.A. system: "Stop where you are!" the voice echoed over. "This is a U.S. Military Installation and–"

By that time, Collinson was already walking around to where he was visible in the headlights of the Ford. He held his rifle high with the white hanky fluttering. There was some electronic confusion from the P.A. speaker. Then Purrington's voice replaced the first one. "Captain Collinson," the colonel asked boldly, "is that you?"

Collinson nodded, his large Stetson silhouetted in the headlamps. "Yeah, Colonel, it's us," he yelled. "Who in hell else did ya' think it was this time of night, anyways?"

A second or two went by while Purrington gathered himself. "My apologies, Captain," said Purrington's loudspeaker voice. "We're just a little edgy out here after what's happened. You may proceed."

Collinson turned and backtracked to the Ford. Biscoe and Turpin were out of their vehicles and trying to calm the horses, moving from trailer to trailer when Collinson signaled them that it was safe to go on. They all climbed back in their vehicles, restarted the engines and drove on toward the fort.

"Sum-bitches were firin' genuine blue whistlers," commented Cecil once they were moving again.

Collinson found the bottle in Cecil's lap and took a long draw. "Now, ain't that a fact," he said, passing the container back to the foreman.

Cecil chuckled nervously, "Hell, I thought we was gonna' have us a real corpse-an'-cartridge occasion." He drained the bottle and tucked it under the seat. "You handled that like an ol' time Buscadero," he continued. "You did, Red." He clucked his tongue. "Yeah, the way you jumped out like that, I thought you was about ta' charge hell with a bucket of water. Reckon you'll still do ta' ride river with, even if it ain't quite like the old days; ain't that right?"

Collinson didn't answer. They were almost to the fort now. He could see soldiers in the darkness surrounding two jeeps with .50-calliber machine guns mounted in place of the rear seats. He could also sense the fear and excitement in the soldiers and he didn't like it–he'd seen it too many times before. The border Mexicans had a saying for it–murder in the air, or blood on the night, something like that. He'd have to have a talk with Purrington. Maybe he could give his men a calmin' down pitch, or something, before they took off after the Germans. Otherwise, Collinson thought, he might just be seeing those dreams he'd been having come to life again–for real.

The entire garrison was on alert. Trigger-happy military police were everywhere with suspicious eyes consuming the small brigade that Collinson led into the echelon. Searchlights swept the three prisoner compounds and the Texans were able to catch quick glimpses of the many rows of German P.O.W.s that were lined up–hands over heads–in the yards between the barracks.

Collinson asked his men to stay put and finally found Colonel Purrington on the porch of the administration building where he was shouting orders, using the P.A. system to make sure that they were being carried out. As Collinson mounted the steps, the colonel turned over the mike to a young piss-and-starch lieutenant, who Collinson figured–by his cock-sure attitude–was the one who'd ordered the machine guns fired. The ranger captain tipped his Stetson to the young officer and got no response; then he followed Purrington into the building.

The clock on Purrington's office wall chimed three A.M. as the men entered. There were two full glasses of whiskey on the colonel's desk and Purrington nodded toward them, "I poured that for you right after we talked," he said to the ranger. "I thought you might need one. God knows I sure enough do."

Collinson winked, picking up the tumbler, "Had a snort on the ride over," he said with a wink. "Sure don't see how another one could hurt though." He took a long gulp and seated himself.

Purrington continued to pace. "I radioed my superiors and told them that it had finally happened," he said. "I'm just waiting for a response. They have to contact Washington and these code things take time."

"Red tape. Yeah, I know," said Collinson. "Those desk-sitters don't understand that each minute lost'll get them krauts that much closer to the Bravo—*and* Mexico."

"I'm sorry," Purrington slurped, almost spilling his glass, "but I have procedure that I have to follow, Captain. I must find out if anything has changed since I was last in contact with my superiors."

Collinson nodded. "How many did you say got out?" he asked.

"Ten," the colonel answered. "Our nose count showed ten missing. That's all."

"Well," said Collinson, "I was able ta' round up six men; an' me makes seven. How 'bout you?"

"That's just it," said Purrington. "I can spare myself, and maybe three others. No more right now."

"Well, that's eleven," muttered Collinson counting to himself silently. "Damn near even, ain't it?" He took another sip and began to pack his pipe.

Purrington frowned out of habit. "Captain," he continued, "I'm as anxious as you are to get on with this thing. If the Germans *do* get across the border it'll look damn bad on my record, no matter what, regardless of my orders. So, I don't really give a damn if O.S.S. has put a damper on my action because I plan on stopping those prisoners even though we have no permission to pursue, not enough men, or whatever."

Collinson scratched a Blue Diamond on his boot-sole and puffed, "Eleven men," he repeated. "That's about enough, I 'spect."

Purrington turned, "Just bear with me, Captain. I'm only trying to better our odds. I'd like to have some extra men," he said. "if that's at all possible. Now that this escape has actually taken place, headquarters just might feel–" The phone rang. Purrington's eyes flicked over to the instrument on the desk then back to Collinson as he added, "I'd feel more secure with some extra men, that's all. I'm not General Pershing." He picked up the phone. "Yes?" he said. "Yes, this is Purrington speaking."

Collinson listened to the one-sided conversation, took another puff and guessed that it must have been his seventh because the pipe was out. He raked another Blue Diamond on his boot-sole and re-lit.

When he looked up again, Purrington was hanging up the receiver and the officer appeared to be somewhat disappointed as he drained his glass before relaying what he'd heard to Collinson. "It's still the same. Nothing has changed. Damnit," he spat. "We're on our own. High Command refuses to acknowledge that they had any prior information concerning the escape. We're still to treat it as if it were a complete surprise to us. That way, the Nazis won't know that our O.S.S. boys have broken their code. I'm sorry, Captain," the colonel continued. "I'm sure that these military details don't interest you."

Collinson took another puff and stood up; he still had his own thoughts to deal with. "Well, I still 'spect eleven'll be plenty 'nough ta' do the job. 'Sides, we do know the land and the layout of things in these parts a mite better 'an they do."

"Oh," Purrington hesitated, "I forgot to tell you, Captain. It looks like they took a hostage—one of my men."

Collinson lifted his eyebrows slightly, "A hostage, you say?"

"Well, either a hostage," Purrington went on, "or one of my men was in on it with them all along. His name is Bowman. And I'm told he was acting rather strange as of late."

Collinson finished his glass and set it down. Turning to the door, he said, "That would make it eleven of them, too." He turned back and winked at Purrington, "I like my odds even, don't you, Colonel?" He took another puff and his eyes narrowed, "Oh, by the way, Colonel, how many guns did they take with 'em?"

The question caught Purrington somewhat off guard. "Why, none," he said, shaking his head. "Not even Corporal Bowman's shotgun. No weapons are missing from this fort."

"Well, then," Collinson grumbled, scratching his nose, "it's another good bet then that there was someone waitin' outside the gates with some weapons for 'em." He shook his head and smiled. "Odds're gettin' better all the time ain't they, Colonel? C'mon," he said, turning to go. "We got a trail ta' pick up 'fore it grows too cold."

"Tracks head off toward the Presidio road, Captain," yelled Biscoe from down below the Mesa. "Looks like there were two trucks big enough ta' hold all of 'em. That's what it looks like."

Collinson, Cecil and Purrington stood on top of the bluff, squinting down to where the young cowboy's voice was coming. "Quad trucks. Those are four-wheel-drive vehicles," said Collinson fingering the large tire-tracks at the top of the rise that led down past Biscoe. "Most likely they won't be stayin' on the road for too long. They'll head off inta' the brush, try an' lose anyone who might be followin' 'em."

Purrington held a flashlight to the Army map of the Big Bend that he had brought along with him. "It seems to me, Captain," he pointed out, "that they'd make a damn B-line to the border, straight down here to Presidio then cross the river there, into Ojinaga."

"I don't think so, Colonel," said Collinson in a casual tone. "That's too easy. If they think someone might be trailin' em, an' I 'spose they do, then the easiest thing ta' do would be for us ta' radio down ta' Presidio an' have someone waitin' for 'em. No," he continued, "they got some other plan in mind, fer' sure. Otherwise, why did they go out of their way to get those quad trucks in the first place, if they ain't proposin' ta' cross some hard country?"

Purrington pondered. "Well, I really don't think that makes much—"

"Colonel," said Collinson, cutting him off. "Right now, we best be gettin' on their trail. Why not let's let the sign they left show us the direction they went instead of arguin' about it."

"Sign?" blurted out Purrington. "Do you really think that they're going to be fool enough to leave us a trail to follow?"

"Cars leave tracks," answered the ranger. "Trucks leave even better ones— *if* them krauts were dumb enough not to cover 'em up. Still, I ain't never found a human being that don't leave some kind of a mistake behind–even Injuns."

"These are not Indians we're following," Purrington interjected. "They're Germans; Desert rats; Afrika Korps. Trained in deception; Taught to be expert in leaving false trails."

"C'mon, Colonel," grumbled Collinson, "let's jest' get a move on, OK? We'll continue our talkin' on down the road. Maybe you might wanna' ride with me so we can—"

"No thank you, Captain," Purrington cut in. "I'll stay in my jeep. *And* I'll also continue leading this little expedition, if you don't mind." He turned to his driver and motioned for him to bring up the jeep. Then he climbed in and took a position in the rear behind the .50-caliber gun and waved the driver on.

Collinson turned to Cecil. "Let's go, amigo," he said with a wave of a hand. "We don't wanna' let the Army get too far ahead of us, now do we?"

"Ya' know what, Red?" said Cecil. "I think we're gonna' be in fer' a good one this time out."

"Let's jest' play it for what it is, OK?" said Collinson. "The old colonel's jest' feelin' a mite perky right now. Remember, one of his men was just killed."

The other jeep with the second .50-caliber swung in behind Purrington's vehicle and moved off toward the Presidio road. Collinson and Cecil climbed back down the rise. They collected Biscoe then went over to where their cars were idling. When Collinson gave the order, they all moved out in the same direction the jeeps had taken.

Raller sat huddled in the bed of the first truck and scratched a match, lighting half of a cigarette. He took a long draw and handed it to Iggy who sat beside him. Raller rubbed at an imaginary smudge on the barrel of the gun that he had been issued and toyed with the safety catch. "Have you ever fired one of these, Iggy," he asked. "A Schmeisser?"

The young officer took another drag from the cigarette and handed it back. He brushed his own weapon with his fingertips and appeared to study it. "No," he answered, "just bolt-action weapons. These type of weapons were issued only to S.S. troops." He threw Raller a friendly smile, "This must make a lot of noise when it goes off, no?" he asked.

"And a lot of blood when the bullets strike home," said Raller, trying not to mock him. "Hold it like this, my friend." He gripped the weapon for Iggy to see. "It will counteract the kick."

Dreshler nodded, attempting to align his weapon in same way that Raller had shown him. "Is this correct?" he asked.

Raller reached over and re-set the angle of Dreshler's gun, "Like that," he said. "That is the proper position. Then you just squeeze the trigger. You do not have to aim this gun, Iggy, just point it and God help whatever is in your sights."

Raller set his own weapon carefully to the side and concentrated on the cigarette. Dreshler watched him for a moment then he too set down his gun. "You do not care much for war, do you, Herr Raller?"

Raller handed the cigarette butt back to the younger man and chuckled, "You have noticed, finally," he smiled. "No, Iggy, I do not care much for war. At least not for this war if you wish me to be honest with you." He leaned back and looked at the sparkling black velvet sky above. "Whether it is this particular war, or quite possibly just my age, I cannot be sure, I really do not know. But I do know that I am tired, young Dreshler, I am definitely looking forward to its end." He took the butt back from Iggy, squeezing another puff from the glowing bud; then he extinguished what remained on the floor of the truck bed. "No matter who is the winner," he added.

"Your words flow as if they were from the mouth of a traitor, Herr Raller," said Iggy somewhat bitterly. "I am sorry. I refuse to believe you."

"And you will, more than likely, never think any different until you have gone through what I have," said Raller. "And even then," he continued, "the way in which you are affected may contrast entirely. Men do not always react the same to what they experience, even when they go through the exact encounter side-by-side. Come to me in a few years, young one. Tell me of your feelings then."

Dreshler nodded. "I will, mein Herr," he said softly. "For no matter what you say, my respect for you will never diminish. It will always remain the same. You are a hero to me, Herr Raller. And you will always be a hero–no matter how hard you fight it."

"Would you care to know what makes a hero, young Iggy?" Raller asked in all seriousness. "To know what glory–seen first hand–is like?"

Dreshler shrugged. He really didn't know if he did. But he eventually nodded, for he knew that Raller would tell him anyway.

Raller laced his fingers around his knees and drew in a long breath. "To be a hero, Iggy," he began, "you must first be afraid. So afraid, in fact, that your subconscious will take over completely from your conscious. It does this to protect you, because your cognizant being is no longer able to function as it should. That is because all of its energy has been directed entirely to your sphincter muscle, to keep you from filling your trousers with the churning liquid that burns inside your quivering bowels." Raller drew in a deep breath then continued. "So your subconscious supersedes and aids you in killing. And to save you from being killed yourself, it aims your gun for you. And it pulls the trigger, because the conscious–You–is in no condition to do that, because the conscious–You–has been drugged on your own inner fear with a poison so potent it will freeze you in your tracks–making you immobile and completely incapable of acting of your own will. Except the subconscious continues to keep on functioning, and you continue to kill and kill and kill. And when it is all over, you find that others have put you on a pedestal for doing something that you do not even remember having done. And soon you start believing what they say about you; what they tell you you did; and how heroic you were. Later the dreams come–the nightmares. And only then do you begin to recall the truth. Dreams are born of your subconscious and the same fear explodes inside of you once again as you re-live the death and destruction. Then you finally awaken to find yourself swimming in a vast pool of your own guilt. Over and over again and again this happens. And you beg and plead to God that it will stop. Only you know that it will not, for the dreams never cease. They just keep reminding you of the giant lie–the lie that slowly consumes you, destroying your life." There was a long moment as Raller realized that others were listening to him, too. He found the cigarette butt he had put out earlier and began toying with the remains. "That is how a hero is made," he added. "It is something that I do not wish even on my worst enemy."

Dreshler's eyes were fixed on the cigarette butt that Raller twisted in his fingers. He did not have a reply. Raller settled back even more, attempting to make the best of the uncomfortable ride. The vehicle began to slow down.

The two trucks had reached the Plata cutoff where they stopped for a moment because they had almost missed the side road in the darkness. Now they backed up until there was room for both of them to make the sharp turn. Raller once again turned to Dreshler and vocalized his thought. "Where we go now," he said softly, "our destiny takes us, young Iggy. And I prefer a peaceful trip. Pray with me, if you will," he asked, "that there will be no heroes. For if there are no heroes–there will be no killing."

Iggy would still not look at him. After a moment, Raller let his eyes close: more pleasant thoughts–images of his woman, his wife, and that green hill in the Fatherland. Those precious visions of oh so long ago began to filter in under his tired lids once again.

CHAPTER FIFTEEN

The road to Plata, Texas was a rough and irregular piece that had quite a few twists and turns in it that had never been drawn on any map. By the time the Germans skirted the little town–which was nothing more than several rag-tag adobes and two barking dogs–the sun's glow was already beginning to flair on the eastern horizon–an hour before it would rise.

At Plata, the two quad trucks also met the end of the road. From there on, it was to be a series of mule-trails and wagon-ruts until they would pick up the Terlingua creek-bed which they planned to follow all the way through the rocky hills to the Alpine Road near Study Butte. From there they would pick up another gravel road that would take them to the base of the Chisos Mountains. What the Germans had not planned on was the rear axle of the second truck snapping from the strain. It happened a little less than three miles out of Plata, bringing them to an abrupt halt halfway up a narrow switchback.

The sudden lack of movement awakened Raller immediately. It was Spengler, shouting commands that snapped both he and the others out of their degrees of sleepiness. As the grey dawn sprinkled its dew on the blue wildflowers that clung alongside the seldom-used trail, the men stumbled out of the trucks to mumble and mull as Pachter and Kuft moved back to the disabled vehicle. First, there was a short-lived attempt at fixing the damaged shaft. Then two men were chosen to walk to Plata to see if they might find a replacement part. But Spengler vetoed that idea, saying that it would take too long–even if they were in no danger of being followed. Not being followed was the part of the scheme that Spengler had never been too sure of anyway and he'd expressed this doubt to both Pachter and Kuft when they'd first met on the mesa above the fort.

Spengler had told them of his experiences with the Americans, of their cunning use of their own free wills–some actually opposing their superiors on occasion, disobeying direct orders. His theory was that even if the Nazi High Command in Berlin had truly succeeded in fooling the American Government with their plant in Washington–the very important, non-existent top spy that the O.S.S. thought they were so close to apprehending and maybe changing the course of the war–just maybe the Americans really had been duped. Duped into thinking that in order to capture the bogus secret agent, they must let a small group of unimportant prisoners slip across the border so as not to give away their secret. Even if the American Government had fallen for the ploy one hundred percent, Spengler had told Pachter and Kuft, there was nothing to keep one or a dozen of the "crazy," self-willed Texas Americans from trying to halt the Germans' flight of their own accord. "That is why we brought with us, the weapons, Herr Spengler," Pachter had chuckled. "For just that kind of an emergency. In case some local heroes become too bold."

But now, there on the rocky hillside, quite vulnerable, with one transport truck completely out of action, Spengler put his foot down. He would not stand by and watch as another precious hour passed when he knew good and well that they would find no replacement part for the truck in a village the size of Plata. "We must all fit into the other truck," he ordered. "If the going becomes too strenuous, then some will have to walk."

Eventually, Pachter and Kuft were to reluctantly consent. But to themselves they had agreed, what a relief it would be once safe in the plane with their prize, when they would finally be able to leave that fat sleazy pig behind.

Coming down the small incline that led into Plata, Colonel Purrington, riding in the first of the two Army jeeps, failed to note that the tracks of the Germans' quad trucks had veered off and left the small road before it petered out. Collinson and the deputized rangers–who had just about caught up by then–continued following the sandy vestige on into yucca country as a matter of course. By the time Purrington realized his mistake, the rangers had put themselves about a quarter of a mile ahead. So it was a very ruffled and somewhat embarrassed Purrington who held tight to the jeep's windshield as the two Army carriers raced and finally caught up with the Texans; pulling around the trailers at the rear of the column and honking to a stop beside Collinson's Ford.

Collinson threw a look to Cecil and pulled the brake before climbing out to greet the red-faced colonel. As he did, he reached for his pipe and tobacco and was packing the bowl as the two met in front of the Ford. The ranger's casual manner kept Purrington from expressing his feelings, so when the two men eventually fell into conversation, it came out as gentlemanly chatter.

"I think, Captain," began Purrington, "that from now on, we should try and stay in a closer formation, don't you agree?"

Collinson struck a match and puffed. "Sounds OK ta' me, Colonel," he casually replied. "We sure don't need no hairs in the butter with them krauts hankerin', like they are, ta' sniff Gulf breeze." Collinson pointed. "See over there?" he said. "That's their tracks. They couldn't've bin' through here more an' a half hour ago." He struck a match, re-lighting his pipe. "So as long as they keep layin' down the sign, we can jest' keep on followin' 'em like jackmules to the bell-mare."

"What we want to do, Captain," said Purrington, ignoring Collinson's slight jab, "is to *catch* them!"

The ranger captain nodded casually. "They'll be makin' horse-hair bridles soon enough, Colonel," he said unemotionally. "We just don't wanta' spook 'em, that's all. 'Else they'd run like a Nueces steer an' just make things that much more difficult fer' us. We'll catch up to 'em," he puffed, "an' we'll put a good sized spoke in their wheels when we do."

Purrington slapped his quirt against his boot. "Very well, Captain," he said brusquely. "I see we can agree on some things. Shall we continue on?"

Collinson squinted off in the direction of some low hills, shaking his head slowly. "Let's give 'em a few more minutes, Colonel," he said. "Right now, they're up there on that rocky outcrop." He pointed. "Looks like there's somethin' wrong with one of their vehicles."

Purrington swung around, his gaze following Collinson's finger. It was still dark enough to make the mountainside look fuzzy so he moved to the jeep where his driver already had the binoculars ready. He put them to his eyes and scanned the horizon. "Yes, I do see some movement," he mumbled almost to himself. "I suppose it could be the Germans."

By that time Collinson had moved in beside him. "It's them, all right," he told the colonel. "I've had my eye on 'em for some time now."

"Well then," commanded Purrington. "What are we waiting for? Let's get after them."

Collinson set a hand on the officer's arm. "Colonel," his voice was firm, "the other side of that mountain is all down hill. I'd sure hate ta' give 'em that advantage. If they see us now, they'll take off like the heel flies are after 'em down that hill while we're chuggin' our fannies up this side. It'd be right smarter not ta' let 'em know we're behind 'em just yet, don't ya' think? Least not 'til we get ourselves atop that climb."

Purrington pulled away, shaking his head vigorously. "I'm sorry, Captain. Now *I* must disagree." He stepped back into the jeep. "The sooner we let them know that we're here, the better our chances for a showdown." He motioned for his driver to move out. "You follow as best you can, Captain," he shouted as the jeep took off in a cloud of dust.

Collinson turned and went back to the Ford, shaking out his pipe and climbing back in. He released the brake and gunned the engine, shifting then signaling the others to follow. He did not say anything to Cecil. He didn't have to. He knew Cecil had overheard the last of the conversation so he didn't have to open his mouth. Cecil just settled back and held on to the seat as Collinson let out the clutch and the Ford V-8 rumbled ahead.

Wallace Bowman saw them first. He had not been issued a weapon and therefore had begun to feel less a part of the group. To make up, he'd been acting as self-appointed rear-guard. His rhetorical whoops of, "Here they come!" and "It's the gawddamned enemy on our ass!" brought Pachter, Spengler and Kuft on the run. While Spengler quieted the American's alarm, Kuft, who was carrying the spyglasses, surveyed the situation.

"Yes," the S.S. man said slowly. "It is the American Army. But, only two transports," Kuft observed. "I can make out only four soldiers." He handed Pachter the binoculars and continued with his comments. "And there seems to be several civilian vehicles pulling trailers of some kind at a distance behind them."

Pachter lowered the glasses. A nod between he and Kuft confirmed the findings then Pachter turned back to the prisoners. "Every man into the first truck," he ordered. "Check your weapons and make them ready for combat."

Pachter and Kuft marched abruptly back past the disabled vehicle and to the first truck, passing by Raller and Iggy who were now standing near the rear of the bed of truck number two. "We are certainly in for it now," whispered Dreshler to Raller as he released the safety catch and cocked his weapon. "Now there will surely be a battle, I can smell it."

Raller fit the clip into his own weapon and smiled softly. "Be patient, young one," he told Iggy. "First we will play cat and mouse. Our number one priority in this escape is not to fight them on their own ground. You can rest assured of that. Not even heroes are that brave–or foolish. For the present, just do as the S.S. order us to do. They are in charge. At least for now they are." Iggy nodded and the two moved off with the others to the first truck.

Bowman and Spengler brought up the rear–the last to reach the first truck. Bowman's fear had turned close to frenzy as he still anxiously glanced behind him and continued pointing. "They're coming, damnit," he warned. "They'll kill us all. We've got to do something." Spengler–who had Bowman somewhat restrained–dragged and finally pushed him to the rear of the truck where several others helped lift the struggling American into the truck bed.

"Hold him, and watch him carefully," Spengler told one of the other prisoners in a low voice. "We will more than likely need him later." The fat Nazi climbed in the back and signaled the two S.S. men who were now in the cab. The truck growled on up the hill. As they cleared the top, someone with the advancing Americans chopped off a burst of machine gun fire. The shots went way wide of their intended target and the Germans never even saw the blue tracers sing into the dawn's light above them. They were already speeding, hell bent for highwater, down the other side of the mountain, headed for Terlingua creek in a ball of swirling dirt and shale.

It took three of them to roll Elmo Johnson's moth-balled deHavilland out of the barn and across the short stretch of desert to the end of the runway where McComb's D.H.4 stood ready and waiting. Once the two planes were side by side, there was almost no distinction between the two aircraft, right down to the newly added machine guns–the twin-Vickers fixed in front of the pilot's seat, and the Lewis .303 mounted in the rear cockpit.

Jim-Bob Pelliteer, with McComb's dog following, drove out behind them on Elmo's utility road grader. He had loaded several 55-gallon drums of gasoline on the large machine and would be fueling both planes as soon as he reached the runway. By the time Josh and Katherine had finished checking out the two aircraft, Jim-Bob had begun hand-pumping the fuel into the Johnson plane. Jim-Bob alone had worked all night on the engine and he'd had the Eagle III chirping sweet and mellow way before the others had the machine-guns in place and secured. Finally, everything was ready. The guns were loaded and the fuel tanks filled and topped off. Extra ammo belts, drums and cartridges had been located in the loft of the barn and were now stored in the rear cockpits of both planes. All that was left was to wait for the sun to come up. Josh feared that too early of an attempt to navigate the Chisos window and then to try and set down on a makeshift strip without adequate light might be asking just a little too much.

He and Katy had talked all the while they worked assembling the machine-guns and Katherine's story now flowed much better for Josh. Katy Faver had been a victim: exploited by both the Nazis and that greatest of all iniquities–greed. *It is amazing,* McComb thought, *what money or the lack of it could do to a person's soul.* Josh knew that deep down inside–where a person really lived–that Katy Faver teemed with goodness. But that her outside shell, that skin called the human being, had, as Monroe would say–fallen from grace. Fallen, for the moment, and was now bound with tremendous guilt. McComb truly hoped that by letting Katy come along–letting her be a part again, giving her the chance to stand beside him in the name of justice, to fight if they must and as they had in the past for the sake of the United States of America–just might help bring Katy Faver back to the reality that surrounded them all: that they were, indeed, only human–and that the Lord God forgave all in the end.

Josh lit a cigarette, glancing toward the horizon, which now glowed with an expectant pink. It would be a good day. Puffy clouds hung scantly against the deep of the sky and silent vistas began to shimmer as the sun's early rays reflected the minerals that tinged the sand and rock. He drew in a volume of smoke and let it sift through his nostrils. It was time to go. He nodded to Monroe. The big Negro nodded back. Monroe appeared to know McComb's every thought. Josh turned, crunched the cigarette under his boot and pulled his leather cap from his back pocket, slipping it on. Katherine did the same. In less than a minute, both pilots were behind the controls.

Before Josh signaled for Monroe and Jim-Bob to spin the props, he threw a look to the mute boy and got a positive response. Jim-Bob had his job to do–as soon as the sun was high enough he would be sending an aviso to Don Miguel Maldonado in Ojinaga–a message to be delivered in the ancient method of the Indian. Using the piece of a mirror that he always carried with him, the boy was to send out a reflective dispatch to be relayed all the way across the border badlands, over the rocks and desert of the despoblado, almost one hundred miles up the winding Rio; a communication that would reach Don Miguel faster than any phone line or local carrier. A summons for Maldonado and the two Brits to "come-a-runnin'" to the Chisos basin and to bring along all the help they could.

Josh twirled his finger in the crisp air then switched his magneto. Katy did the same. Monroe and Jim-Bob spun the propellers.

They took off together, side-by-side, as they had so many times back in those old days when they'd flown together before. Nothing had been forgotten through the years. The two planes left the ground at the same precise moment and once airborne and climbing to a sufficient altitude–with exact inches between the wing-tips–they peeled off: Josh to the right and Katy to the left;, both making corresponding loops in the slick blue sky. Swooping back across the flat of the airfield, dipping their wings in unison to their comrades on the ground, they headed off together toward the foreboding Chisos.

CHAPTER SIXTEEN

The rear wheels of the '36 Ford dug into the loose rocks and gravel, spinning more than they grabbed, spitting sand and small stones against the front of the horse trailer it towed behind, blasting at the peeling paint and rusty metal with abrading consistency. The noise was quite aggravating to the animals inside and their kicking and snorted whinnies just added to the ruckus.

By the time the ranger company reached the rim of the mountain, the Germans were nowhere to be seen; plus, the two Army jeeps had sped on ahead in pursuit and were also gone from sight. Both parties had left plenty of sign and Collinson appeared to be in no hurry to make it a chase.

At the top of the incline, just above the position where the Germans had left their disabled truck behind, Collinson pulled clear of the others and set his brake. He climbed out of the Ford followed by Cecil, yelling to his men. "Gonna' stop here fer' a mite, boys," he said. "If we don't, we may as well be barkin' at a knot. Take a few minutes an' water up the horses–and the radiators. Roll yer'selves a paper-collar stiff, if yer' a mind ta'." He was referring to a cigarette, which gave him the excuse to pull out his pipe. Then he and Cecil walked over to the edge and looked down the trail on the other side.

"Looks like they all got a pretty good go on us, Red," muttered Cecil. He pulled out a dusty, brown hunk of tobacco and began to whittle off some makings with his pocket knife.

"Yeah," said Collinson. "I ain't gonna' worry, though. We're just gonna' follow the krauts' trail like we was gonna' do all along. Now I weren't raised on too much prunes an' proverbs," he went on, "but I'd be willin' ta' wager that the good Lord'll put us right back up with 'em in the next few hours." The ranger knelt down and scratched a match on a rock, then set himself down, wadding up his bandanna and tucking it under one cheek to protect his piles. He looked off over the incline while he lit the pipe. "Hard country, that," he said softly while puffing. "Them Germans not bein' familiar with it, they'll more 'an likely end up comin' 'fore they go. I reckon I'm talkin' 'bout them Army boys, too," he added.

Cecil moved in beside the older lawman, rolling his own and twisting the tips. He bent down, sharing the flame, "D'you think that ol' duffer knows what he's doin', Captain?"

"Colonel Purrington?" puffed Collinson. "Hell no. Way he talks, you'd think he knew everything from soda ta' hock, wouldn't ya'? But the minute I seen him with real dirt on his feet, I knew why his boots was always so clean." He puffed on the pipe again and then re-lit. "Oh, Purrington's entitled to a warm corner somewhere I reckon. He's bin' in the Army longer 'an Jack's got sleeves. He just ain't that acquainted with our way of doin' things, I 'spect."

Cecil shook his head. "Don't reckon the Army ever did understand this big country, Red." He took in a long draw on the cigarette. "Even when they was runnin' those strings of mules down here they ended up havin' ta' hire the local ranahans ta' learn 'em the proper end of a choke-rope."

The two men laughed softly, smoking quietly for next few minutes, as older men do, then Cecil glanced up at the ranger, his deep concern showing a little more. "Red?" he asked.

"Yeah, Ceece," came Collinson's amiable reply.

"What's gonna' happen if we *do* catch up with them Germans anyways?"

Collinson ground his pipe stem with his teeth and shot a look over to the cars where he could see his two deputies and the three young cowboys talking. "Well, Cecil," he began, "I 'spect those three young waddys over there'll get a real thumb whippin', that's what."

Cecil nodded. "Then we're gonna' be unravelin' some cartridges with them krauts fer' sure," he said, now quite serious.

Collinson shrugged. He took some time to bang his pipe on a rock, mashing the embers with his thumb, one by one. "They ain't a bunch o' wetbacks with the chili-chasers on their tail, Ceece. They're trained German enemy soldiers, an' they're runnin' scared. Least they will be once we put some miles up their butts. You can figger' there's a pretty good chance that they won't give up without firin'a few rounds our way, that's fer' sure."

Cecil glanced toward the others then back to Collinson. "Oh, I was jest' thinkin'. Those young rannys of mine're still so wet behind their ears an' all."

"No younger 'an most of the kids that's already fightin' in this war, Cecil," Collinson reminded him.

"I know, Red, but–" Cecil found it hard to complete his sentence.

Collinson put a hand on his arm. "Cecil," he said, "they're growed up boys, now. They're gonna' end up doin' their part fer' Uncle Sam one way or another anyway. 'Sides, didn't you always say that if you were gonna' get gravel throwed on yer boots, better it be Texas gravel?"

Cecil chuckled. "Yeah," he sniffed, "reckon I did used ta' say somethin' such."

Collinson put away his pipe and got to his feet, pocketing the bandanna and holding out a hand for Sitters. "You an me," he said, pulling the other man to his feet. "You an' me'll just have ta' make sure those boys keep a stick 'tween them an' the snake." He winked. "Make sure that they don't make any of the mistakes you an' me did when we was their age."

"Yeah," nodded Cecil, brushing off his seat. "Yeah, Red, guess we all gotta' grow up some time or another."

Collinson started moving toward the Ford. "We'll just see to it that they stay behind us," he called back to Cecil. "Use 'em fer' backup, in case we need 'em. You an' me'll do all the straight shootin', if there is any. Now c'mon, time's a waistin'. That ol' buck colonel's probably bustin' a gut wonderin' where the hell we are by now."

"Where in the hell are those goddamned rangers, anyway?" Purrington's irritated voice raked across the several yards to where his driver, Francis Hatfield, stood atop a large boulder searching to their rear for sight of Collinson's caravan.

The sergeant lowered the binoculars and shook his head, "Still no sign of them, sir," he answered.

"Damn," spat Purrington, sitting back in his seat and whapping the frame of the wind-screen with his quirt–the slap echoing on the flat morning air, bouncing back and forth between the flagstone walls of the wide draw that had abruptly narrowed, narrowed enough to cause Purrington some concern. Because on up ahead, it was obvious that the draw turned into a still narrower canyon with many hidden twists and turns and that from this point on, if the Germans felt like turning on their pursuers, an ambush could possibly be more than a likely supposition. "We'll just have to go on then, Sergeant," Purrington said bluntly. "Take our chances."

"Are you sure that's a good idea, Colonel?" the driver asked cautiously.

"Damnit, Hatfield," the officer replied gruffly. "I can't just sit here while they run all the way to the Panama Canal, can I? Let me see that map again," he commanded.

"Yes, sir," said the driver, saluting. Hatfield jumped down from the rock and crossed back to the colonel's jeep, pulling a 30-year-old chart from his blouse that was already showing some signs of perspiration. "Right here, sir." He unfolded it, spreading the map across Purrington's lap.

Colonel Purrington's confusion was quite apparent to the sergeant as the officer's manicured finger searched the wrinkled paper. He eventually found the town of Plata. Then he located Terlingua creek. "My guess is that they are somewhere in the middle–maybe there, or there. Or even there," the colonel said. "Hell," he grumbled, haphazardly folding the map and jamming it in Hatfield's direction. "Get rid of that useless thing, Sergeant. From now on we'll have to rely on our own common sense. Go tell the others that if those rangers don't show up in ten minutes, we're going on into that canyon." The driver nodded, threw a half salute, turned and walked briskly over to the second jeep.

. When he reached the other two M.P.s, he spoke softly, quietly enough so his voice wouldn't carry back to Purrington's ears. "The old fart actually wants us to be heroes now," the sergeant whispered. "He wants to go on ahead without the rangers for a back up. You two had better pray that those local boys catch up to us in ten minutes, or we all just might be goin' home toes-up with Old Glory for a blanket."

"Ah, shit," coughed the driver of the second jeep. "I didn't work my ass off to get stationed down here just to get it shot off."

"Yeah," the machine-gunner cut in. "They did kill ol' Skuggins back there, didn't they. Probably won't bother 'em none to shoot us either."

Hatfield lit up a cigarette, shielding his action from Purrington, then taking several quick puffs in a row. He glanced back at the old man and said: "I think the old sonofabitch has finally gone off his rocker."

Added the other driver, "Hell, we ain't soldiers. I mean, not the trained, fighting kind."

"Well, I don't want to die," said the gunner, "at least not in this fucked-up, miserable place."

"Me either, soldier," said Hatfield, crunching his cigarette underfoot while still looking at the back of Purrington's head. The old man appeared from behind to huff like a waiting locomotive as he continued to tap with his quirt. "I'll have to admit," continued Hatfield, "that he's probably more than a little nuts over this thing. He really means what he says though, I know that regardless of whether he's crazy or not. So like I said, you guys better start prayin' for those Texas Rangers."

"Hatfield!" came Purrington's shout.

"Yes, sir!" the sergeant shot back automatically.

"Get over here on the double," ordered Purrington. "I think I've come up with a plan."

Climbing through The Window on Katy's deHavilland's tail brought back some memories of the excitement that Josh McComb had damn near forgotten over the years. Misplaced, would be the better word for it. The updrafts; the wind direction changing abruptly; the tricky air currents before the rather rough landing, took him back a few moments to his teaching days at the Johnson Ranch. He'd flown The Window back then, too; only he'd never really attempted to land in the basin. Not even on that day when he'd flown it in the Douglas Attack Plane with a new recruit behind him in the rear cockpit, manning the .50-caliber. They'd swooped through The Window on a run-of-the-mill training flight and had come across a local cockfight in progress approximately where the main cluster of C.C.C. camp buildings now stood. One of the gamblers, an old borracho, had taken a potshot at the plane, most likely thinking it to be the local constabulary, and damned if the kid in the back seat hadn't cut loose with the .50. It turned out that a small portion of the assemblage down below had belonged to the Cano brothers' gang and they immediately returned an avalanche of gunfire. All this had happened before Josh even knew what was going on and he was damn lucky to be able to duck and dive his way out of there before anything more serious took place. The only thing hit that day was a local boy's prize roosters and Elmo Johnson ended up taking care of that matter later. As for the rest of the locals, they never again held a rooster match in the Chisos basin. From that day on, they moved their arena to Lajitas–to the little island claimed neither by the U.S. nor Mexico that sits in the middle of the Bravo near that tiny village–where if ever another surprise visit by an unsuspecting plane was paid while poultry were in the midst of battle, they would better be able to hear it coming and retreat to the cover of the Mexican foothills until the danger had passed them by.

McComb taxied in behind Katherine once they were on the ground. They rolled along to the far end of the dirt road that had been cleared by the Nazis for a landing strip. When they'd turned both planes around they shut down and climbed to the ground. The engines sputtered to a stop. The silence was immediate–just the soft, cool wind whispering above them. A sound reminiscent of an empty seashell slithered through the leaves and needles of the junipers and pines that grew from the mountainsides that girdled the green bowl in which they now stood. Near-distant slaps from unlatched shutters swung their attention toward the vacant C.C.C. camp where several decaying clapboard buildings, some adobe shacks, wooden barracks, tent-frames and wasting corral fencing marked the site of the government ghost town.

The two aviators exchanged glances. No words were spoken. They seemed to know the other's thoughts. Katherine turned and started up the slight incline that led to the camp. McComb followed.

Josh had been afoot in the basin only once before in his life and that had been back in the year when the camp was being built. He had come on horseback up that dirt trail, as it was back then, through Panther Pass to see Monroe Leaton, who was helping the government people with some carpentry. Josh had taken the long ride because he'd been afraid he was going to pick up that bottle again and he'd been filled with fear over some now forgotten problem and had ridden to 'the basin to ask his old friend for help. He desperately needed to find out how to stop the craving that had come back into his body and mind after several serenity-filled, dry years. Monroe's words from that day were coming back to him now. Coming into his mind just as crisp and clear as the day the large Negro had spoken them. Monroe had said, "Be still—and know that He is God." Those were the words. That was all he had said. Then Monroe had turned back to his hammering as if Josh hadn't even been there.

McComb had then walked his horse down to the spring for some water, taking some needed time to just lie back and relax his eyes for a few minutes. It was only then that the words had begun to make some sense. *Be still and know that He is God.* Monroe's words rang again in the present. Why wasn't he doing that now? thought McComb. It worked for him before, hadn't it? Hadn't he just made up his mind that day, after he'd talked to Monroe, to spend the afternoon in the same spot by that spring, not moving, but just lying there and concentrating on his own concept of a Higher Power? Hadn't he felt a spiritual uplifting of sorts? And hadn't the craving for the booze somehow vanished that day? God, he thought, why hadn't Monroe's words come back to him before all the confusion with Graylin? Before he had planned and picked up his renewed affair with John Whiskey. Maybe if he had, he would still be with her this very moment and the whole trip into the Bend would be something that had never happened.

Be still and know– That was it. *Be still and know that He is–*

"McComb! Over here, quick!" It was Katy.

Josh's brain whipped back to the now and his eyes found her on a low porch of one of the clapboards where a screen-door swung from one hinge.

She was motioning for him to come over and the expression she wore was that of urgency. "What's goin' on, Katy?" he shouted.

"Just come over here, will you, McComb," she said in an insistent yet inanimate voice. "See for yourself."

McComb dashed across the silent compound and on up the low steps to where Katherine was standing. "What's up, Katy?" he asked.

Katy went on, her voice in a quiet monotone, "When I flew up here with the weapons the other day, and when I first dropped the Germans off here, there was someone living in this camp. Government folks–three of them I think. The Germans never let me see them, or them me, but I knew that they lived here because I had seen them shopping down at Lajitas before–two men and a woman.

"What do ya' think, Katy? You think the Germans took those folks along with 'em?"

Katy shook her head. Josh noticed that her face was somewhat ashen. "No," she said somberly. "That's not very likely." Josh's eyes followed her pointing finger through the half-open door. "That's what I want to show you," she drew in a long breath. "In there."

The bodies were still bound hand-and-foot. They sat–tied knees-to-chin– on the floor just inside the door and each contained two bullet holes–one at the base of the brain and the other in the right temple. Josh took in the whole scene. A short look was all he needed then he stepped back out onto the porch. "Damn," he uttered as he felt the bile churn in his stomach. "The bastards killed 'em all." The words came dry and clammy.

Katherine leaned back against a post, her complexion still draining. It was obvious that she felt fault–it spilled from her pores. "I," she paused, "I didn't realize–"

McComb reached for her shoulder. He turned her to him, pulling her closer, speaking firmly, "You are not responsible for this, Katy. Forget it, OK?"

Her tears were moments away. "But I brought those Germans here. I flew those Nazi killers into our country to do this terrible thing."

"You might have brought 'em here, Katy," said Josh, now in a much softer voice, "but you didn't know that they would murder anyone. OK," he said, "you made a mistake; but you're not responsible for any killings, you got that? Just get those thoughts out of yer' mind, damnit. You've already admitted that you did wrong and you've started to make amends. Don't go tryin' ta' make things worse for yourself. Jest' be happy that you made that realization when ya' did. Now, c'mon," he urged compassionately, "we have ta' hide the planes before those Nazi bastards come back–put 'em both in a position where we can catch 'em in a cross-fire–give us the advantage in a firefight."

Katy nodded slowly, wiping some perspiration from her forehead. "Yeah," she said softly, "I know you're right, McComb. From now on I'll do my best– honest I will."

Josh nodded, understanding her feelings.

"McComb?" Katherine said as they started down the steps. "You know I could sure use a drink about now."

McComb found himself stopping for a moment as he searched inwardly for a feeling he knew should be there. It wasn't. There was no familiar craving at all. He could hear Monroe's words in his mind again. "Be still, and know that He is God." Then he turned to Katherine Faver who was watching him quizzically and said, "We'll see if we can find you something, Katy. We'll find you a drink, if that's what you need."

CHAPTER SEVENTEEN

"Captain, it looks like the soldier-boys follered them Germans right inta' Diablo Canyon without us," yelled Turpin. The ranger caravan had stopped for a brief reconnoiter at or about the same spot Purrington's group had waited just twenty-minutes earlier. Turpin and Plunker Hancock had just arrived back from a two-hundred-yard "on-foot" expedition into the narrow canyon and Turpin was reporting their findings to Collinson. "We saw jeep tracks on top of the quad's tracks," the young cowboy continued. "An' by the looks of the sprayed sand them Army boys was movin' pretty damn fast."

"Those dumb bastards," mumbled Collinson. "That's a godamned box canyon. Now, even if they don't want ta', them krauts'll have ta' make their stand. Those sons-o-buck Army boys shoulda' jest' stayed here an' waited 'em out—starved 'em, if they had ta'. Godamned military thinkin'."

"We gonna' go in after 'em, Captain?" asked Hancock.

"Looks like we'll have ta', don't it, Plunker," replied Collinson quite simply. He slid out his hog-leg and checked the chambers from habit. "We'll go on in on foot," he said. "No use bein' a bigger target than we have ta'. Boys!" he shouted. "C'mere! All of ya', on the double!"

Doors slammed as the rest of the men moved up to join the others. "Are we goin' in after 'em, Captain?" asked Biscoe as he reached the Ford.

Collinson nodded. "Make sure everyone has a loaded rifle and a pistol, will ya', son?" He turned. "Lester," he yelled. "Bring yer' car an' trailer up a little more; make 'em all like a circle of wagons, if ya' can." And turning to Sitters: "You, me, Lester an' Plunker'll go on in. Turpin, Biscoe an' Shorty'll stay here as backup." He winked to Cecil. "So, find a bush an' drain yer' crankcase, or whatever else ya' might have ta' do, 'cause ya' might not get a chance ta' water the flowers fer' a long while."

The men nodded, then moved back to the other vehicles to prepare. Collinson turned to the driver's side of the Ford where he found two rifles and several boxes of cartridges in the back seat. He handed one of the carbines to Cecil and dumped a handful of brass into his open palm. Then the two men began loading up.

"This could be it, couldn't it, Red?" said Cecil.

"Jest' might, Ceece," answered the ranger. "That is, if them bohunks haven't blinded that trail–left false tracks for Purrington an' his soldier boys ta' folla' after."

"The ol' colonel will be all horns an' rattles if'n they done that, Captain," said the Marcy foreman.

"Yeah, I imagine so, Ceece," uttered Collinson. He took a long pause. *"If* they done that."

Cecil toed the dirt at his feet. "An' you don't think that they did, do ya' Red?"

Collinson shook his head slowly. "No. No, Ceece, I don't. I think that them krauts is down that canyon an' I don't think that they know it's a deadend. So, if I was all of us, I'd start learnin' how ta' say 'howdy' in kraut talk."

Cecil chuckled then slid his last shell into the Winchester, levering a cartridge into the chamber then lowering the hammer carefully. "I'm as ready as I'll ever be, Captain Red."

Collinson nodded, turned back to the others. "OK, boys," he said. "Let's get-a-goin'. Follow me an' keep yer' danged heads down, will ya'?"

The men fell in behind the ranger captain and they moved out down the draw, slow and steady–all of them on alert. The only sound to be heard was that of their boot-soles crunching over the dry sand.

The young cowboys, Biscoe, Shorty and Turpin, waited near the Ford as the four older men disappeared around a bend in the canyon where the walls narrowed even more than before, and the flagstones appeared stacked like books, one on top of the other. They watched as the last man visible dropped from sight, engulfed in the blue tinge of the canyon's shadows.

The first action of the firefight was short and sweet. The Germans came to the end of the deep draw and were stopped by a sheer wall. They realized their predicament immediately. Spengler and Pachter promptly ordered every man out of the remaining quad truck as Kuft struggled to turn it around in the cramped space. When the truck was in place, the men were positioned strategically around the area, some behind large rocks and the others beneath outcroppings and under the truck. Raller and Iggy were instructed to follow the S.S. men to a well-concealed pocket in some boulders. Bowman was also brought along. It was from this location that they were to observe what happened next.

The low hum of the two American jeeps crept anxiously into the Germans' ears several long minutes before their actual appearance. It gave every man present the precious time needed to make ready. Silent prayers were mumbled and reassuring nods were passed from one position to another as the engine noise grew louder and louder, reverberating up the walls of the canyon. Every eye focused on the sandy trail that ran the floor of the steep, flagstone draw–the only place that the approaching Americans could come from.

Because of his position, Iggy saw them first. He recognized the unsuspecting driver of the first vehicle as an American who had given him an occasional cigarette. Although the two of them had experienced a language barrier, he remembered the soldier as a very pleasant fellow. Within seconds, Dreshler's thoughts were all but dashed as the initial burst of automatic fire filled the air. A large, crimson, unwieldy mass appeared, replacing the American driver's face and as glass shattered, the jeep careened and flipped over on its side.

The other American manning the machine-gun in the rear of the jeep Iggy recognized as the commander of the fort. They had never really met personally, but on occasion, the colonel had given the prisoners several long-winded talks, which Spengler had interpreted for them at a later time. And now, as the jeep slid along on its side, digging sharp edges into the sand to the damp, the officer was thrown out. He rolled and came up to his feet in a crouch with an automatic pistol in each hand. There was just a slight hesitation from the Germans–as if to let the man collect his bearings–then a fusillade of bullets hit him from all sides. As the American officer turned and twisted, kicking and jerking in six directions at once, Dreshler could not take his eyes from the scene. The fright, the fear in the man's face, whatever it was, etched deep into the young German's mind, as blood, sand and the reverberating gunfire obliterated all.

The driver of the second jeep must have seen what happened and he used the confusion to slide his vehicle into a 180-degree spin, as the second American machine-gunner raked the walls with ricocheting lead. The tracers made geometric patterns within the small confinement and two of the German soldiers, Enno Wilming and Tilman Schroer, were cut completely in half by the piercing spray of bullets.

When the smoke cleared a little, it was replaced by the screaming sound of the second jeep's high-pitched whine. Rooster-tails of sand shotgunned the canyon's walls, half-blinding several of the Germans as the remaining American vehicle swung around and raced away back down the draw in the direction from which it came. The gunner still fired sporadic bursts until the jeep was gone from sight.

"Get that American vehicle upright," yelled Spengler, indicating the overturned jeep. "We must get out of here at once!"

It had only taken seconds, now the coughing and stunned prisoners crept slowly from their various points of cover, moving carefully past the remains of their dead comrades, and the pieces of the two Americans, on out into the middle of the still smoking battle area.

Raller helped Iggy to his feet and the two of them followed the S.S. men down the slight incline to the sandy floor. The American turncoat, the one called Bowman, moved along beside them and Dreshler noted that there was a strange look in his eyes–it was if he were almost joyful about what had just taken place, as if he were actually pleased with the instant death of his own countrymen.

When they reached the others, the American jeep had already been uprighted and Rossmeisl had the engine running again. Pachter jumped into the rear of the vehicle and checked out the .50-caliber machine-gun. A nod from him to Kuft signaled that it was still in working order as Spengler dispatched the rest of the men into the rear of the quad truck. When all were aboard, Rossmeisl turned the jeep and with Pachter's permission, moved on out of canyon and up the draw. Iggy almost lost his balance as the truck lurched ahead to follow. He wasn't paying attention to the quickness of the move. Instead he was staring intently at the American colonel's torn body that lay face down in the mucky sand–still draining blood. As he took one last look back, he thought to himself, how ironic that the American officer's boots were still so clean and polished.

Collinson was aware of the jeep coming back in their direction. The rangers had all heard the gunfire and now one of the jeeps was speeding back up the blind canyon at full bore. "Get yer' butts up the sides of them canyon walls an' take cover!" he hollered.

The four men scattered and boot-toes and two-inch heels stabbed for footholds as they scrambled to higher ground, diving for cover behind boulders and craggy overhangs. Within seconds, the jeep carrying the surviving M.P.s slid into view and passed by beneath the Texans, going like all hell. "Sum'bitches're really heading home ta' Mary, ain't they," remarked Cecil as the dust boiled up to where he was perched next to Collinson.

"Keep yer' mouth shut an' yer' head down, Ceece, damnit!" hissed Collinson as he bellied down and took careful aim back up the draw. Just as he did, the second jeep, manned by Rossmeisl and Pachter, skipped around the bend in a four-wheel crab, followed immediately by the quad truck. "Wait 'til I fire first," Collinson barked above the swirling din. And he sighted in and thumbed back the rifle's hammer. His first shot caught the left-hand edge of the driver's seat, just missing Rossmeisl who pointed wildly to the rim of the canyon. Pachter swung around with the .50-caliber and cut a quick thirty-rounds in the rangers' direction, arcing with the gun's torque and firing again. Ricocheting bullets sang in every direction as the jeep passed by below. Then every armed man in the speeding quad truck that followed opened fire on the rangers as their vehicle lumbered by. The lawmen were pinned behind a slew of ricochets and spiraling dust-tails that rendered them incapable of returning any lead until the two vehicles had careened on up the draw and out of range.

Collinson half-slid back to the bottom of the canyon followed by the others, in a rain of shale and loose rocks. "C'mon, you beef-heads," he shouted, as they gathered themselves. "Them kids're all there is back there!" He took off at a dead run that would shame a twenty-year-old. The others followed as best they could under the circumstances.

The two M.P.s' arrival back at the mouth of the canyon had given the young cowboys ample warning. Within a minute the Germans burst from the draw with guns still blazing. Biscoe, Turpin, Shorty and the soldiers used Detroit steel for cover–having put the engine blocks and radiators between them and the fleeing enemy. One of the reasons that no one else was killed was that the rangers' cars had been parked sideways to the canyon entrance–in a half circle– with each vehicle pulled up beside the horse trailer in front of it. They had all done more ducking and diving than shooting as the jeep and the quad truck skipped past. Even though they were dodging a hail of lead, they were still able to empty their carbines and the jeep's .50-caliber after the escaping Germans.

They were already reloading and attempting to calm the animals when Collinson, Cecil, Lester and Plunker Hancock stumbled out of the canyon and hurried to their side. "You boys all right?" puffed Collinson.

Turpin stepped out from behind the shattered nose of Collinson's Ford and brushed his forehead with his hat. "I reckon we are, Captain," he said. "But I don't think yer' automobile done too well."

The other two cowboys stepped out into the open and by the proud smirks on their faces Cecil knew that they had somehow enjoyed their little experience. As for the two M.P.s: the gunner had taken a shoulder hit and the driver wore a head scratch. When they had both been bandaged up, Collinson told them that they'd better drive on back to the fort for further medical attention. The .50-caliber was out of ammunition anyway and Collinson felt that someone should be told about the colonel's death; and also that a detail ought to come out and collect the bodies. The two M.P.s were more than happy to agree with him.

An examination of the ranger vehicles put the casualties at two engine blocks, four windshields and six tires, all total. There would be no more vehicular pursuit. After the men had watered up and calmed down about as much as they were going to, Collinson gave his next order. "OK, boys, break out yer' chaps an' chinkaderos, an' strap on yer' spurs! Then unload them fantails an' put some leather on em. We're gonna' finish ridin' down them sourkrauts—Texas style!"

CHAPTER EIGHTEEN

Don Miguel Maldonado–almost a hundred-miles away–received the message from Josh McComb at 6:20 A.M., approximately four minutes after young Jim-Bob Pelliteer flashed the first reflection into the Mexican Mountains across the Bravo from the Johnson Ranch. The Don's spacious hacienda sat atop a sleepy bluff, overlooking a yucca flat on which the little border town of Ojinaga was situated. A scattered village of mostly dry adobes and flaking cement structures, Ojinaga snuggled up to the river with its sister villa, the American town of Presidio. It was here that the international rails met at a point on the bridge that traversed the Rio Grande between the two towns–and countries.

Maldonado sat at a hand-carved patio table dining with his guests–Edward Blakely and Dennis Fordham: British Intelligence. Both men were still using their cover as two Dutch patriots recuperating after a valiant escape from their occupied motherland and who were now traveling with their friend, Señor Sandoval–from Mexico City–who was in reality, a Mexican Intelligence agent.

The four men were having breakfast on the tiled terrace while the long shadows still let them savor the morning cool. It would not be that long before the rising sun would force all things living inside–the Texican desert border country being one of the hottest spots in the entire world.

A man in peon white refilled their tea and coffee cups as one of Maldonado's private militiamen told them of the aviso's message. They listened intently and understood that McComb might possibly be in some kind of trouble. The militiaman was sent back out to gather Don Miguel's Escopeteros–his personal militia–while the two Brits and Sandoval radioed British Intelligence H.Q. in New York City for further orders. Word arrived back within the hour–confirming the escape, explaining that the American Government was still restricting its action concerning the breakout. The Brits were advised to disregard what they knew about the situation for the time being.

After the communication was discontinued, the Englishmen decided that there was still no reason why they couldn't accompany their host and friend

Don Maldonado if he wanted to take them on another small tour of the area. At 8:00 A.M., three carloads of riflemen drove out of the tiny village and crossed into the United States. They were not questioned at the border checkpoint for Don Miguel Maldonado's position was respected by all–on both sides of the Bravo.

"I realize that you probably think that I should have much to say about what just happened, Herr Raller," said the still wide-eyed Iggy. "But after what I have just seen, there are no words for me to speak."

The Germans had made it all the way down to Terlingua Creek before they stopped for some much-needed rest and to gather their thoughts. Several of the men were suffering from superficial wounds, most of them acquired when the escaping M.P.s' jeep tires had sprayed the blast of sharp rocks and sand. At the creek, they were able to wash their eyes and drink from the cool tributary, while Pachter, Kuft and Spengler planned for the remainder of their vigil. While they waited, most of the men found a place to sit and rest where there was some or little shade, and they made an attempt at regaining some of their strength.

Raller took a drag on his cigarette and blew the dry smoke skyward. It hovered above him in a tranquil cloud for a moment then was dispatched into the still air. He and Dreshler had found a large boulder near a maverick trickle of water that flowed over some flat rocks. The two men had slid down next to it, compressing their backs together in hopes that they could squeeze themselves into the small refuge of the boulder's shadow. And now they sat– smoking and resting–thinking the thoughts that tumbled between them about the infinitesimal piece of war they had both recently experienced.

"You do not have to say anything to me, young one," said Raller. "My eyes, like yours, also extend deeply into your heart." The older man took another puff on the cigarette. He could feel the youngster's body trembling against his own back.

"I just don't understand," mumbled Iggy, attempting to restrain useless tears. "I felt as if I knew that American sergeant, even if he *was* the enemy. And though I had never spoken to him, we had still made some communication in a small manner." Iggy wiped at his cheek. "I knew from his eyes, when I first met him, that he held no animosity for me. Why, Herr Raller, did he have to die like that? Why could not it have been someone whom I did not know?"

"Would there have been any less pain?" asked Raller as he stared out across the creek bed, listening to the music of the water as it flowed over the smooth stones. He closed his eyes. "Iggy," he continued, "I ask you this: What is the difference whether you knew that man or not? Does knowing a man who has died really make it more solemn, or is it just our own *personal* loss? The death of one human being or another is the same in God's eyes. Why not ours?" He took a last puff and flicked the butt into the creek. Both men watched as it followed the flow of the water up, around, over and down. Raller continued: "If you had not communicated with that man before, would you still feel as you do now? If your answer is no, then ask yourself 'Why?' For he would still be the same human being, would he not?"

Dreshler now tossed his own cigarette into the water at their feet and it followed an entirely different route than the one taken moments before by Raller's stub. Finally it joined the other in a small whirlpool a few feet down stream.

"Which cigarette is yours, Iggy?" Raller went on. "Can you tell now? Did your tobacco taste any better than my tobacco just because *you* tasted it? Or would mine have been just as sweet?"

Iggy shook his head. "I am still confused, Herr Raller. Because just knowing that American for that small amount of time has really seemed to make a difference to me. Knowing him made me care."

Raller chuckled softly. "You are no different than most men, my young friend," he said. "In war, they find that they can shoot, kill, maim and some even rape, as long as they do not know their victims. But if it were the same thing befalling a friend, or even an acquaintance, it would somehow be different. You also knew the two German boys who lost their lives back there, did you not?"

Iggy nodded again. "Yes I did, but I had never really talked with either one of them."

"See what I mean?" said Raller as he turned around to face the younger man. "All four men who died back there were our human brothers, Iggy. Why then should we not weep equally for them all? Maybe we shall, one day. Maybe we shall."

"Roust!" Spengler's voice echoed across the sand. "You will load into the truck immediately."

The two men got to their feet and gathered their weapons, then started back for the truck to join the others. Before they climbed in, Raller could feel Dreshler's hand on his shoulder and he turned. "Herr Raller?" said the young man softly. "There is a difference. I still do not know why, but there is."

Raller nodded, "I know, young Iggy. And until mankind can lose that difference, as you call it, there will be more wars I am afraid." He watched as what he'd said was savored by Dreshler for a long moment. The truck's engine and more shouted orders interrupted once again. "Come," Raller continued, "let me help you climb aboard, my friend. We do not want to be left behind, now do we?"

The rangers hit the creek a little less than an hour after the Germans had been there. They stopped at the very same spot to water their horses and to take a quick rest before continuing on. While the others dipped their bandannas in the cool water and refilled canteens and goatskins, Collinson and Cecil Sitters made a roundabout of the area, looking for more sign–something that might let them know a little more about their prey.

Cecil was the first to see something. "Well, we know that they got cigarettes, Red. There's enough butts 'round here ta' start our own tobacca' plantation, I 'spect."

"Don't see no air-tights, though," said Collinson. "Tin-cans'd mean they was plannin' on a long trek. But ta' not see no sign of food could mean that they're headed fer' somewhere closer than Mexico. Someplace right down here in the Bend, if I reckon correctly."

"That don't make no sense ta' me, Captain Red," said Cecil. "They're whippin' some tired ponies now. They done burned powder with Uncle Sam an' us back there an' kilt some men, too. Every one of 'em has ta' know fer' sure now that when we catch 'em, they'll be feelin' the cold side of a 'dobe wall. So why would they wanta' stay up here in the states any longer than they have ta'?"

Collinson hunched down with his back to the sun and Cecil moved in beside him. Both men watched as the horses sucked from the creek while the youngsters and the two deputies went about their duties. Collinson went on: "The closer to the Bravo they get, the more chance they'll run across other people–chili-chasers, rangers out of Castolon, even some of them halfcooked, walk-a-heap soldiers the Army's got stationed down at the Terlingua mine." He flicked at the sand with his finger, then he stood up, "No," he shook his head, "I got an idea that them krauts ain't headed down Mexico way. Least not fer' the time bein', Cecil."

Sitters still sat on his haunches. He looked up at the ranger, squinting against the brightness of the sun, "Where do ya' figger' then, Red?

Boquillas, maybe?" Cecil stood up, wiping his eyes as the sun had made them start to water. "Maybe they's plannin' on crossin' over through the del Carmen Mountains," he offered. "Ain't likely there's anybody patrolin' them goat hoppers."

Collinson shook his head. "No," he said coolly. "They'd need a string of mules ta' do that. Crossin' the Bravo in the middle of them mountains is a straight up an' down feat an' they couldn't do it without the help of some Colorado mockingbirds. No," he went on, "I think they're headed one of two places: either the Johnson Ranch—or the Chisos."

Cecil kicked at some pebbles that lay on the ground in front of him. "Well, the Johnson place I jest' can't figger'. There're always too many folks around that place. And the Chisos, what would them Germans wanta' go all the way up there fer'?"

Collinson pulled out his handkerchief and blew his nose to clear some dust. "One road in. Same road out," he said. "It's private, Cecil. And there's a place ta' land an airplane, too—if they was a mind to." His eyes narrowed and he called out to the others. "That's enough waterin', boys. Cinch 'em up an' let's be on our way!" Collinson started into a slow walk toward the horses and Cecil followed along.

"So it's the Chisos, then, is that right, Red?" said Cecil catching up. "Them krauts is headed fer' the Chisos is what yer' sayin'?"

"Ain't sayin' that it's a fact, now, but I'd bet calf-fries against Hooverhog that that's where they're goin', all right," answered Collinson.

The ranger grabbed the drop-rein, stuck a toe to his stirrup and swung into the saddle. The others did same, reining around and waiting for their next order.

"I got me a feelin' that them krauts is gonna' be follerin' this creek fer' some time, boys," said Collinson to the group. "What we're gonna' do is head cross-country an' I try ta' I put a few miles on 'em." With that, he spurred his animal and took off across the creek.

By ten o'clock the Germans had found that to touch any exposed metal in the rear of the truck would cause intense burning. They huddled away from the sides of the bed, exercising muscle and balance. They continued to inhale the constant dust that was being churned up from the tires while they boiled in their own perspiration.

At the top of a small rise, Pachter—in the American jeep—had his driver pull to a stop. The quad truck came abreast. From this vantage they could look down across a vast, slanting valley, marked, here and there, with rocky outcroppings, and traversed by two gravel roads. Blue smoke could be observed drifting lazily from several locations, indicating the quicksilver mines that dotted the landscape. In the distance, the majestic Chisos mountain range rose from the flat, with deep reds and purples clashing in subtle elegance against a rippled sky.

For Bowman–the King–it was like the Land of Oz. Fields of waving poppies, criss-crossed by sparkling yellow-brick roads, and all of them leading to the Emerald City–sliced the clouds on the far side of the Technicolor setting. *I will build my castle there, atop those splendid mountains,* thought the King. *And my subjects will farm in the valley below and worship me upon high. I have watched them in battle and they have been victorious in my name. For doing that they shall live under my protection throughout eternity in glorious tranquillity in the land that God has so graciously set before me.* He dropped to his knees in thanks, for he knew that all of his dreams had, at last, come true. What he didn't quite comprehend was the annoying tugging at his collar.

"Was fehlt Ihnen?" interrupted the voice. A strong arm lifted the American defector to his feet. Bowman was face-to-face with the fat Ballena–Spengler, the one subject he had already dealt with–and the only one that he still did not trust.

"Get your fuckin' mitts offa' me!" snapped Bowman, spinning sideways and lashing out blindly at the man. Raking fingernails creased Spengler's left jowl. At the same moment a helpful rifle-butt cracked against American soldier's skull, dropping him in a heap.

"No more," shrieked Spengler, "leave him be! He is crazy, yes, but we must not kill him–just yet. Now, everyone out of the truck," he ordered. "Take a few minutes to rest and stretch your legs." Spengler motioned for two of the Germans to take care of Bowman then he jumped down from the truck and moved to the front where he met with Pachter and Kuft.

"There are your mountains, Herr Spengler," smiled Kuft, pointing. "We are much more than half the way now. We can be there in less than three hours."

Spengler answered impatiently: "We are running late, as it is, Herr Kuft. I just hope, for your sake, that this American pilot you have hired will keep his part of your agreement."

Pachter chuckled. *"She* will be there, Herr Spengler."

Spengler snapped around.

"He is a *she,* Herr Spengler," said Pachter quickly. "Do not worry, she is quite competent. She will be there, I guarantee that."

Kuft glanced back toward the truck where the two German prisoners were in the process of tying the unconscious Bowman's hands. "I see that you are having some trouble with your defector," he said to Spengler. "It would be much easier, would it not, if you just shot him now?"

Spengler shook his head. "No, I think not. I wish to keep the American as our security. Somewhere along the way it may well be to our advantage if we keep him alive. Men in your position should understand these things. If," he continued, "if something should go wrong, then he would become a bargaining tool. Americans, I am sure you know, put a great value on human life–or have you forgotten that, Herr Kuft."

Both of the S.S. men nodded in agreement. "Yes, Herr Spengler, you are right," said Pachter. "We will keep the American with us as you wish. It is not that much further, anyway."

Spengler nodded his understanding of the situation. "Then I suggest we be on our way."

"Yes, Herr Spengler," snapped Pachter, with a Nazi salute. "We have already spent too much valuable time here." Pachter turned back to Kuft, "Order the men back into the truck and let us be going." He smiled discretely to his partner, "We do not wish to keep Herr Spengler waiting any longer."

"What do ya' make of it, McComb?" asked Katherine Faver.

"Dunno' yet, Katy," said Josh squinting, "It's pretty bright down there. Lemme' try those field glasses you brought along."

Josh and Katherine had spent the good part of an hour maneuvering the heavy planes into favorable positions–one on each side of the dirt road that led down from the pass, through the basin and on into the C.C.C. camp. They'd angled the two aircraft so that the .303s mounted on the rear cockpits of each plane would have a clear sweep of the road in every direction. They'd hacked branches and underbrush and done their best to camouflage the deHavillands until they were completely hidden from sight. It was around noon when they finished the chore and then decided to climb to the top of *Casa Grande*–the towering flat-topped mountain behind the camp. Josh wanted to try and see if they could spot any sign of the returning Germans.

McComb continued to sweep the valley with his bare eyes while Katy fumbled in the knapsack they had brought along with them for the binoculars. The air at this peak altitude blew thin, pure and crisp, and there was a constant clash of extremes–the warm, almost hot, sun beating against exposed skin, while goose-bumps stood neck-hair on end from the chill. From where they were situated, they almost had a 360-degree panoramic of the Big Bend: the prehistoric lava flows, the domed mountains and the painted sands. In certain directions, there was no indication that man had ever set foot. In others, smoke and several wandering roads, gave faint evidence. Josh and Katherine were casually aware, too, of what appeared to be the Earth's curvature, as the Sierra del Carmen mountain range, beyond Boquillas, appeared to bend, like an earthen bow, into Mexico. And the Christmas Mountains, to the northeast, seemed to tilt away from them, as if seen through a distorted fishbowl. When Josh brought the fieldglasses to his eyes, a more realistic scene unfolded: two silent dust clouds–one within a mile of the other. The first appearing to be on the road that headed toward Panther Pass and the mountains. The second: a smaller blotch, most likely made by a cluster of animals–possibly men on horseback–looked to be moving across the open desert in an effort to head off the first dust cloud.

"Take a look," said Josh, handing the binoculars back to Katy.

Katherine watched through the magnifiers for several long moments. "It sure looks like someone's following someone else, doesn't it?" she said. "That bigger one in front could be the Germans coming up the pass. See." She handed the fieldglasses back to Josh. "There are two vehicles. But who is that following them, I wonder?"

Josh lowered the glasses. "Well," he said, "that's damn well someone followin' 'em down there, Katy. But I got a feelin' that no matter if someone's on their tail or not, those Germans still won't be ready for *our* little surprise."

He started to hand back the binoculars so she could return them to the knapsack. That's when their eyes met. Two sets of eyes that had not looked into the other's for oh so many years–and it brought back just as many memories for both of them. Katherine leaned in. She expected that they would kiss as they had so many times before.

"No, Katy," said Josh firmly. "No."

But they were only words. McComb's emotions eventually won and they embraced in a long kiss. Then Josh pulled away.

"C'mon," he told her, "we got too much to do."

They both got to their feet, he helping her up.

"Josh," she begged, "will it work again for us?"

There was a moment then McComb shook his head. "No, Katy. There's someone else now. I'm getting married, remember?"

Red Collinson held back his horse some, maintaining a steady gallop as he led the others across the brasada. The slope of the valley angled up slightly and he knew that to spur out to a full run would only tire the animals much too soon. The Germans had done exactly as he'd predicted they would. Where the Terlingua creek met the Alpine road, they'd headed due north and then they'd turned east at the Study Butte fork, taking the only other road in the vicinity– the one that would lead them to the Chisos Mountains.

On Collinson's orders, the rangers kept on moving across country in a direct B-line toward the mountain range, urging their animals on in a constant canter, resting and watering them for five minutes every half-hour, then continuing on. The Germans stuck to the gravel roads and though they offered the smoothest passage to the Chisos, they certainly were not the shortest distance. So by the time the Germans were headed up through the lower foothills, their pursuers were less than a mile behind.

As Collinson rode along, his hawk-like eyes following the faint twistings of whirlwinds left by the German wheels, similar flickers commenced to tease at the base of his brain. Paralleling pieces of visionary celluloid working their way into the rusty sprockets; threading their way past the ancient aperture that opened into his consciousness. And the curtain slowly parted to reveal what appeared to be almost the exact image that had been before him. The only thing different–at first–was that there was no color; at least not a true color. For the Chisos had lost their browns and greens and had taken on deep shades of gray and the sky turned stark white while the dust and dirt that swirled around him stayed the same sepia murk. And when he rode his horse up and over a steep ridge, instead of the Germans he had expected to see by that time hightailing it toward the high-country, Red Collinson came face-toface with a sea of sombreros and snapping Mauser bolts.

He reined his horse up so hard that the bit grated on teeth and the animal almost sat down with him as he swung off and stepped away. He was close enough that he could see the faces of every man that stood before him. The barrels of their weapons were pointed directly at him, glistening, white-hot, in the sun. He could also see that each man carried the bullet holes that he himself–Red Collinson–had administered. Black, sticky goo oozed heavily from the gaping cavities. They were the men he had killed–the men whose lives he had chosen to end. And now they were banded together into one. They would soon be Red Collinson's firing squad.

They stood there, all of them, the light breeze whipping at their bandannas and broad-cloth, with their guns raised and cocked and their fingers slowly easing down on the smooth triggers. This was a time for prayer, for sure, Collinson thought. But no prayers came to him. Not even God would back him now. This was surely going to be his last gunfight. In the Bible's own words: his *Time for Dying*.

Collinson felt a sadness creep into his soul; a feeling that should have entered unto him many years earlier. A melancholy that broke like a tear and splashed in bereavement for these men who no longer walked the Earth's face, but if not for Red Collinson would still be doing so. Where had he been given the right to take their lives? Had that circled star he'd worn for so many years given him that special privilege? He had thought so for a long time, hadn't he? And that thumb-buster he wore on his hip. That had sure put him a notch above other men. Why? Why had he felt that way? Why couldn't he have taken them all alive, eaten a little drag dust if he'd needed to; other rangers had. The job didn't have any firm rules that said you had to kill the prey–just hunt it down. But Red Collinson had always shot first. He'd never been second in his entire life–because second meant dead, didn't it? So he had always blown the prey to kingdom come before *it* got him, and that was just the way it was. Everyone had accepted that fact–that it was a ranger's job: killing. But it could have been different. With a little less pride, and a little more regard for another human being's life, it could have been much different.

In his reverie, the bore of every rifle centered on Red Collinson while his eyes passed slowly from one man to the next and then to another and another. He could hear the firing-pins, in unison, as they fell on the percussion caps, and the powder as it ignited, grain after grain, and the gas, as it expanded, expelling the many plugs of rotating lead in his direction. Red Collinson slowly closed his eyes. It was too late now; too late to change a thing.

"Red, Captain Red!" Cecil Sitters' voice brought him back to the present.

Collinson raised his hand and reined his horse to a stop. The others pulled up next to him. "What is it Ceece?" he asked Sitters who rode up beside him.

Cecil was pointing toward a large rock formation about five-hundredyards ahead of them. "Didn't you see that, Red? No more German dust boilin' anymore. Looks like they're up ta' sumthin'. They're up behind that big outcroppin'."

Collinson squinted. He recognized the odd-shaped mountain as a familiar landmark. "That there's *Alsate's Face*, Ceece," he said. "History has it that the Mes'claro Apaches ambushed a whole troop of 10th Cavalry nigger boys from up there behind that hill. Damn near looks like our German amigos got the same idea, now don't it?"

Cecil nodded. "They know we're here, that's fer' sure, Captain."

"And they expect us ta' keep on comin' right on up that road in front of 'em, too," said Collinson, swinging down from his saddle. "Dismount, boys," he shouted, "an' start walkin' yer' animals fer' a spell. Keep our dust churnin' so's they don't know that we're onto 'em jest yet. When we get down to that ravine there, I'll let you know what we're gonna' do.

A small piece of shale slipped loose about halfway up the face of the outcropping, bouncing and dislodging more stones and dried clay, almost growing into a small landslide before it petered out against flat ground about four yards from where Spengler now stood. The bloated German looked up the precipitous incline that made up the backside of Alsate's Face and decided that it was just too dangerous to place any men that high up, although it would have made a fine location for a sniper or two. Instead, he turned to his right, where a mass of very large boulders towered at least thirty feet into the air and he made up his mind that the men would be more than adequately protected by that edifice. He ordered the men into position and had them start digging in. The road would now be more than well covered. When he was finally satisfied, Spengler turned and walked back down to the base of the bluff where the quad truck and the American jeep had been hidden from sight.

The small area they had picked for the ambush was close to perfect in every way. The road passed by the opposing mountain just twenty-five yards from the rock heap where the men were hidden and it was backed by a sheer cut into a tremendous slope that would make escape or entrenchment virtually impossible. On the closer side of the road, the bank fell off into a small gully that would be the only way out–if it were tried. And the entire expanse was still fully in the firing line because the trench slanted up again, directly into the base of the huge boulders where the Germans would be waiting patiently.

The Germans had been aware of the posse coming up on them for some time as they climbed toward the Chisos out of Panther Junction. At first they thought the men on horseback to be local hunters, or maybe just cowboys. The thought of the riders actually being some of the same men that they had encountered back at the dead-end canyon never entered their minds until Pachter, using a high-powered telescope, saw silver flickers from several chests–and rifle scabbards with many bandoleers hanging from the tack.

Just minutes earlier, Pachter had told his driver to stop the jeep and the quad truck had pulled along side. Then he, Kuft and Spengler had observed and remarked on the sturdiness of the Americans.

"How do they cover so many miles with just horses?" questioned Kuft.

"They are extremely familiar with this God-forsaken country," replied Spengler, "and we are not, that is how." Then he turned to Pachter, acting very official. "I suggest, Herr Pachter, that we find some place as soon as possible and eliminate these people, whoever they are. I am sure that you do not wish them following us all the way to Berlin. It would be a terrible embarrassment if these determined Texans somehow kept us from leaving this country."

"I understand, Herr Spengler," said the S.S. man. "I will be looking for such a place." Then all had climbed back into the vehicles and they'd continued on.

As the truck had ground gears to keep up with the jeep, Raller, Iggy and the other men in the rear held to the side-boards and watched the dust of the rangers as it drifted and blew across the shelf a mile below. "They are some persistent cowboys, ya?" one of the men had nervously chuckled.

Raller nodded. "They are terribly smart, these Texans," he said. "I would say that their leader has, what the Americans call, much horse sense."

Iggy cocked his head at the strange expression. "I do not think I understand this 'horse sense,' Herr Raller. What does it do?" he asked.

Raller smiled and settled back. "This leader," he explained, "he knows in advance what we are going to do. He sees where we go before we go there. It is like intuition, even greater than intuition, I believe. I have heard that it is because of this 'horse sense' that the American pioneers were able to conquer this vast country so easily. They do not follow their heads like we Germans do. They just let their heads follow. Like the horse that is many miles from home. Most would say that he is surely lost, but the horse always returns to his stable in time for supper. He does not run in circles crying, 'I am lost, what shall I do?' He just lets go his head, and by some miracle, he is divinely directed."

Raller chuckled to himself. "So these men do not have to follow us, exactly; they just figure out where we are going and they meet us there."

He noticed that Dreshler had turned his attention again in the direction of the horsemen. "What is bothering you, young Iggy?" he asked. "Is it that we may have to fight these brave Americans? They are not from the fort, like the others, you know. They are strangers. You have not met one of them before,

I am sure. So, more than likely, killing them will come easier for you. We will be ready for them. Knowing the way our S.S. leaders think, a coldblooded ambush will certainly be their final destiny."

"Herr Raller," said Iggy. That was all. Dreshler had turned back to him and Raller noticed that the rims of his eyes were damp so he held back further words. Raller knew instinctively that his point had finally been made. The Germans had driven on in silence another quarter of a mile while all eyes remained fixed on the mysterious riders. Then the two vehicles had turned off the road abruptly.

Now they were ready; ready for the cowboys to make their approach. Each man was settled deep between the rocks and they were waiting. The S.S. men hung back near the trucks and they kept Raller close by, and of course Raller kept Iggy with him. Judging distance, the horsemen should have been coming into sight at any second. In several short minutes the rangers would all be dead, and the Germans would be on their way again with no one left to hinder them.

CHAPTER NINETEEN

There was only one position better for an ambush than the pile of boulders that Spengler had chosen for the Germans, and that was from the top of the high cliff that loomed up immediately behind the backside of Alsate's Face. It had walls that shot straight up from the small pocket where the German vehicles were parked. The S.S. men had not even considered the advantage because of the impressive height and the fact that there appeared to be no way up–or down–the sheer rampart.

At the top, which overlooked the entire German placement, there were about twenty-five yards of semi-level ground, covered sparsely with large rocks and pinon pines that sloped back into a partial syncline. This dry runoff crept back down and around the north side of Alsate's Face and then connected into a large ravine that serpentined it's way past and on into the sprawling desert below. This entire route was hidden completely from the Germans and they were never aware of the muffled hooves and the stifled snorts made by the rangers' animals as they climbed to the unseen shelf high above.

With no words between them, Collinson spoke in sign–sort of a monkey-see, monkey-do rendition of old Indian and Army hand signals–pointing out positions for each man along the edge of the rim. Collinson also made sure that the small posse removed their hats and spurs before sliding, belly down, to their assigned tree or rock. Both Collinson and Cecil–Winchesters at the ready– snaked their way over to the base of a pine tree that had roots dangling precariously over the brink. Collinson waited patiently while his men all settled in behind what cover they found, then he sent a "ready" nod from man-to-man. Levers creaked gently and hammers were cocked as brass and packed-lead slipped quietly into chambers. Below, the exposed backs of the Germans presented bizarre targets as they waited for the horsemen to fill their own sights–the horsemen who, in reality, had the Germans themselves in the cross hairs.

The voice echoed between the mountainsides with explosive affirmation. The words were English but every single German knew them all too well. They'd heard them numerous times before in every B-Western that had ever played a Deutschland movie arcade. The voice belonged to Texas Ranger

Captain, Red Collinson–and it said: "Drop yer' guns, boys. Put yer' hands in the air. We got ya' covered."

The Germans heard the voice and they all froze. They simply had no idea, for the moment, from which direction it had come. The German prisoners threw puzzled looks to one another and then to their leaders. Raller looked to Iggy and winked. "Horse sense," he whispered. Then the two of them were hustled to their knees beside the truck by the S.S. men for their own protection.

Spengler was sweating balls of anxiety as his cheek hugged a rear tire. He exchanged a look with Pachter and Kuft, who both shrugged as if to say, we don't know, either.

The voice continued. "We'd be much obliged if you krauts jest' threwed down them guns an' come outa' them rocks. Now, it'll make it a lot easier on all of us, if ya' jest' do as I say."

Pachter's raspy whisper slid along behind the truck to where Spengler was crouched. "Do you see them, Herr Spengler?" he questioned. "The acoustics are so that I cannot tell where they are."

Spengler nodded slowly and the others watched his eyes as they narrowed in on the high cliff. All that could be seen from below was an occasional metallic reflection that presumably bounced from a rifle barrel. "They are up there behind us," whispered Spengler. "How they managed to climb that distance, I cannot imagine."

Kuft held tight to his Schmeisser and systematically cocked the weapon for firing as he slid to the rear of the truck and got to his feet. "I will find out just what their strength is," he declared, stepping out from behind the vehicle in a firing position.

An ugly thud smacked into the gun's mechanism, followed by the reverberating crack of a rifle. Kuft, stunned for a second, dropped the demolished firearm and dove for cover back behind the truck.

The voice called out again. "Now that was about as dumb as a man can get, amigo. Even a pepper-gut Mes'can wouldn't have made a dumb move like that. Now you get yer' butts started tossin' out artillery 'afore I give an order an' have my men Green River every last one of you cabbage suckin' sons-o-bitches!"

Pachter and Kuft edged in closer to Spengler. "Do you think that he means what he is saying? That he will kill us all?" asked Pachter.

Spengler ignored the question. "I believe that they have us at some disadvantage. Maybe it is time that we show them our defector."

Pachter smiled broadly and nodded. "Herr Spengler, I now understand your madness." He found a handkerchief and tied it to the barrel of his Schmeisser. When he'd waved it significantly for the rangers to see, he stood up slowly and began walking around to the rear of the truck where he gently dropped the tailgate. He took the half-dazed Bowman by the arm and dragged him out, forcing the American soldier to his knees on the ground in front of him. Bowman's hands were still bound and as he attempted to gain his balance, Pachter brought down his Schmeisser's barrel level with Bowman's temple with the white handkerchief still fluttering.

"Ya' see that, Red?" whispered Cecil on the ledge. "They got an American soldier down there, lookit' the uniform. The sum'bitches had an ace up their sleeves, all right. Didn't I tell ya'?"

"Quiet, Cecil," ordered Collinson. "Damnit ta' hell anyways, jest' be quiet."

Now Spengler slowly stepped out from behind the truck. From the top of the cliff the rangers could not see his vengeful smile. But when he finally spoke, the newfound power in his voice was carried on the wind along with his special dictum. "Americans! We mean you no harm," he yelled. "All we wish is to reach your Chisos basin without further incident. Neither my men nor I are prepared to surrender. So I suggest that you pay close attention to my offer."

"What's he mean, Red?" asked Sitters.

"Gawddamnit, Ceece," said Collinson with no attempt to hide his annoyance, "jest' shut up an' listen to the man, will ya'?"

Spengler continued: "As you can all see, we have a hostage: one of your own. An American soldier from the fort. His life will not be long in living if you do not consider letting us pass on into the basin. I give you ten minutes to let me know your intentions. And remember, we are prepared to fight to the last man. And if your answer is negative, the boy will be the first one to die. Have I made myself clear?"

"Clear as a bell in a Mes'can church steeple," yelled back Collinson. He turned and motioned the others over to where he and Cecil were.

"What're we gonna' do, Captain Red?" whispered Suggs as they all gathered around.

"They got that poor kid hog-tied. I seen the ropes," said Turpin.

Collinson settled back against the pinon pine and leaned over on one elbow. He casually pulled out his pipe and pouch. "Well," he said in a calmer than usual voice. "That fat kraut gave me ten minutes ta' think on it. I suggest you boys have a smoke, 'cause that's what I'm gonna' do."

Down below, Spengler watched the final seconds tick off; then he moved boldly around to the back of the truck–past Raller and Dreshler, to where Pachter still stood with the Schmeisser held to Bowman's head. He glanced down at the American soldier–the American traitor who had helped him so easily accomplish his end of the escape–and he smiled. He looked up to the top of the cliff and called out once again– "Americans, your time is up. I need to know your answer."

There was the silence of a long moment then Collinson's voice came back with: "Go ahead, amigo. We sure ain't gonna' stop ya'. Yer' free ta' go. We don't want no more dead soldiers we'd have ta' explain ta' the Army. Go on. Ya' got my word that no one up here's gonna' shoot."

Spengler turned to Pachter and spoke in a low voice. "Take him in the jeep– both you and Kuft. Follow behind us and make sure that they see that you keep the muzzle to his head."

He turned to the others and called them down from the rock pile, ordering them into the back of the quad truck. When they were all aboard, Spengler slid behind the wheel to drive himself. The engines were started and the vehicles began to move out, on up toward the narrow road.

From the top of the cliff, Collinson watched the truck and the jeep pull onto the road and move on toward the basin. When both of the vehicles had disappeared around a bend, he swung his look back to the base of Alsate's Face. He could see Cecil, Suggs and the others ride out into the open down below. He smiled to himself. They'd made it all the way to the bottom without the Germans being aware that they were still not at the top with him. He waved his hat and the men waved back. Then he checked the knot in the rope he had tied around the pine tree's trunk, and the other knots that secured the four lariats he'd connected together, and he threw the coil over the edge. He stood up, slipped on his gloves and snaked the rope under the seat of his pants, re-buckling his gun-belt around the rope as a safety precaution. Then, grabbing the rope high with his left hand and low with his right, he turned his back to the open space and let himself over the edge.

The posse watched in awe as Collinson slid down the rope, kicking out, releasing some slack, then bouncing back and kicking out again. Turpin couldn't believe his eyes, "Will ya' look at that ol' man," he gulped, "he's got more stretch in 'im than a pickle-barrel full of chimpanzees."

When Red Collinson's heels finally touched solid ground he removed his gloves, dusted himself off, re-buckled his gun-belt and moved to his horse that Cecil had trailed down for him. He stepped into the stirrup and swung into the saddle with, "Gonna' have ta' come back fer' them ropes, boys," as if nothing spectacular had just happened. And he stuck a spur to some flank and moved out in the direction taken by the trucks. The others followed.

From Alsate's Face, through Green Gulch and on up to the top of Panther Pass, the road narrowed as tight as it could possibly get and still let a vehicle as large as the quad truck navigate. There were also many ups and downs, as well as treacherous curves and switchbacks. Spengler, behind the wheel of the truck, was able to get an initial head start on the jeep, so there was about a quarter to a half-mile distance between the two as they made their way through the pass.

Somewhere along the way, Wallace Bowman's disheveled brain came back to reality—reality, in the sense that he was suddenly aware of his situation. Maybe it was the Schmeisser's barrel tapping out its disturbing staccato against his skull with every bump and vibration the jeep made as it bounced along the road, or perhaps a mind such as his just snapped in and out at will. Whatever the cause, the truth of his plight must have become quite clear to him, because he did something only a man who knew he faced certain death would do.

Somehow Bowman managed to get hold of the cotter-pin that immobilized the .50-caliber machine gun while it was not in use, and at what he felt was the proper moment, he yanked the pin out and flung his body against the gun as hard as he could.

Pachter was taken by complete surprise. Bowman's quick move threw him off balance and his gun went off, spraying a slew of lead past Kuft's head and blasting out the windshield of the jeep. Before Pachter could regain his senses, the barrel of the .50-caliber made a complete arc, rotating fast, catching the S.S. man with all its weight, and knocking him up and over the end of the barrel. Pachter frantically grabbed onto the barrel in an attempt to keep from being thrown from the careening jeep. He was actually hugging the wildly bouncing gun with his arms only while his legs kicked savagely out over the side of the passing ledge. And for one fleet second he was made aware of two genuine, final facts: one, his groin was completely covering the .50-caliber's muzzle, and two, Bowman's hands were loose—and they were reaching for the trigger.

The rapid-fire slugs tore Pachter's body from the gun. The bullets rammed into his torso with such tremendous power he was flung, in several pieces, far out into the expanse of sky beyond the road—where he dropped, like plopping cow-dung, into the mesquite, below.

But Bowman had hesitated for that one second too long and as he attempted to turn the gun back in Kuft's direction, the driver fired point blank into the young soldier's belly with a Luger. The shock and instant numbness dropped Bowman to his knees and he toppled out, over the tailgate of the jeep, hitting the ground hard then rolling to a stop in a cloud of gritty dust and gravel.

Kuft grabbed for the Jeep's steering wheel in a last ditch effort to regain some control, but as he did, the loose .50-caliber swung around again and caught him above the left ear with reckless abandon and the jeep went into an uncontrolled skid. The vehicle shot off into space, nosing down and then burying itself for one instant in the thick brush before exploding into a ball of bright orange fire.

Wallace Bowman felt the intense heat of the blast, but to him it flowed over his battered body as only a warm breeze–and he saw nothing more of this world as he passed on into the kingdom of his dreams forever.

At the first indication of trouble in the jeep, Spengler had stopped the quad truck and tried to back up, but the condition of the road at that particular section, made it close to impossible. All the Germans were able to do was watch as the bizarre scene played out behind them.

When it was all over and the jeep had crashed off the road and burst into billowing flames, all that visibly remained was Bowman's crumpled body lying in the shifting dust. The terrible scene behind them prompted Raller to put a gentle hand on Dreshler's trembling shoulder and say quietly, "Iggy my friend, *that* is what makes a hero."

The young officer turned to the older man with great doubt in his face. He cleared his throat and tried to stop his head from shaking. "But, Herr Raller," he said trembling, "that soldier was a traitor, a traitor to his own country. How can, how can you call him a hero? He was a crazy man."

Raller smiled softly. "As I have said before, a man is only a hero in the minds of others. Others have seen what happened and he will be called a hero. Believe me."

"We must go on," yelled out Spengler from the truck's cab. "There is nothing we can do for any of them." He shifted into gear and the truck rumbled forward. The men in the rear would keep looking back. For as much as they didn't want to, there was no way to avoid the black smoke as it belched its thick column into the deep blue that embraced the jagged peaks.

The rangers had seen the daring escapade, too. They'd observed the fight and explosion from the backs of their galloping horses as they over-and undered their foaming mounts up the perilous passage in an attempt to catch up to the jeep and possibly assist the courageous American soldier.

Led by Collinson, the small posse now cantered through the wind swept smoke and reined up around the soldier's body. Collinson looked down at the boy and slowly removed his hat. The others did the same. "That there's one hell of a man, fellas," he said. "I don't rightly know who he is, or jest' how he come by getting' captured by the krauts, but he sure as hell gave 'em the best lick he had."

"You can say that again, Captain," added Cecil.

Suggs said, "Amen."

Collinson continued: "May God have mercy on his soul." He turned to the young cowboys. "One of you boys use yer' rain slicker an' wrap 'im up good. We'll have ta' leave 'im here fer' the time bein'."

Turpin was the first to swing down. He untied his raincoat and moved to the body, followed by Shorty and Biscoe. They lifted Bowman carefully and lay him down on the coat at the side of the road. They began to fold it around him and button it up. When they had almost completed the chore, Collinson heard Turpin utter, "Oh, my, will ya' look at that."

"What is it, son?" asked Collinson.

"This here boy dyin' like he did is sure gonna' make a little filly cry her eyes out somewhere, Captain," the youngster said sorrowfully. "Lookie here, here on his arm. It says, 'Peggy.' Looks like he done pricked in the ink his own self. Musta' bin' a lotta' love there, Captain. A whole lot of genuine love."

Collinson nodded, putting his hat back in place. "Yes, sir," he mumbled. "Must have bin', son. Must have bin'."

CHAPTER TWENTY

The caravan transporting Don Miguel Maldonado, the British Agents, and Señor Sandoval in the lead car–with the Don's personal militia following in the other two vehicles–pulled into the Panther Junction water station to find Monroe Leaton, Jim-Bob Pelliteer–with Josh's dog–and Graylin, McComb's fiancée. The three were trying to cool down the radiator of Graylin's Plymouth. Elmo Johnson's model-T pickup, which Monroe and Jim-Bob had borrowed from the ranch, sat nearby. Monroe had been somewhat fearful that the aviso sent by Jim-Bob might not have reached Ojinaga in time. So he had appropriated both the pickup and several hunting rifles then headed out for the basin with the boy in case they could be of some assistance to Josh and Katherine Faver. Graylin, in her car, coming from the other direction, had made it as far as Panther Junction where the vehicle had overheated.

"Would you three lovely people care to join us?" Blakely had called out, "It seems that we're off for a brief hunting party. But I can guarantee you, it shall be no holiday."

Maldonado, pointing to Jim-Bob, added: "We received your aviso, Chico."

Monroe grinned from ear-to-ear. "We were on our way to meet you up at the basin, Don Miguel, when we come upon Miss Graylin here. Her car is in pretty bad shape, suh, an' I sure don't want to leave her out here all alone."

Graylin moved over to the Don's touring car and leaned down. "Monroe has told me all about what's going on. If Josh McComb is up there, and he's about to face a bunch of German soldiers, then I want to be with him."

Maldonado shook his head, "Uh, señorita. I do not feel–"

Moving over beside the woman, Monroe cut in with: "Miss Graylin's one heck of a crackerbox shot, Don Miguel."

Blakely leaned out of a rear window with a smile. "We can always use another rifle, Miss. Please feel free to join us."

"Thank you," said Graylin. "I won't be any trouble." Room was made for her in the Model-T pickup. Then the four automobiles roared on up the junction road toward Green Gulch and the basin.

"You know something, McComb?" said Katherine calmly. "If I hadn't been so damn greedy, we wouldn't be in this mess."

"There ain't no use cryin' over spilt milk, Katy," said Josh.

The two of them stood in the middle of the gravel road where they shared a final smoke before going to their separate airplanes where they would each spend the last minutes alone as they awaited the Germans' arrival.

"Oh, McComb," said Katherine as she moved closer to him. "If we'd only been able to stay together, maybe we–"

"It was all my fault," interrupted McComb. "I couldn't handle my liquor. I was drunk most of the time toward the end. I'm sorry, Katy, I really am."

She took hold of his hand, squeezing it tight. "Maybe we could try again sometime," she offered with a soft smile.

The near distant whine of the quad truck's engine broke the silence in the basin as Josh squeezed Katherine's hand in return. "I reckon that'll be our German friends," said Josh.

He kissed her on the cheek then the two of them turned and moved off in opposite directions, headed for the camouflaged deHavillands.

The quad truck cleared the summit and Spengler slowed it to a stop. He opened the door and stepped down, surveying the emptiness of the vast, green bowl that lay before them. The basin was much larger than he'd expected it to be–three miles in diameter, if not more. The mountains that circled the hollow stood as erect and magnificent pinnacles with a few of them towering several thousands of feet above the valley floor, itself a mile higher than the Rio Grande that could be seen winding through the distance, beyond the cleave called The Window; and further still, stretching for several hundred miles to the horizon–the infinite Mexican desert.

There was no sign of the airplane that Pachter and Kuft had said would be waiting. But there were many trees and outcroppings that, most likely, hid it from Spengler's view. There was also supposed to be a government camp of some kind and Spengler wasn't able to see that either. As a precaution, just in case something might have gone wrong, he ordered the men out of the truck. He felt that it would be safer for them all if they traveled on foot from this point on.

From his position in the rear cockpit of his D.H.4, McComb could see the apex of the road where it crested the pass and fell off into the basin. He still had the binoculars that Katy had salvaged and he raised them to his eyes. A truck was there all right, but it was stopped. The Germans were climbing out and milling around a large man who appeared to be giving orders. McComb lowered the glasses and called across the road to where Katherine sat in her plane hidden from view. "Katy," he yelled over to her as soft as he could. "They seem ta' be comin' in on foot."

Katherine nodded through the foliage covering her plane. She could see the Germans, too.

Josh raised the glasses once again and this time he was able to count the number of men. "There're only eight of 'em, Katy. I thought you said there'd be more?" He lowered the binoculars and looked over in her direction.

Katherine shrugged. "Maybe something happened," she called over to him. "I'm only going by what I overheard the two Nazis I was with say."

"Well," McComb continued in his hushed voice, "they're still comin' in on foot. They'll be more spread out now, so keep yer' pistol close by–in case some of 'em get behind ya."

Katherine nodded, holding up the Colt single-action .45 she always wore in the holster around her waist. "All loaded and ready, compadre," she said with a quick smile.

Josh smiled to himself and raised the glasses again. "Hell," he mumbled. "They got grenades, too." He called out to Katherine once again. "I don't recollect you ever sayin' anything about 'em havin' any bombs, Katy."

Katherine Faver shrugged. "I thought I did," was her answer. "Sorry Josh, it was just one of those things. I'm sorry."

"It's too late now, anyway," said McComb. "Nothin' can be done about it."

From where she sat hidden in the foliage-covered airplane, Katy could sense the tension in his voice.

He continued: "OK, they're startin' down the road now. They're spreadin' out some. Don't let go of that gun, Katy, whatever ya' do."

Katherine shot him an unseen grin, gripping the .303 tightly. "It kind of reminds me of the old days, McComb, how about you?"

Josh nodded, gave her a thumbs up.

"I see them now," said Katy. "I'll tell you what, McComb, if we get out of this alive, I'll personally fly you and your new wife to Mexico City for your honeymoon."

"Thanks but no thanks, Katy," said Josh. "I'm afraid I couldn't concentrate if you were at the controls."

Katherine chuckled then became very serious. "You're finally happy, aren't you, McComb?" she said easily.

Even though she could not see him through the brush, he nodded. "Yeah," he answered. "I reckon you could say that my life finally seems to be comin' together."

Spengler had given the order and the Germans were now moving down the hill, spreading out to the sides of the small road, guns at the ready.

After they'd gone a few hundred feet, Raller found he was separated from Dreshler for the first time since the escape had been initiated. And when the small band had traveled another hundred feet, Raller realized that Spengler had fallen back and was now walking almost at his side. "Is there something that I can do for you, Herr Spengler?" Raller asked, trying not to sound sarcastic.

"From now on, Herr Raller," said the fat man with a sly grin, "you shall stay close to me at all times. You and I will be the first out, you understand of course."

Raller answered: "Of course."

Spengler moved in closer as Raller kept his eyes roving ahead. "According to my late associates," he began, "there will be an American pilot waiting with the plane. Part of the original plan was to eliminate this American and then Herr Kuft was to take the controls. But now, due to what has occurred, that will be impossible. So I must ask you, Herr Raller, to pilot the craft. You are, after all, the most famous flyer in all of Germany, so that should pose no problem for you."

Raller could sense what was going through the S.S. man's mind. "That is all right with me, Herr Spengler," he replied, "but, what about the other men? I have my doubts that it is in your plans for me to drop you off in Mexico and then come back for the others, one at a time."

Spengler laughed softly. "Of course not," he said. "The entire object of this escape is to transport *you* back to Berlin, Oberstleutnant. The others will understand. They have all taken the oath to the Fuehrer, and as you already know, Hitler himself sanctioned this entire endeavor. The others will just have to fend for themselves. They are soldiers of the Reich. There have been those who have died with less glory."

"I do not recall you ever making that clear to them," said Raller. "I am afraid that they are all under the false impression that, they too, will be going home to the Fatherland."

"In war, Oberstleutnant," said Spengler, "plans must change every moment. A soldier must be ready to accept whatever fate befalls him."

Raller's hand stopped his flow of air, clamping hard against the fat Nazi's throat. Spengler's eyes bugged out as the blood supply was cut off completely.

Raller continued to squeeze as he pulled the struggling man closer. "You are a foul pig, Spengler," he said gripping even tighter. "And a fool, at that. These men would have not come along with you had they been told the truth. You know that as well as you know I must return to the Homeland if my family is to survive." He pulled Spengler even closer, almost spitting in his face. "But there is one thing that you have forgotten, Herr Spengler, something very important indeed." The next few words were spoken very slow and precise. "No one in Berlin really cares if *you* return or not. You too, are expendable, Herr Spengler. But unlike the others, your death will not be glorious."

` A sweet gurgle crept up Spengler's throat and Raller tightened his grip again just as a challenging charge of machine-gun fire ripped into the dust and gravel four feet from the two of them. Raller had to release his hold on Spengler's throat and he grabbed the man, pulling him into the ditch at the side of the road to avoid the fusillade.

A second series of rooster tails pocked the road nearby and when Raller was able to look up, he saw that the others had all found safe cover and that no one had been hit. A low groan drew his attention back to the S.S. man who lay in the ditch at his side. The dive from the road had knocked him unconscious. There was nothing to do but leave him there for now while he located Iggy and then found out where the machine-gun fire was coming from. He waited a few moments until there was a short span of silence then made a dash down the side of the road.

Chattering bursts of return fire were now being discharged from behind brush clumps and boulders where the Germans had taken temporary retreat. Raller zigzagged his way across the road and slid in behind a stony mound where Iggy had sought refuge. From there, Raller was able to take a better look at the situation and he could see that the machine-guns were set about 70-yards away and across the road from one-another. The Germans had been snared in crossfire, but that had not stopped progress altogether. The Germans were still able to advance, some by tossing grenades and then using the smoke as a screen, enabling them to edge up a little closer with each explosion. The distance was still too great for their nine-millimeter Schmeisers, but they would fire anyway, hoping that the noise and confusion would distract their hidden adversaries.

The thundering hoofbeats of the seven ranger ponies were overwhelmed by the sounds of the firefight as Red Collinson and the posse rode toward the raging battle, reining to a stop at the top of the pass. From that vantage, they could see what appeared to be a scene lifted directly from somewhere in Europe and transported straightaway to the depths of the Lone Star State. Tracers were singing and grenades bursting from every conceivable direction and the pungent smell of burnt powder drifted all the way up and into the horse's nostrils causing them to skitter and blow. The animals showed their distaste for the obstreperous engagement that they somehow knew they were about to become a party to.

Collinson unsheathed his Winchester, cocking the weapon with only one hand in a single action. The others drew their own rifles. Then Collinson turned to them for one last reminder: "Get ready ta' burn powder, boys. Who ever them krauts is tradin' lead with down there is bound ta' be friends of ours—so, jest spread out an' stay low, Injun style, an' make every dang shot count." He turned back toward the basin for another look, raising his rifle overhead as his horse reared high. "OK, you flag wavin' Sons-o-the-Republic," he shouted. "Let's give 'em hell!"

Spurs dug blood deep while hooves and tails showed their undersides. Turpin let out a rebel yell and Shorty and Biscoe followed with horrifying Comanche war cries. The road came alive with boiling horseflesh as the rangers swooped down on the Germans' unprotected rear.

Only those Germans who had served on the Russian Front had ever seen anything like it. Flashes from the past of charging Cossacks caused hearts to bubble with fear. The German soldiers left their hiding places for new ones, turning their weapons, if they could, in the opposite direction, some trying to reload, others blasting away at the turbulent stampede that roared down upon them.

Rifle fire belched from ground level as the cowboys hung from their stirrups and levered their Winchesters as fast they could. Several of the Germans were kissed by .44 caliber slugs and were nosed into Texas soil, caught completely off guard. Shorty's horse took a cluster of bullets in the chest and dropped, throwing the half-pint cowboy ass over teakettle, only to see him come up firing once again.

The other Texans rode on, screaming and hollering, making extremely difficult targets. Biscoe galloped in so close to one German that he was forced to use his rifle butt like a war-club, smacking the man along side the head and bringing him down in a swirl of crimson.

Rosmeisl's weapon jammed and he took off running toward some heavier brush. Right behind him came Turpin, hanging low off the side of his saddle. The youngster leaped from the horse, sailed through the air, and grabbing the

German by the neck in a clothesline fashion, he dumped the German into the soft shale. The two of them rolled down a steep bank in a haze of fine powder, with flailing arms and legs, until Rosmeisl hit his head on a boulder at the bottom, killing him instantly.

Collinson reined up with Cecil at his side and the two swung off their snorting mounts near some ground cover. They ducked in behind, continuing to fire and reload. Suggs' horse rode directly over an exploding grenade and was lifted several feet into the air by the blast. The older ranger came down a few yards away with no injury except to his backside, the horse's body having protected him from the flying shrapnel. He crawled as best he could to a boulder, pulled his pistol and kept on shooting.

Raller and Iggy made their way through the confusion down the ditch toward a stand of oaks on the near side of the road. When they were much closer, they could finally make out the shape of a plane behind the natural camouflage, and the figure of Katherine Faver behind the Lewis .303 in the rear cockpit. She wasn't shooting, but preoccupied with reloading the gun.

Raller tapped Dreshler on the shoulder and whispered, "I will draw her attention while you move around behind." Iggy nodded; then the two men split up, moving out on their elbows and bellies in opposite directions.

Katy saw some movement in the brush close by and she slammed the breech and was swinging the .303 around when a voice from behind stopped her before she could pull the trigger. "Achtung!" the voice said. "Halt!"

Katy froze. Somehow one of them had managed to get around behind her. She glanced across the road and could see McComb through the veil of oak leaves as Josh continued to fire, completely unaware of her dilemma.

"Mach schnell! Steh auf," the voice commanded. Katy wrapped her hand around the butt of her .45 Colt and started to stand up. As she turned, she cocked the gun and swung around fast. She did not fire. Neither did the German. Their eyes locked for a quick moment, each realizing that to pull the trigger of their own weapon would mean instant death.

A brief moment passed with Katherine suddenly finding the circumstances amusing—and somehow, the joke that tickled at her anxious brain just trickled out. "Well," she said slowly. "What do you know, my first real, honest to goodness Mexican standoff—and you're a dreamboat."

Dreshler, in his awkwardness, assumed that the American woman was telling him to drop the weapon and he answered, "Nine." So the two just stood there, guns at the ready, and remained motionless.

Raller could partially see what was going on from his position in the high grass, but he feared that to make a move might cause a nervous finger to flinch. So, he lay low for the moment, hoping that one of the two would back off.

"What's your name?" asked Katy in a gentle voice. She was thinking, *Why not? The kid is young. Maybe he's never shot anyone before. Just maybe I can talk him into putting the gun down.*

"Wir fahren nach Berlin," answered Dreshler, figuring that the American woman had most likely asked where he wanted to go.

Katy shot back, "No, kid, I asked you your name. What's your name?"

"Ahhh," Iggy said nodding, finally realizing that the woman just wanted to know who he was. "Dreshler," he answered with a slight smile, "Ignaz Dreshler."

"I'm Katherine Faver," said Katy, "out of Lajitas. I guess you probably don't know where that is," she added. "I'm sorry about all this trouble, but I just can't let you have this plane."

Dreshler motioned cautiously toward the aircraft with the barrel of his gun. "Das Flugzeug fliegt nach Berlin," he said.

Katherine halfway caught the meaning of what Dreshler said and she had to chuckle. "Oh no," she shook her head, "this plane is staying right here where it is. You can just–"

The stray bullet invaded Katherine Faver's skull with a small, hollow thud. There was an instant of realization on Katy's face and her eyes dropped to Dreshler's gun where she saw that the young German had not fired. Katherine Faver's whole life shut down, whirring to a stop, and she plunged from the cockpit, head first, landing at the astonished Dreshler's feet.

Raller was up and to the young man in moments. "Come quick, Iggy," he urged. "Help me move this brush and–" Dreshler was not responding. Raller turned back to him, taking his arm firmly. "Iggy," he shouted, "the woman is dead, killed by a wild bullet. You must not feel that you are responsible. Come and help me start this plane. If we can get it airborne, we may still be able to assist our comrades before it is too late."

Still Dreshler did not move, so Raller stepped around in front of him, looking directly into his glazed eyes. "Listen to me, Iggy. I saw what happened between you and this American woman. Both of you were aware for an instant of each other's similarities. You saw that the enemy was just a human being like yourself. Be thankful that you were able to experience that, young one. Most people do not find that out in their entire lifetimes. But she is dead now. There is no more that you can do for her."

For a split second, the years rolled back to 1917 for Raller. To that certain day long ago when he too had been made aware of every man's responsibility to his brother man; that day when he, like Iggy now, had come face-to-face with the enemy and found him to be the perfect reflection of himself. And from that day on, Raller had changed his entire outlook toward living, and had reset the positions of his values. "Iggy, please," he now begged, "I need you to turn the propeller."

There was another moment then Dreshler looked up and spoke. "The propeller. Oh, yes," he stumbled, coming back to reality. "I will assist you, Herr Raller. What must I do?"

Raller stepped up onto the wing, "Grab hold of the blade, my friend, I'll let you know when to give it a turn."

From McComb's position in his plane, he could see Maldonado's caravan come racing over the pass. The remaining Germans saw them too and Schmeissers and hands were thrown high into the air. Josh hit the ground in a run, leaving the machine-gun while yelling over to Katherine, "C'mon, Katy, they're givin' up!"

Raller watched as the American jumped from the other plane, shouting something in his direction. He waved back, knowing that the oak trees and the camouflage around the plane he was in would make him out to be no more than an outline from the distance between them. He waited until the American was out of sight and then glanced down at the instruments. He would have no trouble figuring out the controls of the deHavilland, and it felt good to once again be sitting in an open cockpit. He quickly made the contact then nodded to Iggy. In just two attempts, the huge propeller danced backwards then whirled into churning ferocity.

Dreshler ducked then dashed under the blades through the backwash, preparing to climb aboard. He was stopped in his tracks by the lethal muzzle of a Luger pistol that was pointed and waving at both he and Raller, held by a very austere Dankwart Spengler.

"I must order you both to drop your weapons," the Nazi barked above the engine noise, "and for you, Herr Dreshler, to stand back." The two tossed their Schmeissers at his feet. "There is only room for one more in that plane," Spengler continued, "and I am sure that you will understand when I tell you that *I* will be that single passenger. Now stand away!" He waved the gun in Iggy's direction once again and the young officer backed away one cautious step.

Raller tried to object but the gun was redirected toward him. "Do not underestimate me, Herr Raller," Spengler continued, "I could shoot you without hesitation for no other reason than our personal differences. But that would be foolish of me if it can be avoided. So, if you both would please cooperate with me, do what I say. And you, Herr Raller–think only of your family, your wife and children, then you may eventually be reunited with them. But refuse to cooperate and I will end this entire operation right now."

Raller's eyes gravitated beyond him to Iggy who–when Spengler had focused his full attention on Raller–had begun to edge slowly toward the S.S. man. Raller wanted to scream "NO" to his young comrade, but he knew that a warning from him would only thrust Spengler's attention back to the boy. It was too late anyway. Dreshler heroically, but clumsily, threw himself at the larger man who turned at the onward rush with his Luger extended, firing point-blank. Raller could see from the cockpit the spume of chunky red as it sprayed out of Iggy's lower back as the young man was flung against the fuselage and then to the ground. It all happened too quickly then Spengler had the Luger pointed back in his direction before Raller even had a chance to unbuckle his safety strap.

"It can end that fast for you, too, Herr Raller," spat Spengler from behind his pistol. "So you must continue to remember, your death will only result in the same for your family. It will only be when the *living* Oberstleutnant Erich Jurgen Raller sets foot in Berlin that the S.S. will release them." He chuckled at his threat. "That is my protection," he shouted again over the engine noise, "my insurance that you will fly me out of here and to Mexico. For if you refuse – I will simply kill you and report that it happened during the escape. By that I swear, Herr Raller. My superiors will believe me if I tell them that, you know. So remember, only you, in the flesh, can save your loved ones."

There was a long moment then Raller motioned for him to get into the plane. Spengler hesitated, took one step toward the rear cockpit and was slammed face first into the side of the fuselage. He dropped to his knees and turned, trying to lift the Luger again but was hit with another horrific impact that sent his corpulent body rolling under the wing toward the front of the plane where he attempted to stand once more, aiming the Luger. Three more .45 slugs smacked into blubber, impelling the fat Nazi straightway into the dissecting blades of the deHavilland's whirling propeller.

Raller had to look away. And when he did, he saw Iggy on the ground where he had fallen. In the youngster's hand the pistol that had belonged to the American aviatrix. The young man was not yet dead, and his eyes were open and blinking blindly. He tried to speak, but the words had no breath behind them to push out what he wanted to say. Blood had filled the passage. But in the boy's face Raller could see that his fear was gone, and the muscles in his cheeks were trying to pull the corners of his mouth into a half smile. Iggy's eyes closed, he slumped back. Raller knew that he was dead.

Raller pushed forward on the throttle, maintaining his look toward the boy's body. Just before Raller released the brakes, he sent young Dreshler a final salute. "Iggy, my special friend," he said somberly. "Inside my heart you will always be the hero you so wanted to become. And I promise you that I will carry your beautiful memory home with me to the Fatherland so that others will remember also." Raller drew in a long, long breath. "Goodbye, Ignaz Dreshler," he continued, "it was most rewarding having known you."

"Mister McComb! Captain Red," shouted Suggs. "Lookie over there, someone's started up one of them airplanes." McComb and Collinson had been overseeing the roundup of the surviving Germans while watching the arrival of Maldonado's caravan. Now they glanced back down the road toward the oaks just as the Johnson deHavilland broke through the underbrush and swung out onto the road with Raller at the controls. The sound of the engine was now free from the natural baffling of the oak grove and it screamed its departing presence.

"One of them danged krauts is stealin' the gawddamned plane," yelled Plunker Hancock from the other side of the road where he was rousting one of the Germans. McComb broke into a run, heading back toward the other plane as Raller gunned the engine, gaining ground speed, moving up the road toward the posse.

Collinson raised his rifle and took careful aim bringing the pilot into his sights, swinging his aim with the machine as it roared past his position. The others waited anxiously for the crack of the Winchester. It never came. The heads that should have turned with the passing deHavilland, remained fixed on Collinson.

"What's the matter, Red?" asked a puzzled Cecil. "Why didn't ya' shoot?"

Collinson watched as the plane continued on up the road, headed straight for the Don's three approaching cars that had to veer off to avoid a collision. It was only after the wheels had lifted from the ground that the militia men realized what was happening and fired several rounds after the departing aircraft.

Collinson turned back to Cecil and the others. He shrugged. "I dunno', Ceece," he said quietly. "Maybe I'm jest' gettin' soft in my old age."

Josh McComb was running on instinct now. He raced back to the grove, searching for Katy Faver and stopped suddenly when he found her lifeless form lying between the bodies of the two dead Germans. "Katherine?" he said softly, kneeling beside her, brushing her lifeless cheek with his hand. He knew there wasn't time. Revenge pushed him back across the road to his D.H.4 and he had the propeller whining in less than two spins. He swung into the front cockpit, securing himself, pushing the throttle and checking the flaps. He released the brakes and moved out onto the road.

Monroe and Jim-Bob–with McComb's dog–joined Collinson and the others just as McComb accelerated past them. Monroe raised a hand and a thumb in his direction. "God bless you, Mr. Josh. No matter what happens, I'll be a' prayin' fo' ya'."

Maldonado, the two Brits and Graylin came running through the backwash, having left Sandoval and the militia to assist in securing the prisoners. "Isn't that Josh McComb?" asked Graylin, pointing to the deHavilland as it lifted magnificently into the air and banked toward The Window in the same direction taken by Raller only moments earlier.

Collinson nodded. "Yes Ma'am," he said. "That's Josh McComb, all right."

CHAPTER TWENTY-ONE

The steady drone of the Eagle III engine sent reverberations bouncing off the sheer walls of the mountains, growing then shrinking in McComb's ears, causing the drums to pulsate; echoing louder and louder as the passage narrowed with his approach to The Window. He could see the distant silhouette of the Johnson deHavilland as if it were pinned to the Mexican sky; drifting motionless above the pinks and deep browns of the horizon's subtle flexure. The German was headed straight for the Bravo, directly toward Santa Elena Canyon.

A warm thermal seized McComb's deHavilland as the plane shot through The Window, catching Josh off-guard. By the time he'd adjusted and leveled off once again, he'd lost sight of the other plane. His eyes scanned the cloudpocked sky along the Bravo–from the faint tracings of the Johnson airfield to the south, to the low hanging smoke over the Terlingua mines in the west–and he could see no sign of the other aircraft. The German appeared to have simply vanished. He must have dropped lower, thought McComb, hiding out against the desert's lineaments, trying to blend into the discordant landscape. Josh pointed his deHavilland's nose toward the Santa Elena slice–which was the last place he'd seen the German. He trimmed and leveled off; all he could do now was keep his eyes open. All he could possibly hope for was that the other deHavilland would appear again sooner or later and that he would be lucky enough to spot him first when that happened.

Josh had been in similar situations many times back in the Great War. Back in those early days, soaring over European soil, when he'd practiced this highly individual form of combat until it had flowed naturally through his veins. Back when the casualty rate for flyers like McComb had been as high as one hundred percent a month. Back when the fierce duels raged daily in the air over the battered Western Front. And when you flew those missions, you never knew if the multicolored Fokkers of the Deutsch Luftstreikraft would be lurking behind the next cloud, or if they might be waiting right on top of you, their backs against the sun. *Beware of the Hun in the Sun*, the pilots used to say. Yeah, those were trying times–those days.

Something in his deep thoughts must have made McComb look up as he had in the old days because while squinting into the white glare, he saw the German–the faint outline, the tiny speck–waiting there immediately overhead, like an arrow at the ready, directly in line with the blazing star. And while he watched, the German dove headlong, swooping down on him with everything he had.

McComb changed his course quickly, making a sharp turn to the left. The German's diving deHavilland was then forced to level off in an attempt to move in behind him. Josh kept his plane turning in a tight circle and the German had to follow until the two planes were eventually opposite one another.

Over his shoulder, Raller had seen the other deHavilland take off as he'd sped out of the basin through The Window. He knew that he would now have to face this other pilot, this American flyer. Raller was no stranger to the chase and he recognized that his chances in an air battle would be much better than if he tried to outrun the American.

They were both flying the same type of plane. Presumably, they both had an equal amount of fuel, and in a direct run to Mexico the American would be constantly on his tail with the shooting advantage. No. Raller knew he must chance a dogfight; he had to hope that he could surprise the American and knock him down before the American could get a firm bead on him. The deHavilland flew similar to several other aircraft Raller had piloted in his career and the twin Vickers machine guns mounted in front of his windscreen were comparable to the guns he'd known in Germany as Spandaus. What he had to do then should prove easy. *Besides,* he thought, *this American behind me would in no way have had a like experience to mine in air warfare.*

McComb swung to the left into another circle. Raller followed, having to give the American some credit for intelligence. Neither one of them were gaining on the other. Neither could fire their weapons, for the guns were "fixed"– they had to be in a direct line with the target. As long as Josh stayed in a turn, there was no way that Raller could use his guns. But there was one problem: In doing this both planes were losing altitude. In the next few minutes, one of them would have to make a move.

They continued, tail-after-tail, for several more lingering minutes then Raller suddenly broke from the circle and was able to maneuver into a position behind and above. *Now the American will run for it,* he thought. But McComb did not. He just tightened the circle into a more confining 100 yard diameter. And though he was closer than before, Raller was still unable to fire his guns with any accuracy. If he dived, the Yank would obviously climb. If he attempted to drop some altitude, he would incur a loss in air speed and they would be back where they both had started. For the moment, all he could do was look down on the other D.H.4. *So close, yet so far,* thought Raller.

In the early days of the Great War, before either side had mounted machine guns, they'd carried rifles and pistols. *What a shot I'd have with a Luger,* thought Raller. He could actually see the hair flutter on the Texan's neck, the whisps blowing in the wind. And he could almost make out the American's facial features behind the goggles whenever the pilot turned to catch a quick glimpse of his adversary above.

The American was older than Raller had guessed–maybe forty, perhaps even as old as himself. From the way the man was handling the deHavilland, it was quite possible that this Yank had flown with the Lafayette Escadrille.

For a moment Raller flashed back those twenty-some years. The other plane below became a French Spad, and the joystick between Raller's knees momentarily belonged to a brightly painted triwing Fokker. Two shining Spandau machine guns replaced the fixed Vickers' and the sand and rocks of the Texas desert below blurred into the greens and browns of the French countryside.

For those few precious seconds Raller flew in the languishing clouds of his past, those days when proud gentlemen splashed their private duel of death against a vast canvas of blue, using chivalry as their only brush; those days when he had first known Anna, so young, so fair; and the both of them, so in love with each other. But the S.S. had her now, didn't they. And they also had his two sons and his daughter–all of them now being held somewhere by the dreaded Gestapo. Held captive by men like Spengler, Pachter and Kuft: depraved men, with absolutely no moral fiber, no thought for human dignity. Men who basked solely in self with unrelenting regularity, men who climbed over anything and smashed underfoot what or whomever they had to while advancing their evil dreams of power and prestige.

If there were men who should die in this war, Raller thought, it should be those who lived by the skull and bones, not the innocent Iggys of the world; not the Yank down below, who was only doing what he considered right. And surely not his beloved Anna, so far away; nor his children who had been taught so different than he while growing up–their childhood games having reflected the tenderness and love of their mother's upbringing, not the Prussian severity of their father's. So unjust, so unfair, he thought. But they will be all right. As soon as he could get back home to them, they would be all right. He knew that.

Unexpectedly, the American pulled his plane into a loop, letting off a wild burst of machine-gun fire zipping into the blue nowhere near Raller's position. But the American's evasive maneuver had caught Raller completely off guard and all he could do was watch as the Yank continued in the loop, heading straight for the ground. Then at barely seventy-five feet from the soil, the American pulled out and ran for the river. Raller had to smile to himself and admit that this aviator had pluck. Raller dived away steeply, leveling off several hundred yards behind him.

McComb poured it to the deHavilland as he'd never done before, almost kissing the desert floor with the wheel carriage as he headed for the Santa Elena slice. "Lord Father," he said under his breath. "I know this ol' day-bomber wasn't never designed ta' fly like a Spad, but if ya' got it in yer' heart, Lord, would ya' please reach out an' put a hand or two on my butt an' gimme' a good push."

He took a quick glance back and could see the other plane behind him. He knew that the German had the advantage now, but that was the chance he'd had to take. He was still out of shooting range. If the German did fire, there was nothing to keep a flock of lead sprayed too high from catching him with a wild shot.

McComb began to slip a little, throwing the tail left then right. The maneuver would slow him some, but it would make him harder to hit. Ahead, the Sierra Ponce Mesa de Anguilla loomed higher and higher as he drew closer. From the level they were flying, Josh had to assume that the German couldn't see that the colossus cut was there—the 1700-foot palisade, chiseled, from top-to-bottom, by the carving of the Rio Grande.

Raller was gaining now. The Yank was slipping and sliding to avoid his guns and that was slowing the American down sufficiently. The distance between them was closing and Raller could see the sheer wall of rock ahead. He knew that soon the American would have to start climbing. Raller fired off a swift burst—about twenty-seven bullets; just enough to bring up a tracer or two so that the Yank would know he was still there.

Raller watched the phosphorescence burn way wide of American's plane and was surprised that the pilot didn't veer away. Only the best remained that calm when under fire. This Yank must have flown with a crack fighter squadron at one time or another. The two planes skimmed along for another minute and that was when Raller realized what the American was going to do.

They came up over the tops of some low cottonwood trees and there it was: a canyon with walls so steep Raller's neck cracked looking for their tops. A giant slice, cut by the river over the centuries, directly in front of them in the sheer rock face that towered toward heaven from the flat desert sand. The American dipped to the left and flew straight into its mouth at about fifty feet above the river's surface.

Raller did not slow one bit as he swung right, then left, following the other plane directly into the shadows of the tremendous gash.

The intense repercussion made by the engine noise resounding off the steep walls was ear shattering. Both men were deaf to the thunderous pandemonium, their concentration directed entirely to their toes at the pedals and their hands on the stick. The path, though narrow, was nowhere close to straight, having been a design of nature begun millions of years earlier. Santa Elena Canyon was a recurring series of twists and turns, lefts and rights, sometimes narrow then widening, expansive to confining–beyond every blind turn, a totally new sequence of obstacles.

Every so often Raller would sight the American's tail, and after they'd flown the maze about a mile, he chanced it and fired off a few rounds from the twin Vickers'. The bullets went wide, riddling the cliff-side, blasting away some loose rock and shale that plunged then bounced directly into his path, grinding through the propeller blades and spraying him with a storm of pebbles that peppered his windscreen and speckled his cheeks with a shower of burning sparks. *Damn,* he thought, *this American is proving to be some match.* He almost ate those words as he rounded the next bend and saw the first deHavilland already in a steep climb to the top of the canyon. A quick glance showed him why: The Yank had been leading him into a natural trap–the advancing walls narrowed abruptly into a space through which no aircraft could ever pass.

Raller shoved a full throttle and pulled back hard on the stick, nosing up in a desperate climb. He could see the American above, silhouetted against the white-hot blue, already clear of the jagged death-snare. Blurred outcroppings accelerated at him from both sides as his engine furiously screamed its escape. Two gut-twisting rasps shot through his ears to his bowels as the upper wingtips scraped the volcanic masses and he was popped free–sky all around. The plane damaged but still air-worthy.

Beads of perspiration bubbled through every available pore as Raller leveled off, his eyes searching anxiously for the Yank. He heard the lead puncture the canvas of his fuselage, followed by the dull staccato of machinegun fire. He could not dive. The top of the canyon's walls below now leveled out into mesas on both sides and he didn't have altitude. He heard the guns again as blue tracers sped past on the right in a downward angle, producing dust-puffs on the plateau beneath. All he could do was backtrack to the canyon entrance and dive for the river–try to shake the American any way he could.

As Raller raced back in the direction from which they'd come, McComb turned and sprayed again; then he dove on the German's tail, running with him, about one hundred yards behind. McComb poured out two more quick streams of lead before the German went past the edge of the mesa, rolled to his right and dived.

Josh throttled back, sideslipping hard, almost flying laterally; giving him that instant to spot the German down at the water's level skipping on down the Bravo. He poured on the power and dove himself, angling his machine parallel with the river's surface, following the German as fast as the D.H.4 would go.

Raller was looking back when the American slid over the top of the mesa and dropped in behind. He'd only seen that done once before, by an Allied pilot in a French Spad over the Western Front battlefield twenty-six years earlier. He'd brought that one down, though–through sheer luck. The Spad's pilot had suffered some engine trouble, giving Raller time to turn and fire. He'd knocked a wing-tip off the Spad and the crippled plane was forced to hedgehop with Raller right behind, until he shot out his opponents control wires and damaged the cowling, causing the Spad to bury its nose into a muddy French field.

That had been the day Erich Raller had stopped the killing. He had already earned the highly respected title, "Grosse Kanone"–The Big Cannon–"Ace." He was one of Germany's top air-heroes, one of the select few who wore the Blue Max. But something had happened to him on that day. Maybe some words his Anna had said to him during one of their many discussions had finally made some sense to him; or possibly the hand of God had reached out and simply plucked the hatred from his heart. Whatever it was, the killing stopped that day. And though he'd flown once more for the Fatherland in Spain and then again in this present war, Raller had only shot to wound, never to kill intentionally as he had before that personal day when he watched the battered pilot crawl from the flaming wreck of the French Spad.

Back then, Raller had circled overhead several times and then–as he'd been doing with every kill he had made before–he dove on the wounded man, his finger at the ready on the Spandau's trigger. Raller was seeking any revenge he could on the downed pilot for all of his friends and fellow comrades who had faltered and fallen in battle with their planes spurting flames–victims of enemy bullets. But on that day something had told him, "No." He'd simply given the fallen pilot a thumbs-up along with a gallant smile as all flyers had done in the very early years of the war. Then he'd flown away. And Eric Jurgen Raller had never killed again.

The two deHavillands wound their way along the Bravo, hedgehopping, in a sense, over outcroppings, cactus and cottonwood groves. Sometimes so low the wheels made brief wakes on the river's green surface. The two planes skimmed past adobe jacals and Mexican goatherds, startling shepherds and causing dogs to bark. They flew over sandy beaches and rock-strewn tributaries ever turning with the steady flow as the great river crooked gently one way then bent again in another direction. When there looked to be a chance, McComb pressed his advantage, sending bullets ripping through canvas, bracing-wires and struts.

Raller knew full well that another stratagem was required–a tactic that could erase this pestering Yank from his tail. What came to his mind in that brief moment was the "Immelmann Turn"–a maneuver that called for a short, swift climb, while at the same time, performing a half-roll. With that extremely difficult maneuver completed, he would be headed in the opposite direction, where, with any luck, he could pepper the Yank from head on, hoping to hit his engine–a coup that would put the American down for good.

Another slew of bullets whistled by and Raller went for it. He throttled forward and tucked the stick as far back as he could. As he started into the half-roll he knew that it was all over. Some spars and wires had taken some fatal hits and there was a lot of twanging and creaking. The bottom left wing broke off and Raller lost control.

McComb pulled away sharply and watched as the German's day-bomber came apart in the sky before him. Pieces of wings and fuselage disintegrated. The plane slowed to a complete stop in its climb. For a split second, the airplane remained motionless; then it arced back slowly, like a toppling pin and nosed into a spin, twisting and turning in a headlong dive.

Somehow Raller managed to belly it in on a sandy beach, smashing through clumps of greasewood and roughly bouncing for what seemed like forever, until the remains of the fuselage fished around and turned on its side, throwing Raller clear just before the gas tanks caught fire–exploding.

McComb circled the smoking wreckage twice before diving in for the kill. He could see the German crawling desperately for the river's edge, with blood clearly visible. McComb knew that once the German hit the water, he would be swept away with the current and that the escape would have been complete. There was just no possible way for an airplane to continue to follow him through the heavy Mexican brush. Josh would have to stop him now if he was to have any chance at all.

Suddenly, compelling thoughts surfaced from within Josh McComb. Thoughts that recalled in detail the day he had lain there, like the German, only on French soil. He had felt so terribly helpless and alone that day in the past as the triwing Fokker had dived in on him. And he recalled that exact moment when the German pilot had smiled and pulled out of the dive to circle over him. The German had given him the "thumbs-up"–a tradition that had all but been lost in those last years of the Great War.

McComb had never given too much thought over the last twenty-six years as to actually why the German had not killed him that day. His life had been spared, and by all rights, he should be dead.

What had gone through that German pilot's mind in those last seconds before he'd pulled away? There was absolutely no plausible reason why his fingers shouldn't have squeezed the trigger. At that point in the war atrocities were being committed every other minute by both sides in the name of vengeance. Vengeance. *My God,* thought McComb, *I was actually about to commit murder using Katy Faver's death as his excuse. Oh my loving God,* the words tumbled in his brain. Who in the hell was he to judge that helpless German on the ground? Who was Josh McComb to drop the gavel and condemn that helpless man for what was nothing more than basic human ignorance? Men kill men out of fear–ignorance and fear. Katy Faver was shooting at them and they were just shooting back. Or perhaps it was the other way around–whichever way one wanted to look at it. Hell, there were two German bodies lying back there beside Katy, weren't there. Shit, he didn't even know for a fact just who had killed Katy–he probably never would. It didn't matter anyway because he felt his hand pull back on the stick through no means of his own. *I will not judge.* The words converged on the center of his brain. *I will not judge another human being again for as long as I live.*

Raller flattened out as the wheels of the deHavilland swooped in so low over him that several small twisters were whipped up on either side. The American had not fired his guns. In those final moments, when the plane had been so close that Raller could actually see the Yank's face, the American had just smiled; then he had pulled out of the dive, swooping over him and then turning into a circle overhead.

Now the American was coming back. Had he some second thoughts? Would the final bullet come now? Raller slid another few feet toward the riverbank. Then for some reason, he turned and looked back at the approaching plane. As the deHavilland flew over, he saw the distinct outline the American's thumb. It was extended skyward. At the same time, an object slammed into the sand beside Raller. Not a bullet, but a metallic object of some kind. The American pilot climbed a few hundred feet and while turning toward the Chisos Mountains, he dipped his wings.

Raller painfully crawled to the spot where the object had landed. His fingers groped and searched, finally grasping something that he carefully lifted from the sand. It was an enamel and gold Blue Max medallion. Raller recognized the German medal immediately. He slowly turned the award over to its reverse side and what he had been expecting to see was there: Engraved in very small lettering was his own name–E.J. Raller.

Slowly Raller raised his hand and painfully put up his own thumb. He watched for as long as it took for the American pilot's plane to disappear against the rugged contour of the mountain range.

When there was finally silence, Erich Jurgen Raller slid into the soothing waters of the Rio Bravo. After a moment, he struck out as best he could with his injuries, toward the Mexican side.